A ROADSIDE ACCIDENT. A YOUNG GIRL FLUNG THROUGH THE WINDSHIELD OF A CAR. BLOOD STILL POURED FROM HER CRUSHED SKULL.

"Help her, Michael," the old woman said. "If you can do what you've been telling me, then I want proof. Bring that girl back to life."

Make it look good, he told himself as he approached the corpse. *You know that old bitch is watching you. The laying on of hands—that always got them. Try the laying on of hands. You've got nothing to lose. . . . Make it look good.* Without knowing why, he closed his eyes.

And then it began. . . .

LIGHT. PURE LIGHT. WHITE LIGHT. INTENSE. SO BRIGHT IT HURT. THE FEELING. LIKE A FAINT ELECTRICAL CURRENT IN HIS HANDS . . . SPREADING UP HIS ARMS . . . TO HIS CHEST . . . HIS HEAD . . . LIFE!

He felt a trembling in the still, dead body.

And then he heard a scream. . . .

CAIN'S TOUCH

Saul Wernick

A DELL BOOK

Published by
Dell Publishing Co., Inc.
1 Dag Hammarskjold Plaza
New York, New York 10017

Dell ® TM 681510, Dell Publishing Co., Inc.

ISBN: 0-440-13468-4

Printed in the United States of America
First printing—November 1978

For Julia Stratton Wernick

PROLOGUE

July 1951. Harbortown, Massachusetts.

The old man had dark brown hands, weather rough-ened and mottled by age, that tied new knots in the ripped seine so fast that the boy couldn't see how he did it, only that the knots appeared, and that in a few minutes a whole section of the mesh was mended, with new twine showing where the old had been torn.

The boy liked to sit beside the old man and watch him. Sometimes the old man talked to him. The boy liked that, because the old man never talked down to him or treated him like a child. But the boy would never start the talking himself. He always waited for the old man. Some days the old man wouldn't say a word and paid no attention to the boy.

The old man liked to sit on the end of the wharf in the heat of the sunlight, warming his old bones. Small waves splashed against the pilings supporting the broad, timbered dock. The wharf was next to the one that most of the fishing vessels tied up to, and there were always two or three broad-beamed draggers or trawlers tied up to the wharf the old man liked to sit on.

The inner harbor was a deep, narrow inlet, the wa-ter dirty from the offal thrown overboard and from the sludge pumped from the bilges of the fishing fleet. Overhead hundreds of seagulls wheeled and soared, beating their way up from the water, caw-cawing at each other. The air smelled more of gutted fish than of salt water, especially when there was an on-shore breeze.

Today the old man hadn't spoken at all, and the boy was content just to rest and watch him and say nothing. When he finally spoke, the boy was startled.

"Out there," said the old man, in his hoarse voice, jerking his head sideways toward the ocean beyond the breakwater, "that's where it began."

"What began?" the boy asked.

"Life."

His rheumy eyes were fastened on the netting piled in his lap; he sat with one leg bent under him and the other extended, his feet bare so that he could stretch the net with his toes while he worked on it. His fingers were stiff and ached all the time. So did his knees, but he'd mended nets since he had first begun fishing, and now that he was too old to go on the boats, he was still able to mend nets ashore.

He said, "First there was heaven and earth and there was darkness on the face of the deep. That's what it says."

"In the Bible," said the boy.

"That's right. It's all there. An' it's still goin' on. It'll go on long's the earth's here. Come from the fish is where we come from. All of us."

"I read in the Bible," said the boy eagerly. "Not much of it. I skipped the *begats*, but I read the first part a couple of times."

"Why'd you do that?" asked the old man.

The boy squirmed uncomfortably. The old man continued mending the nets while the boy squatted near him, watching him for a while, then turning his face away to stare down at the weathered planking of the wharf, then looking up to examine the grayish brown of the chipped and splintered pilings, and, finally, he watched one particular gull beat its way off the water and pull itself into the sky and lose itself in the soaring, circling mass of gray-and-white gulls' wings. He wondered what it would be like to be able to fly like the gull.

"You gonna answer me?" asked the old man.

"I killed my brother," said the boy, looking down at the old man's thick hands. He saw how swollen the knuckles were and how the twine unreeled from the shuttle which was almost hidden in his cupped right hand, how the knots seemed to spin themselves into existence, and how the mesh was built up in the net, one side at a time until the four knots lay evenly, one in each corner, and then the shuttle went on to the next square.

The heat lay heavily upon them. The boy wore only shorts, but the old man wore a heavy shirt and old, frayed corduroy trousers. The sleeves of his shirt were rolled up just past his wrists. The boy wondered how he could stand the heat.

"You really did?" asked the old man.

"That's what my mother told me. She got mad at me one day, an' started screamin' at me an' yelled that I killed my brother."

"How old was you when it happened?"

"Three," said the boy. He said, "He was my twin," as if that explained everything.

The old man sniffed, then wiped his nose on the sleeve of his shirt.

The blaze of the sun seemed to get brighter and the

heat heavier and the sounds of the harbor seemed to die away.

"When she got over bein' mad at me, she tried to take back what she said. Then she said it wasn't my fault it happened." The boy spoke carefully; he wanted to make the old man understand what had happened and that he wasn't to blame. "She said it was supposed to be our birthday. Three years old. An' she come into the bedroom. We was sleepin' in the same bed. I was just lyin' there with my eyes open lookin' at her while she come into the room an' over to the bed. He was lyin' at the other end of the bed with his eyes closed. She said she didn't know he was dead until she picked him up to wake him, an' I was watchin' her all the time an' she said she just knew I had done it."

His throat was very dry. He stopped talking. He still couldn't bring himself to look directly at the old man.

The old man said dubiously, "It's kinda hard to believe a three-year-old kid got enough strength to kill another three-year-old."

The boy nodded seriously. "That's what she said later on. She said she was sorry she yelled at me an' didn't ever mean to tell me how she felt. She wouldn't have, except she got mad."

"What do you think? You think you did it?"

"Oh," said the boy, knowing this was the hardest part to say. He'd never been able to tell any of this to anyone else. "I think it happened. I think I killed him."

The old man was silent. He'd expected the boy to deny it, and was prepared to reassure him.

"That's why I read that part about Cain and Abel a couple of times," said the boy, in explanation.

"Three years old an' you had strength enough to kill him? That what you believe?"

"I didn't need no strength," said the boy. "I put my hands on him."

"You put your hands on him?"

"Uh-huh. An' everything got dark. I don't know for how long, but when the dark went away, he was dead an' he was lyin' at the other end of the bed."

"An' you remember all that? You remember from the time you was three years old?"

"Sure," said the boy.

"Then how come your mother had to tell you about it?"

"Oh, I remembered," said the boy. "I just didn't know anyone else knew about it."

The old man had nothing to say. He sat and mended his nets in the sunlight, and the boy watched him until he got bored and then he got to his feet and wandered away. He felt much better for having told someone about what had happened to him.

The old man kept on mending his nets, thinking about how youngsters could tell you a straight-faced lie; how it became real to them even while they were telling it. And then he thought that it wasn't just youngsters who did that; a lot of adults he knew could do the same thing. Lying wasn't just for kids.

The thing was, he was disappointed in being sidetracked. He'd wanted to tell the boy about the ocean and the things in the ocean and what it was like to have spent your life on the ocean fishing for the life beneath it and thinking about all the mysteries of the deep sea; how we didn't know much about it, except that life came from it.

The boy was there the next day, as if nothing had happened and sat and watched the old man mend his nets. But it was different, and the old man couldn't bring himself to talk about the sea. He did ask the boy his name.

"Michael," said the boy. "Michael Hietala."

After that the old man said nothing, hoping that the boy would go away, but he didn't. He sat and watched the old man mend netting. Late in the afternoon the boy said abruptly, "I can heal people, too, you know."

"Sure," said the old man sourly, "sure you can."

The boy heard the sharpness in the old man's voice.

"I can, too," he said defensively.

"Arthritis," said the old man.

"What'd you say?"

"I said I got arthritis. I'd sure as hell like to see you cure that."

"You really mean that?"

"I'd like to get cured of arthritis, that's what I mean."

"All right."

The boy got up and went around behind the old man and put his left hand on the old man's crinkly, gray hair and his right hand on the old man's right shoulder and closed his eyes.

It seemed to the old man, just before it got so bright, that even when he closed his eyes the light hurt him, that everything came to a stop—that the gulls hung suspended in mid-flight, that the sound of the *Dora Jane* turning into her slip faded and the trawler stopped motionless in the water, and that even the water in her wake hung frozen and did not roll over. Everything became intensely, painfully bright. He wondered if he was having a heart attack. When he felt the blood surge in his veins in a massive expansion, he was sure of it, and then there was nothing but the bright, crystal clarity of the sunlight smashing into him.

When he opened his eyes, the boy was standing in front of him, staring at him. Somehow the boy looked different, like a stranger whose face reminded him of someone he knew. The netting was in a pile on his lap, and the shuttle had fallen between his legs.

Carefully the old man flexed his hands, stretching his fingers out wide. There was no pain in them. He couldn't remember how long it had been since he hadn't had pain in his fingers. He looked down at his knuckles. They were no longer swollen grotesquely and they no longer hurt. He moved his arms and his shoulders. He could feel no pain anywhere. Then he put his hands over his face and began to weep.

"You see," said the boy seriously. "I told you I could."

After a while, the old man dried his eyes and looked up for the boy, but he wasn't there. He was standing at the end of the dock defiantly, his head back, his small legs apart. A nun was bent over him threateningly. He could hear the sound of their voices but not the words they were saying. The nun was angry with the boy, scolding him furiously. The boy said something to her. She slapped his face. The old man heard the sound of the sharp blow and thought she shouldn't hit so small a boy so hard.

The boy went running off the docks, and the nun made her way toward the old man. He saw her picking her way over the thick, broken, salt-worn planks of the pier. He wondered how she could withstand the heat of the sun, covered as she was in black from head to foot. The starched white of the linen binding her face was glaringly bright.

When she approached him, he saw a dust stain on her skirt. Somehow, it made her seem less forbidding.

She stood in front of him. He saw that she was young and that her face could have been pretty were it not for the severity of her expression that pinched lines into her forehead above her nose.

"Has he been bothering you?" she demanded.

The old man said, "No. He hasn't been bothering me."

"He shouldn't be here," the nun said. Her voice was sharp and cold. It grated on the old man's ears. Her face, compressed by the edges of the linen cloth, protruded so that her cheeks bulged slightly. Her skin was scrubbed and smooth and red, her eyes were small and angry, but she was still pretty. The old man looked down at his lap.

"He shouldn't be here," she repeated firmly. "If he comes again, you send him away."

He didn't answer.

"Do you hear me?"

"I hear you," he said, not looking at her. She loomed over him like a huge, black bird of prey ready to pick the flesh from his old bones.

"If he comes, you send him away."

When she got no reply from the old man, the nun turned and began to pick her way back through the debris on the wharf.

The old man stood in the warming sun, moving his gnarled hands and fingers. The swelling was gone. The absence of pain gave him a great deal of joy. He moved his shoulders and his arms and his legs. There was no pain anywhere. He would have been very happy, except for the nun. He had wanted to thank the boy.

* * *

That was the summer the boy was nine years old. By the time he was twelve, he had forgotten what had happened that summer, and forgotten the old man. All he remembered was that he liked the sea and he decided that some day he would live beside the sea instead of coming only for a short vacation.

From the sea cliffs off Cape Mary, the darkness in the last minutes before dawn is no longer black nor bluish gray nor gray. In the time before the sun rises out of the long, flat swells of the North Atlantic, the darkness dyes itself with pale streaks of pink along the ocean horizon, and the color seeps dimly through the night murk.

It is just before that time, just before the rising of the rays of the sun that the darkness is at its heaviest, and there is no hope in the world. At that time, it is a world not yet made for man; he has no place in this world. His time has still not come.

CHAPTER ONE

June 1977. Adam's Cove, Massachusetts.

From the beginning, there was something different about this day. He awakened before dawn, and that in itself was unusual.

It was still dark in the bedroom and dark outside, but he came awake quickly, not drifting out of sleep as he usually did or stretching his body for a long time before he opened his eyes.

. . . Michael Hietala . . .

The voice that awakened him was as clear in his mind as if he'd been called by someone standing by his bed. He came awake and alert instantly, his eyes opening, searching the dark quickly but without fright, knowing there was no danger, feeling calm, feeling only curiosity.

It took a while before he realized that the voice saying his name had been in his head, part of a dream he could no longer recall.

The heat from Lisa's nude body stretched beside his own warmed his ribcage and waist. He felt the long, convex slopes of her hip and thigh, but this time he did not put his hand on her groin as he usually did when he awoke before her.

Even without looking at the clock on the bureau, he

knew that the night was almost over and that the day would begin soon. He felt that he could not lie in bed any longer; he was too much awake.

He swung the covers away from his nakedness, slid out of bed and padded barefoot on the shag rug to the window to pull back the drapes and to look out into the darkness. He could see the twisted black of the stunted pines on the edge of the cliff and the lighter darkness of the sky and the dim stars of the eastern constellations.

After a moment he turned away. In the faint, greenish glow coming from the face of the digital clock, he made his way across the room to the hallway and down the stairs to the lower level. The polished hardwood of the stairs was cold to his feet. He did not turn on any lights as he went; he felt comfortable in the dark. He did not stumble once.

He went into the kitchen to make a cup of coffee, but the sliding glass door to the sundeck was open and the breeze wafted through it, bringing the salt smell of the ocean to him. The smell disturbed him. It was strong this morning. He knew that it must be deep low tide, with the kelp and seaweed exposed and the barnacles and the mussels on the rocks lying open to the night air.

The distinct smell and being so wide awake so early gave him a vague sense of dissatisfaction—not dissatisfaction exactly, but a feeling of not quite understanding what was going on, of not being in total control of himself. He wasn't sure he liked the feeling.

He never put the coffeepot on to boil. Still barefoot, he wandered out to the farthest corner of the sundeck, where he could see between the trees to the ocean.

As he stepped out of the house, the muted, roiling

susurration of small waves breaking on the shore and around the base of the cliffs grew louder in his ears. The ocean was black all the way to the horizon; the sky above it was a dull gray and the clear, crisp air lent clarity to the minute, blue-white flicker of the fading stars.

Orion was always the easiest for him to find. He made out the three stars of its belt and saw which way the constellation was lying. He never had trouble finding Orion, except for the stars that were supposed to make up its arms.

He wondered why he didn't feel sleepy. That was strange. He'd never been an early-morning person. Nights were different. He could stay up all night and feel good; but he never felt good if he had to wake up early. He'd never felt this way before—wound up, expectant yet not knowing what to expect, only to expect something. Something was going to happen.

And he was aware of himself. He was aware of his body, of the way he was standing naked in the blackness at the edge of the sundeck, the wind sighing on his skin. He was aware of the way his muscles moved under his skin, of the bones in his arms and wrists and the tendons that held his bones together and how they moved so smoothly and surely.

When he touched his face, feeling his high cheekbones and the broad bone of his forehead, it was like touching another face, not his and yet familiar to him. When he moved his hand down, his fingers felt the short hairs of his beard. He smiled, thinking how he'd grown this beard on a whim only a few months earlier and how it had turned out to be the best thing he could have done even if he'd planned it deliberately.

The house was on a low cliff. To the east, the sky was beginning to lighten; a thin stripe of light was moving between the night sky overhead and the flat, huge mass of the ocean's darkness, tingeing the sky with the beginnings of pink—as if a keen, enormous flensing knife had been drawn sharply along the horizon, separating the ocean from the sky, the wound opening and the first streaks of blood oozing from it.

He stood there, not feeling the chill, even though he was barechested and the cold air came in off the ocean and touched him so that his nipples contracted into tight wrinkles of hard skin. He breathed deeply, trying to rid himself of the strange tension that was constricting his lungs.

God! He felt powerful! He felt he could reach out and take whatever it was he wanted to take. He could see through things and beyond things. He could understand the world.

The strange feeling grew within him. He began to feel apart from himself. It was as if he were standing away from his body, able to observe it from a distance, able to view himself with a frightening, unemotional objectivity.

He saw himself as he stood there on the sundeck, a lone, naked figure of a man, wind-touched, trying to look into the reaches of the new day, not knowing what it was he was looking for. As if looking at a stranger, he saw the way his hair moved in the wind, saw the brace of his solid legs and the long, flat muscles of his thighs, saw the familiar stranger standing wide-legged on the furthermost edge of the sundeck, his strong hands grasping the thick wood of the railing.

Something was going to happen. He knew.

On the horizon, the knife edge of pink and red grew wider, and the red was an angry red like the red of a suppurating flesh wound. In a little while the whole of the eastern sky was red and pink and the clouds took on shape, dark purple burnt with red and vermilion. He knew that the day had started and knew that for some reason he had been awakened to see it because, in some way, it would be an important day for him.

He didn't want to turn away. He wanted to stand there for a long time, until the sun rose high enough to strike him squarely on the face and to heat his skin and blind his closed eyes with its glare. He wanted to see the whiteness of the glare behind his closed eyes, and feel its scorching heat on the skin of his lids.

Lisa came out of the house and stood beside him. She was wearing a heavy, white terrycloth robe against the chill. She put an arm around his waist.

"Michael?"

"Yes?"

"Why couldn't you sleep?"

"I just couldn't."

Tell her you called out to yourself in your sleep. Tell her you awakened yourself to come and see the day born because you know it will be different from every other day in your life. Tell her.

"Something on your mind?"

"No."

Liar. Tell her everything is on your mind all at one time. Tell her you're frightened and calm. Tell her you know everything that is happening and nothing that is happening. Tell her!

"Aren't you cold?"

"No."

"I couldn't sleep without you, Michael. Isn't that funny?"

"I've left you alone before."

"I know. It's never bothered me before. This morning it did. I couldn't sleep. You weren't with me."

"Yes?"

"I was frightened. It was as if you'd gone away."

He put his arm around her shoulder.

"There's nothing to be frightened of."

"Things are going too well, Michael. Could that be it? We've never had things go so well for us before."

"We've never had a scam like this one before, baby. We've got it made."

"You've said that before."

"This is different. I've got everything figured out this time."

"There's no way it can go wrong?"

He shook his head.

"No way, baby. It's legal. That's what makes it so good. There's nothing to worry about. Not even the IRS."

He felt her body shudder, a quick tremor that rippled through her and was gone.

"Michael?" Her voice was hesitant. "Michael, let's go back to bed."

"I'm not sleepy."

"Neither am I," she said, pressing her face against the flesh of his shoulder, touching him with her lips and then with her tongue. "I want to make love, Michael. Let's go make love."

2.

After they'd gone into the house, the morning sun came up and touched the huge A-frame of the building, shining on the vertical, redwood board and batten sides and on the glass front that soared three stories in the air above the cliff.

From the sea, making a landfall, the house on the top of the cliff was the first thing that came into view. With the sunlight on it, the sharp peak of the A-frame looked like a spire. When it had first been built, the fishermen on the draggers and trawlers out of Harbortown and Hereford had thought it was a church and some of them still thought so, even though the house was now ten years old.

The great, inverted V of the building rose out of the side, planked sundecks that ran around all four sides of it, so it was easy to see why they would think it was a church.

It was for that reason that Michael Hietala had rented the building almost immediately after he came to Adam's Cove.

He named it "The Church of the Second Life."

3.

"When's the old lady coming?" Lisa asked, turning on her side to reach for a cigarette on the table beside the bed.

"Around eleven," he said.

She lit one cigarette and gave it to him and lit another for herself. The covers had fallen away from their bodies. She liked to look at him naked. She put her hand on his stomach, feeling the hair flatten under her palm.

"Be honest with me, Michael," she said. "How does it look?"

"I told you it looks good."

"She's a tough one. They told us how tough she was. Carl thought he had her a couple of years ago. Right up to the last minute, and then she took off. Without a word."

"Someone will get her. I think I can do it."

"There are easier marks. Why her?"

Almost cruelly, he said, "Because this is my kind of con. It was made for me. I spent four years with that fucking evangelist preacher. I learned every one of his tricks. Carl's a fake. He's all surface. It doesn't take much for a mark to see through him."

"And Madame Orlovski? And Eugenia?"

"She won't go for a spiritualist con. It's got to be straight religion. You know that. Christ! We've spent almost a year checking out the old lady. We know everything there is to know about her."

"Mike, we've got every penny we can scrape together invested in this. If it doesn't work, we're tapped out."

"I told you it'll work. Now, shut up about it!"

Angrily, he rolled off the bed and went into the bathroom. She heard the shower running. He ran it for a long time.

When he came out, he pulled on a pair of soft gray slacks and a wine-red cashmere turtleneck. His dark brown hair was damp and looked almost black. There were still water drops in his short beard.

He came over to the bed and looked down at her.

"This is the big fish, Lisa," he said. "Believe me, this one will work. And we won't have to run. She's going to pull in others for us. You know what it's like to open mail week after week and pull out dollar bills? And tens? And twenties? Even hundreds? All in cash? If that pea-brained, redneck evangelist can do it pounding his goddamned, limp leather Bible on television, then I can pull this off! Only it won't be for tens and twenties! The old lady alone is good for a couple of hundred grand. Maybe more. And she's got friends, baby. Don't ever forget that."

He grinned down at her.

"You just stop thinking this is a con we're pulling. You think of it as a new religion, because that's what we are. We're The Church of the Second Life, and you're a deaconess. And the goddamned Commonwealth of Massachusetts has issued us incorporation papers. We're as legal as the Catholic Church or the Baptists or the Universalists or the Christian Scientists!

"Now will you get your ass out of bed and make breakfast for us?"

4.

Sarah Cameron Flint was seventy-six years old. She did not like being seventy-six years old. She was the widow of Augustus James Flint, who had died at the age of eighty-five, leaving her more millions than she knew what to do with. She had been seventy-two when he died, and his death frightened her terribly.

She didn't like the idea of getting old, nor did she like the idea that like her late husband, she, too, would be put away into the ground and that there would be an eternity of nothingness ahead of her.

When she thought of dying, which was often, she felt cold fear gnaw itself ratlike into her guts. The fright came from knowing there was nothing she could do to prevent her death.

When she entered what had been the living room of the A-frame house that was now The Church of the Second Life, she walked slowly, leaning on the cane she held in her left hand. Her pinched, wrinkled face wore a look of suspicion.

Michael Hietala waited for her. He held out his hand. To her surprise, she found herself taking it.

Usually she did not shake hands. Her own hands were too fragile; her bones too delicate. She worried a great deal about falling down and breaking her bones or being bruised. She bruised easily.

Now she found that her hand, almost of its own volition, was in his, and she felt the strength of his fingers. They were very strong hands, she realized, but they were gentle. Her hand felt protected in his grasp. She liked that.

When she looked up into his eyes, he let his face break into a smile. She felt warmth and gentleness. They were very brown eyes, and they were very kind. She suddenly wanted very much to be loved by those eyes because there was so much love in them.

She smiled back at him, which was surprising, because Sarah Cameron Flint was not known to smile at many people. Her hand was still in his two hands, warmed and cosseted. Reluctantly she took her hand away from him.

"I'm Michael Hietala. Thank you for coming."

She liked his voice. It was a very personal voice. It came softly to her ears.

"Please sit down," he said.

She let him help her into an armchair. The armchair was in the center of the huge living room. The cathedral ceiling soared almost three stories into the air before its angled walls butted solidly into the span of the rooftree. The vertical wall of glass at the end was hung from rooftree to floor with a drape made of wide-mesh, rough knotted trawler netting, so she could see through it to the twisted trees growing on the edge of the cliff and to the ocean beyond.

Opposite the armchair was another, smaller straight-back chair. To one side was a white leather couch. Aside from two sideboards along the right wall and two polished wooden teak chests, there was no other furniture in the room. She had expected many chairs, candles, and perhaps an altar. Certainly an altar. Always before, in every one of the places she'd gone to, there had been an altar draped in rich cloth. Here there was no altar. There was not even the usual tall candelabra with the obscenely fat candles in them, as if she could be impressed by wax and weavings!

She liked the openness of the room; it was as if Michael Hietala had nothing to hide. Leaning her cane against her skirt, she settled herself into the armchair.

"This is Miss Fialho," he said. The girl had been standing quietly off to one side. Sarah Flint nodded her head. Miss Fialho smiled tentatively at her and sat down on the couch.

"Well," said Sarah Cameron Flint bluntly, "tell me about yourself."

Her voice had always been slightly sharp and nasal; from the time she was a young girl she had been used to giving orders.

"I could call myself a minister," Hietala said. "I'm ordained, if that means anything. At the moment I don't have a congregation, nor do I want one. This is The Church of the Second Life. There are only a few of us. We do not congregate to pray. Each session is with one individual and private."

She liked the sound of his voice. It held her as his hands had held her, with great strength and assurance, but cradled in gentleness. She didn't let her face show her approval. There would be time enough for that later.

"Go on."

"How old are you, Mrs. Flint?"

"Seventy-six."

"Do you think much about death?"

Her hands had been resting on the rounded head of her cane. Now they clutched the ivory carving in an involuntary spasm of fear. The familiar, hateful chill flooded through her chest. She saw Michael Hietala watching her face and knew that he was aware of the acid fear splashing inside her. She disliked him for knowing that.

"Yes," he said, looking at the tired, old, wrinkled face and the small, tight eyes staring angrily at him. "I see that you do. It frightens you, doesn't it?"

She refused to answer the question. Her thin, bloodless lips pinched together. Almost every day now she thought about death. Most of the time it was bad, but it had never been as bad at it was at this moment. Only the thinnest membrane of self-control kept her from screaming out her fear.

"It frightens most people," Michael Hietala said comfortingly, and, surprisingly, she felt comforted. The fear began to recede. It was manageable once more.

"Especially," she heard him say, "when a person gets along in years and she is alone and has too much time to think about death."

Sarah Flint found her voice.

"Why are you talking to me like this?" she demanded.

"Because this is what you want me to talk about," he said. There was such ease and sincerity in his voice. And honesty. She responded to the honesty. "Anything else would be hypocritical. Do you want me not to talk about it?"

The silence lengthened. The sun angled in through the huge window wall and through the rough, wide-mesh of the fishnet, spilling light along the polished oak planks of the floor. She liked that. She liked the openness of the room and the space and the light. Everywhere else they had talked to her in dimness and darkness, and there were those thick wax candles heavily dripped down their sides, and it was shoddy and cheap. Artificial. Not like this. Not clean and honest, with the hard glare of daylight scouring the room.

He waited.

She gave in.

"Go on."

"You think about death a lot," he said. "Because you know you don't have much time."

Again she hated him for putting it into words. At the same time, she respected him. Augustus James would have talked to her like that. He'd been a realist. *Whatever else you do,* he'd said often, *don't fool yourself! Don't hide from the truth!*

She said tartly, "I've heard everything there is to say about death. One of these days, I'm going to die. So are you."

"I don't want to talk about death," said Michael Hietala. "I want to talk about life. But I have to talk about death to talk about life. The fear of death. The fear of death is unnecessary. There's no reason to fear death."

"Are you going to tell me I can find peace of mind by praying with you?" she demanded, her voice biting at him in scorn. "I'm too arthritic to kneel."

"To *pray* with me? I don't believe in prayer."

"You don't believe in prayer?"

"No."

"What do you believe in?"

"People who are intelligent. Myself. You."

"And death. You believe in death."

"I believe we all die sooner or later, whatever the

word means. Death is a stage in life. It's the prelude to birth."

"You'd better explain that," she said sharply.

He said: "Have you ever wondered why we are so afraid of death? So instinctively afraid of it that this fear transcends centuries and cultures? So afraid that we have created religions with shamans and priests and rituals and rites to comfort our fears?

"We refuse to accept the fact of death, that's why. *We believe that we will live again!* We build pyramids and tombs and catacombs and mausoleums *because we know that death is not a finality*. We are going to live again!

"We don't just fear dying. We resent it! Somehow, we know it shouldn't have to happen. And we're right. It shouldn't. Not if death is the end of everything."

He had begun to pace across the room, walking closer to her so that now the old lady had to look up at him.

"Is death a nothingness that we must sink into? I don't believe it! Was there a nothingness before birth? I don't believe that, either! I do not believe that the mind must cease to exist merely because the body wears out!"

If he heard her gasp, he paid no attention to the sound. He was striding back and forth across the width of the room, not looking at the old woman, talking as if to himself.

"The body remains alive although every one of its cells ages and dies over and over again. Why shouldn't the mind continue to exist even as it replaces the body that serves it? Do you understand what I'm saying?"

The old woman forced herself to remain silent. What she was beginning to feel was hope; she was afraid of hope. She didn't want the savageness of disappointment that always followed hope.

Michael Hietala said: "Death is a natural end only to the body. Man is destined to be born again and again. Of all the lessons that Christ preached, of all the lessons He tried by His example to teach us, that is the one we ignore!

"Lazarus was not the only one Christ brought back to life. *Death is conquerable!* Each of us can do what Christ did for ourselves. *Ye shall be born again* does not mean only in spirit!"

He turned to face her, pointing a finger at her.

"You don't have to die, Mrs. Flint! That's what I'm telling you. This is The Church of the Second Life. There is no death if you don't want to die! But you must learn to believe in yourself! Not in Christ! Not in me! Only in yourself! If you can do that, you do not have to die."

Because it was so much what she wanted to believe, she became angry with him. Enraged that he should be standing in front of her in the prime of manhood, young, flushed with strength, telling her with such certainty everything she longed to hear and have faith in.

He was telling her what she desperately wanted someone to say to her, and she was afraid that he would turn out to be a fake like the others. She could have screamed her rage at him! It wasn't fair! It wasn't right for him to say what he was saying!

Her hands trembled on the head of her cane. Her face contorted.

"Do you think I want to live forever?" She spat out the words.

"Don't you?"

The old woman gave a harsh bark of a laugh; a concentrated rasp of bitterness and frustration, spewing out all of the soured hopes of the last dozen years.

"Like this? Look at me! I'm seventy-six years old. I weigh a hundred and nine pounds. My hair is white and beginning to fall out. My skin is wrinkled like an elephant hide! My breasts are flaps of flesh. When I bathe I hate to look at myself! I'm in constant pain. I live on pills. How do you think I'd look at twice my age?"

She drew in a deep, furious breath.

"What the hell is the matter with you, asking me a question like that?" she demanded fiercely.

Resentment boiled out through her monkey eyes and her voice, resentment and hatred and bitterness.

Quietly Hietala asked, "How old do you think Miss Fialho is?"

Sarah Flint turned her head to look at the girl seated on the couch. Light blond hair hung in thick sheaves down to her shoulders. Her skin was fine and taut; pearly with the glow of youth. Her legs were slender; she wore no stockings to cover the supple musculature of her calves.

"No more than twenty-eight," the old lady snapped bitterly, hating him because he was forcing her to compare herself with the girl, wanting him to know that once she was even more beautiful than this chit of a girl.

"And I?"

"Thirty-five . . . thirty-six."

He said: "Miss Fialho's body is twenty-seven. Mine is thirty-six. It is her second body. It is my third."

He waited for her to grasp what he'd said, and suddenly she did. She drew in a quick, sharp breath.

"I don't believe you. You're lying!"

For a moment they stared at each other, not in hostility but as if she desperately wanted to say something and couldn't bring herself to say it, and she wanted him to help her say it. She wanted his help so much. She knew she wanted to say the words.

"It's true," he said. "You know it."

She would not let it out. She tried to fight it. She refused and refused until, finally, her head nodded and she said in a small voice, "I—I think so. It's insane. If I said it, people would think I've gone out of my mind. That I'm senile."

"Yes, they'd say it," he agreed. "But it's true."

The idea outraged her. It destroyed everything she'd ever been taught. A lifetime denied everything he was saying. In the way of proof, all he offered was what was in his eyes and in his voice and the way he looked, and people lied to you with their eyes and their words. So many of them had lied to her!

She couldn't take her eyes away from his. They were so soft. There was so great a warmth and such deep understanding in them. And love. *God! There was such love!*

She closed her eyes, trying not to think, trying only to let the turmoil in her mind settle. She couldn't think. Not now. It was hard enough to breathe. Her heart was pounding. *Oh, God!* she thought. *Please let it be! Please!* She found herself beginning to cry, felt the wetness of tears slide down the crevasses of her face, through the deep, wrinkled skin of her cheeks. The hurt was so beautiful!

When she opened her eyes, he had turned away. He was standing at the far end of the room at the glass wall, looking out across the cliff at the green-blue ocean.

"Michael?"

He heard her call him by his first name, and he knew then that he'd won.

He'd known that she'd either do that—call him by his first name—or get up and walk out.

They'd told him how tough she was. They'd told him about her visits to the mediums and spiritualists and cultists in Manhattan and London and Los Angeles and San Francisco. About the crackpot groups she'd corresponded with, the gurus she'd gone to see or who had come to see her. Each of them had tried to get her; some of them thought they'd had her. Each time she'd shied away at the last minute. They never saw her again.

She said his name a second time.

"Michael?"

You're not home yet, he warned himself. *Don't get overconfident! She's too damn wary to take any chances with! Slowly! Go slowly. Let her do it herself. Don't push.*

"Yes?"

"Will I . . . "

She stopped, still not able to bring herself to put it into words. Words that would make a commitment.

"Yes?"

"Will I . . . can I . . . really be . . . be born again physically?"

He put a look of surprise on his face as if she hadn't understood what it was he'd said.

"I didn't say that," he said, feigning a deep disappointment. "I didn't say that you'd be born again. Not the way you mean."

Resentment flared in the old woman. *He'd tricked her!* What kind of game was he playing with her! Her face distorted with rage, she struggled to get out of the armchair.

He came close to her. She lifted her cane, flailing blindly at him with weak, ineffectual blows. Deep, racking sobs clogged her throat.

"Let me out of here! Fake! Charlatan! Liar!"

He ignored the outburst. He let her strike him with the cane; the blows weren't strong enough to hurt.

"They all promised you re-birth, didn't they?" he asked, his voice gentle and compassionate. "Yet who'd want to be born again—to have the body of a baby? Infant diseases? Childhood torments? Puberty? Adolescence? Even worse—*not to know who you'd been in your previous life!* Not to have all the knowledge and experience you've accumulated so painfully up to now! You'd have to be a fool to want that. I don't think you're a fool, Mrs. Flint!"

The old woman looked up at him, confused, not knowing what to say.

"They told you that so many times, didn't they, Mrs. Flint?"

She let her tired head nod.

"Yes."

Her voice was an old linen thread of sound—faint, fragile, ready to snap apart.

"They promised that you'd be born again, didn't they?"

"Yes."

"But you always wondered how you could tell if they were telling you the truth. If you come back in the body of an infant, not knowing you'd ever lived before, let alone who you were specifically—how could you ever prove they were right?"

"Yes," she said, "yes, that's it! Charlatans, every one of them!"

She tried to look at him through the film of tears that filled her eyes. It was like trying to look through a rain-spattered window. His face blurred and wavered in her sight. *But, he understood! God! He understood what she'd been through!* She felt a flood of guilt. She'd misjudged him completely. She had denied him. She had struck at him in anger to cause him pain.

"What . . . what do you promise me?" she managed to ask.

"Nothing."

She heard him say the word, and her heart sank.

"I *promise* nothing. Yet I can tell you that it is possible for an adult—one of the spiritually elite—to take over the body of a young person. To take it over completely and fully and totally! Just as Lisa Fialho did! Just as I did!"

He paused for a moment, long enough to move so close to her that he was almost touching her skirt. She had to crane her neck to look up at him.

"If you have courage," he added. "Do you have enough courage, Mrs. Flint?"

Augustus James would have liked him, she knew. He was saying what her husband had always said: *You have to have guts enough to reach out and take what you want! You get nothing for nothing! Damn the consequences! Let others look out for themselves!*

Yes! Augustus James would certainly have approved of Michael Hietala!

The morning light came in through the expanse of glass window wall, striking him from behind so that a nimbus of light lay around his head and a burst of shining sunlight lay on his shoulders, and his face was arrogant and strong and kind and loving and beautiful, and—*Oh, God! What a lovely thing he was offering her!*

The old lady reached out with both of her hands,

taking his right hand in hers, bringing his hand toward her face. She lowered her face so that her lips pressed against the skin of his hand. Tears ran down from her eyes to wet her cheeks and wet the back of his hand and her hands holding his, and she cried because it was all so lovely and the rat gnawings of fear inside her would go away, and . . . *Oh, God! it was happening! He hadn't come along too late!*

CHAPTER TWO

They sat in the back of the Bentley, in the high, soft
seats that were so unlike the low, deep seats of Ameri-
can cars. The automobile moved quietly, at even
speed, along the wide, curving stretch of Route 128.
Mrs. Flint was on the left, her cane in her left hand,
her right hand touching Michael Hietala's left hand
on the seat beside her. There was a great soaring happiness in the old woman.

They'd come out of Adam's Cove, through Harbortown, where the beltline, the divided Route 128 began, and they were moving south, keeping in the right
lane at a sedate fifty-five miles an hour. The pickup
trucks and the Volkswagens passed them on the left
doing seventy and seventy-five miles an hour. For the
first five miles, the traffic was light. Then the cars
ahead of them slowed to a crawl in a long tight line.

Through the windshield, Hietala could see the
flashing blue lights of the Massachusetts highway patrol cars and a group of autos pulled into a cluster off
to the left side of the road along the grass of the highway divider.

Mrs. Flint leaned forward and asked, "What is it,
Arnold?" and her chauffeur said without turning his
head, "It's an accident, Mrs. Flint."

"It looks bad."

"Yes, ma'am."

Highway patrol cars were spaced along the side of the road. The police were standing along the road, keeping traffic moving, jamming it into a single lane beginning a hundred yards or more before the accident. The Bentley allowed a car to slide in to the right and move ahead of it.

There was glass all over the highway, and thick streaks of rubber were laid down on the cement. The Bentley came up to the accident and moved past it. The wreck had been a late-model sports coupe. It was overturned now, lying on its crumpled roof, the side pillars collapsed so that it lay squat and heavy, its tires ugly in the air. One wheel still spun. It lay diagonally across the grass of the divider strip.

To one side of it, parked at an angle, was the white ambulance with a broad orange stripe around it and the name of the hospital on one side. Its double rear doors were open. A stretcher, still unopened, lay on the ground by the opened doors. The two ambulance crewmen stood beside the front doors.

Small flames were licking around the engine compartment of the overturned car. Two police officers were spraying streams from fire extinguishers onto the flames.

They saw the white-coated figure of a man leaning over a body on the ground, pulling a sheet over the body, and then they were past the accident and beginning to move freely. Suddenly, Mrs. Flint said, "Arnold, stop the car. Pull over to the side of the road."

The Bentley moved out of the traffic and off to the grass on the right side of the road and came to a stop.

"That was a girl," said Mrs. Flint.

Michael didn't understand.

"That was a young girl," Mrs. Flint said again. "I saw her clearly."

"Yes?"

"She's dead," Mrs. Flint said.

Michael looked at her.

"You've got to help."

A highway patrolman came up to the car. Arnold slid down his window.

"You can't stay here," the cop said. "Let's keep the traffic moving."

The old lady leaned forward and raised her voice. "I'm Sarah Cameron Flint, officer. Does that mean anything to you?"

"Yes, ma'am," the cop said. "I'm sorry I bothered you."

"We'll try not to block the highway."

He touched the brim of his cap and walked away.

"I'm not a doctor," Michael said.

"She's past a doctor's help," said Mrs. Flint, settling back in her seat. "I saw him pull the sheet over her face. The girl is dead."

"What do you want me to do?"

"Bring her back to life."

"Mrs. Flint . . . "

Stubbornly she cut off his protest. "No," she said firmly. "If you can do what you've been telling me you can do, then I want proof of it. Bring that girl back to life, Michael!"

He was watching her face. She wasn't looking at him. She was staring fixedly ahead of her, her small, wrinkled features set and hard. He cursed silently, not letting his emotions show.

"Very well," he said, and opened the door to his right and got out of the car. He left the door open and began to walk back toward the accident, swearing out loud now that she couldn't hear him.

Of all the goddamn times for something like this to happen! Everything had gone exactly the way he'd planned it. The old lady had been like putty in his hands. Especially at the end, after she'd broken down and cried, and then, when she'd taken his hand in hers and kissed it, he knew that he had her. Goddamnit! He had her!

She had stayed another hour. They'd had coffee together. She'd told him about her husband, Augustus James, and how much like him the old man had been.

She hadn't wanted to leave him so soon, but she was very tired and wanted to go back to her estate in Hamilton and nap for a while and then talk to him again. He'd agreed to go along with her. Arnold and the Bentley had been waiting outside.

And now this! Of all the damn times for an accident to have happened! And how the hell did she get the idea that he could bring dead people back to life? It wasn't at all what he'd told her!

Well, maybe he could fake it. Maybe he could put on an act and come back to the old lady and tell her that because the girl hadn't known him while she was alive he couldn't do anything for her.

He knew she'd be watching him. The act would have to be good. But he was good at that. Good at putting on the religious act. Hell! Four years of ass-kissing that fucking revivalist, evangelical preacher had taught him everything there was to know about it. He'd even been ordained by the Reverend Orbus Killigrew; he'd conducted services for him. Coat off, collar torn open, shirtsleeves rolled up, standing on the rough, wooden planks of the temporary platform

under the sagging, worn canvas of the big tent,
torches blazing away and adding to the heat of the
Southern summer night. His voice exhorting and
shouting and quoting the Bible and praying and exhorting them again and screaming at them, then his
voice dropping and cajoling them and flattering them
and scorning them and scathing them with the flay of
his accusations—oh, yes! He knew how to preach to a
mob!

And he knew how to preach to just one person, too,
because that's what you did on television. In those
small, Southern television stations on Sunday morn-
ings. That camera was one person. One man. One
woman. You talked right into the eye of that lens with
the little red light glowing on top of the camera to
show it was the one taking your picture, ready to turn
to the second camera the minute the light winked out
and the other red light winked on.

You didn't shout and you didn't exhort as you did in
the tents. You talked quietly and then louder, but not
too loud, and you got down on one knee, the sweat
pouring off your face so they could see it, and the
Bible open in the flat of your left hand and you held
out your other hand to the camera and you asked it,
you pleaded with it, you prayed with it, with that
lens!

Well, it might not be exactly the same thing up here
in the North, in New England. But, basically, it was
just being able to put on a good act, and he could put
on a good act, certainly good enough to fool an old
lady like her.

He crossed the road, dodging between the slow-
moving cars, and came over to the accident, the police
letting him go through the cordon. They'd seen him
come from the Bentley. They knew he was with Sarah

Cameron Flint. The name meant something to them. He wondered about it, but only for a second.

As he came up to the wreck, the stench of raw, spilled gasoline filled his nose, along with the smell of the fire and the smell of the extinguisher fluid and the smell of the crushed, wrenched metal. The car had skidded off the highway at high speed. From the length of the skid marks, the girl must have been driving at better than a hundred miles an hour. He guessed that a tire had blown, because that's the way the skid marks looked. The car had hit the slope of the divider strip and flipped over and skidded on its rooftop, the columns collapsing, glass spraying out, the car tearing up the grass and the turf.

As he came up beside the white-sheeted body, the intern got to his feet, his stethoscope hanging from his neck. The intern had a scaly, thin face, still pocked with acne scars, and a suspicious look.

Michael Hietala looked down on the sheet covering the girl's body.

The intern stared at his bearded face and said, "You a preacher?"

"Yes."

"You don't want to pull back that sheet," the intern said. "She's pretty bad. She went out through the windshield when it went over. It cut her up pretty bad."

"I don't need to look at her," Hietala said, and knelt beside the body on one knee. He rubbed his hands together slowly, working the bones of his right hand with the thumb of his left.

Make it look good, he told himself. *You know that old bitch is watching you!*

Kneeling, his right knee on the grass, his left leg bent, his left arm supported by his left thigh, he clasped his hands together. He closed his eyes and lifted his head and looked upwards.

It isn't enough, he thought, even as he did so. *She won't be satisfied with what you're doing. You damn well better make it look better, or you've lost her.*

Goddamnit, he couldn't lose her now. Not when he'd put so much time and money into it. Every cent he had. Not now! He couldn't lose her now.

What you've got to do is the laying on of the hands, he thought. That always got them. That was the best act he had. It worked every time. They'd broken down and cried and screamed *hallelujah* and come shuffling and then running up to the altar to throw themselves down and scream out their faith. And the poor, fucking, ignorant cripples that came to him for the laying on of the hands! Some of them in wheelchairs, some of them carried by their relatives.

The fervor and the fever had worked in them too. One girl had been brought to him on a homemade stretcher improvised from an old camp cot. She'd looked at him out of her wasted face, her eyes enormous with fear and faith and hope and belief, and when he'd prayed over her, she'd cried aloud and screamed, *I believe! I believe!* and then, she'd scrabbled around and clawed at him for support and raised herself to her feet and stood there on her wasted, twisted legs, her thin face, exultant, shining, in pain but *standing. Yes, standing!* While all her relatives shouted hosannas and *Jesus. Lord!*

She hadn't been the only one. God, but they could talk themselves into anything! He was good at making them believe in him.

Well, he didn't have a crowd going for him now. He didn't have a tent or flaring torches or a two-hour exhortation to bring them up to fever pitch.

And this girl was dead. Not crippled. Not maimed. Not lame or burnt like some of them or harelipped— but *dead*. Goddamnit! What do you do when they're already dead!

Now there was an audience of only one. One old woman with a tough, sharp, shrewd mind, who might have gone overboard when he'd had her alone to work on. But they were out in the open air now, and there were cops all around, and the intern and the ambulance crew and the people in the passing cars.

Play to her, he told himself. *Forget the others. Play to her. This time it counts. Try the laying on of the hands. You've got nothing to lose.*

So he put his other knee on the ground and bent over the body under the white sheet. He put one hand on the mound where the head should be. He felt for the roundness of the skull, ignoring the red blood that had soaked through the whiteness of the sheet and put his left hand on it, feeling the wet stickiness of the blood.

He put his right hand on her groin. He hadn't meant to touch her there. He'd meant to put it on her waist. He could feel the pubic mound under the sheet, but he didn't want to move his hand. They wouldn't know why he was doing it and it would look bad if he moved his hand. It would look awkward and things had to look smooth. Now that his hands were in place, he bent his head. Without knowing why, he closed his eyes.

He envisioned the scene.

The car, the smoke in the air, the police standing around watching him, the intern standing beside him watching him, the ambulance driver and his assistant standing now beside the open rear doors of the white and orange ambulance, watching him. The cars moving slowly past on the highway, the people in them straining for a glimpse, watching him.

Everyone was watching him, wondering what he was doing, and only Mrs. Flint knew. Only Mrs. Flint, sure that he could bring a girl back from the dead.

That was the revelation that came to him. The old woman really thought he could do it!

Or she wouldn't have sent him out to do it!

It isn't so bad after all, he thought. *Just make it look good, and maybe you can get away with it.*

He felt the sun beating down on him, and even with his eyes closed, he was aware of the brightness and the cleanness of the day.

What a hell of a day to die, he thought. There was so much life all around. There was life in the leaves of the trees, in the grass under his knees, in the soil, in the breeze that came in from the ocean only a few miles away, still rich with the smell of salt and fish and seaweed. There was life everywhere.

And then it began.

He felt the feeling in his hands first. Like the faint tickling of a tiny electric current, and the feeling, the trembling spread up his arms and reached his chest and then his head, and it went down his thighs and his calves and into his feet. It came back out of the ground and went through him in alternating waves, and he felt good. God! He felt so good and so alive and so powerful with life! There was life everywhere, and it was flowing through him and flowing out of his hands, flowing into the body under his hands, flowing into the girl through her head and through her groin and flowing in a powerful, pulsating aura all around him.

Everything was light. Pure light. White light. Intense light. Light so bright that even with his eyes closed, the white light hurt.

Light and life. Life and light. And clean. And pure. And good.

There were no words in his mind. There was no thought. Only feeling. Only the feeling that had taken over his body and made it one with the clean, pure, bright, white luminescence that shone on him and through him and from him.

It went on and on, until finally he felt a trembling in the still, dead body underneath his hands, and he knew, without any surprise, that the body was not dead anymore and that the girl had come back to life, had stirred under his hands. He knew! He knew what he had done!

When she screamed, he wasn't surprised. When her body moved so violently that his hands were thrown off her, he accepted it because he knew it was going to happen.

She screamed again and sat up. The sheet fell away from her face. Bone showed through the strip of flesh where the glass of the broken windshield had slashed her face. Blood was still pouring out of her torn scalp, out of the vicious wounds on her neck, from the broken, smashed nose, from the gaps in her mouth and gums where her front teeth had been, and from the crushed skull of her forehead.

There was blood, and there were her screams and there were the shouts of the intern and the policemen all yelling at the same time.

The intern was shouting for the ambulance crew to get over to her with the stretcher, and he had flung himself at his black satchel, tearing it open, searching for the hypodermic needle and the vial of morphine.

The ambulance crew came running up with the rolled stretcher, fumbling at the straps, ripping them open, snapping the stretcher apart.

"Careful with her! Goddamn it! Be careful with her!" the intern shouted at the ambulance crew.

The girl tried to fling herself about. The two crewmen threw themselves down on her and held her down. The intern ran over, grabbed her right arm and shoved the needle into the vein of her elbow and pumped the clear fluid into her until the glass tube was empty, and all the time she was still screaming.

Michael Hietala got to his feet and walked away from them.

He walked across the road, the cars stopping for him. He walked slowly on the grass on the far side of the highway back to the Bentley. His hands were bloody. He took his white handkerchief out of the hip pocket of his light gray slacks, staining the pocket with the blood, and wiped at the blood with the handkerchief.

He got into the car and shut the door and leaned back in the seat.

Sarah Cameron Flint stared at him, crying. He sat there, in the backseat of the Bentley, totally and utterly exhausted, stunned, drained.

Arnold started the Bentley and moved it onto the road and down the highway.

Sarah Flint had turned so that she could look at Michael Hietala. She looked at his bearded profile, at the dark, wavy hair that swept down over his ears and over the collar of his jacket. She took in the bent, arrogant nose, the firm, well-defined lips, the short, jutting beard. She saw the pallor of his skin. It was as if there were no blood in him, as if, under his skin, there was only a ghostly glowing of light.

She wanted to touch his hand, but she was afraid to. She wanted to speak to him, but she was afraid to disturb him. She wanted to say his name in awe.

Most of all, she wanted to cry out, "I believe! Now, I truly believe!"

Exhausted, Michael lay back in the deep, soft seat of the Bentley. He was aware of Sarah Flint at his side. He was frightened by what he'd done. Images raced chaotically through his mind. Then the voice came to him, gentle, with ineffable kindness and deep love, and even though he'd never heard it before, he knew immediately who it was and knew that he'd spent his life longing to hear that one, particular voice.

—*Hello, brother.*

He wasn't surprised, not since he'd waited so long to hear it, even though he hadn't been aware of waiting.

—*Hello, Aaron,* he said in his mind. *You've waited a long time.*

—*I had to wait. You weren't ready for me until now.*

Michael said, *Aaron, I'm sorry for what happened.* And Aaron said, *No, you're not, Michael. You never were. You had to find out if you had the power.*

—*I didn't know I had the power!*

—*But you didn't stop,* Aaron reminded him gently and without resentment. —*Even when you could have.*

—*I was three years old! For God's sake! What does a three-year-old child know?*

—*It doesn't matter.*

—*It mattered to me! I remembered! I couldn't get it out of my head for years! You don't know how I suffered!*

He heard the reproval in Aaron's voice. *Oh, Mi-*

chael, please! I'm your twin! The other half of the same egg. I know you! You're part of me, just as I'm part of you.

—But I have the power, Michael said stubbornly. *That makes us different.*

—*No*, said Aaron, *because it's not the only power.*

Michael thought about it for a minute.

He said: *I can kill. Does that mean you can heal?*

—*More*, said Aaron. *I bring life. You saw it.*

—*And you've been with me all these years?*

—*From time to time*, said Aaron.

Michael thought of the old man mending nets. He hadn't thought of him in twenty-seven years.

—*The old man*, he said, knowing Aaron would know whom he meant.

—*He's one.*

—*Who were the others?*

—*Don't you know?*

—*No. I don't know.* But he did and waited for Aaron to name them.

—*What did you call them just a few minutes ago?* Aaron asked. *The poor, fucking, ignorant cripples who came to you for the laying on of hands?*

—*The girl on the camp cot?*

—*She was one of them. There were so many, weren't there, Michael? Hundreds of them in just four years.*

—*I thought—hell! I don't know what I thought!*

—*What do you think now?*

—*All right*, said Michael, defensively. *So it was you. Why?*

—*Because you kill.*

—*And that's the only reason?*

—*Of course not*, said Aaron. *I can only live through you, and then only for minutes. I want more.*

—*Say it*, said Michael savagely. *You want my body!*

—*Only to share*, said Aaron. *Will you let me? You need me, Michael.*

—*No! No, I don't. I don't want you! Go away, Aaron. Go away!*

He pushed the voice into the darkness of his mind. He thought Aaron would protest, but he faded away without a word of remonstrance. It bothered him that Aaron would go so easily. Now he knew that Aaron would be back. He would have to be on his guard against Aaron.

Sarah Flint saw the tense lines on Michael's face. She wanted to stroke them away, but she didn't dare touch him. If only she could hold him in her arms, she thought, she would be completely happy.

CHAPTER THREE

Mrs. Flint said, "You must take care of him."

"Yes," said Lisa. "I will."

"Have you looked at him? Have you really looked at him?"

"Not since he came back."

"He's not the same."

"In what way?"

"I don't know," said Mrs. Flint, her small, old face filled with concern. "I can't put my finger on it. It's just that he's not the same at all. I only met him this morning, so I really don't know him well. But he's not the same as he was this morning. He doesn't say anything, for one thing."

They looked out through the window onto the sundeck as if they could see him standing there. The deck was empty.

"I wish you'd been there," Mrs. Flint said. "I was blessed. I was present at a miracle."

Lisa waited for her to go on, but the old woman fell silent, wandering back in her mind to what she had witnessed.

After they'd driven away from the accident, Michael had been silent for a long time, and Mrs. Flint hadn't said anything. When the car was almost to the Hamilton town line, he spoke. "I'd like to go back," he'd said quietly, and Mrs. Flint had told the chauffeur to turn around and they'd driven back to Adam's Cove and the house that was The Church of the Second Life.

Michael had gotten out of the car without a word and had gone into the house and upstairs. After a while, he'd come down again, dressed only in shorts and sandals and gone out onto the sundeck to stand and stare at the ocean. Then he'd gone down the steps to the path cut along the cliff edge and made his way down to the small, pebbled beach at the foot of the cliff to stand among the boulders at the water's edge.

"Would you like some coffee?" Lisa asked.

"Tea, if you please."

"You look tired," Lisa said. "Don't you think you should lie down?"

"After I have the tea," Mrs. Flint said. She was sitting on the couch. "You're right. I'm very tired. I haven't had my nap."

She began to cry. She took a small handkerchief from a pocket of her dress and pressed it to her face. She cried into it as quietly as she could. Lisa went into the kitchen and made a pot of tea and brought it out to Mrs. Flint.

The old woman was staring out at the empty sundeck.

"He hasn't come back," she said.

"He will," said Lisa.

"It's been several hours. Does he do that often? Go off by himself like that?"

"Oh, yes," said Lisa, lying. "I think you ought to go upstairs and lie down."

"As soon as I finish my tea," said Mrs. Flint.

In a while, she put down the teacup and said, "Will

you help me? I don't think I can make it by myself. Stairs are very difficult for me."

Lisa helped her to her feet. Holding on to the girl's arm and with the help of her cane, Mrs. Flint moved slowly up the stairs, stepping on each one first with one foot and then bringing the other up beside it, then taking the next step the same way. It took her a long time.

When Mrs. Flint sat down on the bed, Lisa knelt and took off the old lady's shoes and rubbed her feet. The old lady touched Lisa on the top of her blond head in a gentle gesture. She let Lisa help her lie back on the pillows.

"There are pills in my purse," she said. "I can't sleep without them."

Lisa brought her a pill and a glass of water and the old lady sat up and swallowed and lay down again.

"You must take care of him," Sarah Flint said, as if she had forgotten she'd said it before.

"I will."

"You promise?"

"I promise."

"Is . . . is this the bed he sleeps on?" Sarah Flint asked, letting her eyes close.

"Yes."

"He really does sleep on this bed?"

"Yes," said Lisa. "This is his bed."

The old woman smiled and after a few minutes the smile went away from her face as her mouth relaxed and she was asleep. She had wanted to put into words what it was she felt about Michael Hietala, but she couldn't, and anyway, it didn't make much difference.

Lisa went downstairs and out onto the far end of the sundeck. Leaning over the railing, she could see Michael standing on the rocks at the edge of the beach, the waves foaming white around the base of the rocks. From above, the perspective was sharply distorted; she could see the top of his head and his shoulders.

She went down the steps to the path and down the path to the pebbled beach and went over to him, slipping on the wet rocks, scrambling to keep herself from falling down.

When she was beside him, she put her arm around his waist and hugged him.

"You did it, Michael!" she said, exultantly. "You really did it!"

His body felt cold to her, even through his thin sweater.

"I didn't think you could. I really didn't. I was worried all the time. But you brought it off! I don't think anyone but you could have done it. Not in one session."

Her arm didn't feel comfortable. He felt different to her. She pulled away and asked, "Michael? What's the matter with you?"

He didn't answer. His head didn't move, his body didn't respond to her touch. He stared out at the horizon but he didn't see the horizon. Or the ocean. Or the waves. He didn't feel the sea breeze.

Lisa moved around so that she could look full into his face. It was pale; his features were fixed and tight. His eyes held an expression so deep and so lost that she wanted to cry for him.

She said: "Michael? What the hell happened while you were gone? The old lady tried to tell me some crazy story about an accident and a dead girl and how you put your hands on her and brought her back to life. She didn't make any sense. What really happened, Michael?"

His body shivered. She touched his face. It was cold, so cold that her fingers felt the chill coming off his skin. She moved a step away from him, almost slipping on the rocks.

"Michael . . ." she began, and knew that she shouldn't talk to him, that he was to be left alone, because whatever it was he was feeling, there was no place in it for her. The feeling frightened her.

"Michael . . ." she said one more time and felt as if she were committing a terrible, sacrilegious act by saying his name aloud to him.

She wanted to talk to him, to let him know how excited she'd been when the car had come back to the house and she'd seen him get out and seen the old woman get out right after he did and she knew then that everything had gone well.

Only now the excited feeling was gone; some of his coldness had gotten into her. The chill seeped into her bones, making them feel cold and brittle. She didn't know why she should be so frightened, but she was. She knew that she shouldn't be close to him, that he should be left alone. After another moment she turned and went back up the pebbled beach, her shoes slipping on the small, smooth stones and made her way up the narrow path to the top of the cliff and up the steps to the sundeck and into the house.

2.

Long after it was dark, Sarah Cameron Flint awoke and washed her face. Lisa helped her downstairs and into the car, and she was driven off by Arnold.

Michael came up from the beach. He stood at the railing of the sundeck where he had stood that morning. He watched the moon rise slowly out of the water where the sun had risen earlier that day to make dawn. Now the moon was high in the night sky; an enormous, round ball of white light on which faint, gray lines made a semblance of features. The moon was bright. It was very bright.

After a long time, he came inside and went upstairs and showered. He put on jeans and a navy blue turtle-neck sweater and loafers and came downstairs.

Lisa asked, "Where are you going, Michael?" almost in fright as he went out the front door, but he didn't answer her.

He hadn't heard her. He hadn't heard anything all afternoon, except for the roaring in his mind and the tumbling of thoughts and the memory of the intense, white, bright, burning light on his eyelids and in his brain. He had heard nothing all afternoon, not since he'd gotten back into the Bentley after wiping the blood off his hands.

He hadn't been aware of standing at the railing or of standing on the rocks at the edge of the water or even of watching the moon come up.

When the darkness came, the bright light left his mind along with the festering, kaleidoscope images swarming maggot-like in his brain: the rich, thick, red blood seeping through the white sheet; the curves of the covered body; the feel of his hands on the smashed skull and on the soft, dead flesh under the white sheet covering her pubic mound; the dark blue uniform trousers and gray, epauletted shirts of the Massachusetts state troopers; the twisted, overturned, crushed metal of the sports coupe, the glass sharded and splintered on the roadway and on the grass; the white ambulance with the broad orange horizontal stripe around it, its rear doors patiently open, expecting a victim, waiting for a corpse; the girl sitting up, the sheet falling away from her flayed, distorted face, the white bone and the red blood and the pink tissue of her torn mouth. And always, always, the screams coming out of the gaping holes ripped from her gums.

The images and the sounds were gone now as he left the house. The soft, absorbing blackness of the night cradled Adam's Cove like the deepest of all fogs, curling into every crevasse. His feet crunched on the gravel driveway as he walked to the garage and got into the Toyota coupe. He backed out of the garage, turned in the drive, and roared out into the street.

3.

Adam's Cove is shaped roughly like a diving tern, its head pointed toward the southeast. It is almost an island, but because of its link to Harbortown by a narrow stretch of land, it is a peninsula.

Adam's Cove forms a protective arm of land that makes Harbortown one of the finest small-boat anchorages along the Atlantic seacoast. The inner harbor of Harbortown consists mostly of piers and wharves from which the trawlers and draggers go out into the North Atlantic, and two- and three-story wooden frame houses in which the fishermen and dockworkers and fishpackers work. There is a three block Main Street, two cathedrals and several churches, and bars and restaurants along the waterfront.

Harbortown occupies a large land mass, extending further inland, only here the land is sparsely settled because of the salt marshes. Where the land rises in hills, the base is mostly solid granite, almost impossible to build on.

To the north of Adam's Cove, connected to it by a causeway, is Turtle Neck, an artist's colony which is empty most of the winter months and swollen with tourists in the summer.

On the far side of Harbortown, to the northwest, there is a great bay and along the shore of this bay are scattered small towns: Lawton's Race, Bay Cove, Barrett's Cove, Gale Harbor, Crab Inlet, and Pinchon's Bay. Most of the people living in these villages are descended from the original settlers, except in Lawton's Race. There most of the houses are large and expensive; the very rich have moved to Lawton's Race because of the yacht anchorages and the enormous estuary that connects Hereford Bay with the Atlantic Ocean just to the south of the main part of Harbortown.

All of this area is called Cape Mary. There are a great number of cemeteries in Cape Mary. Each village has at least two; some have as many as six. The towns date back to 1630 and 1635, and in more than 300 years a great number of people died and had to be buried.

There are more cemeteries in Harbortown than in any of the other villages. For one thing Harbortown is larger, and also most of Harbortown's population are fishermen. Almost half its population are Italian or Portuguese who settled there to work on the boats. Many of them died at sea, and there is a memorial stone in a cemetery for each one of them.

In Harbortown, the street along the waterfront is Atlantic Avenue. There are a lot of bars on Atlantic Avenue. The trawlermen and dragger crews go to the bars in the late afternoon and early evening. Some of them stay until late.

So do the few girls that frequent these bars. Most of the girls are young; the dropout rate in the Harbortown High School is over thirty percent. There isn't much for young people to do in Harbortown. The young men go out on the fishing boats if they are lucky. Or they work as lumpers, moving fish from the ships into the packing and quick freeze plants and moving the frozen fish cartons onto trailer trucks. The girls go to work in the few small stores, or they get married and then go to work in the fish-packing plants.

Most of them don't work. The unemployment rate in Harbortown is high. But somehow the girls all seem to have a dollar or two, and there is always Rosario's or The Dolphin or The Crow's Nest or Jack's.

Rosario's is a small bar on Atlantic Avenue, in the middle of the waterfront area. It has a twenty-seven-inch color television set mounted over the bar so that it can be seen by everyone in the room. There is a long, dark mahogany bar along one wall. The booths are along the opposite wall.

There are almost always girls in Rosario's.

CHAPTER FOUR

Mary Palumbo saw Michael Hietala come into Rosario's and stand in the doorway and look around. It was dim in the entranceway where he stood. She saw that he was tall and that his hair was dark and that his sweater and jeans were dark. The small light in the entrance shone on his bearded face.

It looked to her as if he were staring across the room at her; that he'd picked her out. She tried to move her eyes away and couldn't. Not only couldn't, but didn't want to.

Her boyfriend, Joe Balzarini, sat next to her. Ruthie Olivieri sat in the booth across from her, next to Vito DeLuca, who said protestingly, "Hey, Mary, you're not listenin' to me."

"I'm listenin'," she said, her eyes still on the doorway where Michael Hietala was standing. She felt her chest tighten. It was hard to breathe. She felt a warmth in her. Christ! It was as though he were touching her with his fingers, stroking her slowly across her stomach. She felt herself get wet between her legs.

Ruthie Olivieri put her hand on Vito's shoulder and slid it down his arm so that her palm was on the back of his hand.

"C'mon, Vito, don't spoil the story. T'hell with her! You know Mary."

Vito made an expression of disgust.

"What the hell," he said sourly, "she ain't my girl."

"Look, just tell the story or shut up," Joe Balzarini said. He didn't like other guys making cracks about Mary. He turned to her and said, "You want another beer, Mary?"

She took her eyes away from Michael Hietala.

"Yeah," she said. She was sitting on the outside of the booth. She got to her feet. Joe started to get out of the booth. Mary put a hand on his shoulder and pushed him down.

"I'll get the beer," she said. "You want one, too?"

"Yeah. You got enough money?"

"Gimme a buck."

Joe took a dollar from his pocket. Mary took it from him and walked away.

"What's the matter with that broad?" Vito asked.

"Tell your fuckin' story," Joe said curtly. "Leave her alone."

None of them looked after her as she walked away from the booth. Vito started on his story again.

She walked past the bar to the doorway where Michael was standing and came up to him. She smiled at him. She knew she looked good when she smiled. She had straight white teeth and long black hair and her teeth looked good against her olive skin. It looked to her as if he smiled back at her.

Jesus, she thought, *the son of a bitch doesn't know what he's doin' to me with that smile. He's turning me on!*

"You got a cigarette?" she asked.

She stood directly in front of him, hipslung, her weight on one leg. She knew she looked good standing that way. It showed off the lines of her body. She had good legs. Her head was cocked to one side so that her long hair could fall in a straight line on that side of her head. She thought it made her look sexy.

He took a pack from his pocket and flipped it so that a cigarette jumped partway out.

She took the cigarette.

"Got a light?"

He lit it for her. In the flare of the flame she saw his face and the deep brown of his eyes staring into her. He wasn't smiling at all. He was just staring at her as if he owned her. It gave her a funny feeling. She'd never had anyone look at her like that before. She wanted him to put his hands on her. She wanted to feel helpless under his hands.

She said, "You wanna buy me a drink?"

"You old enough to drink?"

"I'm here, ain't I?"

He shrugged.

"I asked if you wanna buy me a drink."

"Not here."

"I don't care. I don't like it here so much anyhow. Let's go."

They went out through the door. Only Joe Balzarini saw her leave. He hid the quick, hot spurt of violent anger that arose in him and tried to push away the dirty words that he was thinking about her. *Screw her!* he thought savagely.

Vito went on with his story. When he finished, Ruthie Olivieri laughed, even though it wasn't a funny story.

Vito looked at Joe Balzarini's tight face and said, "Hey, Joe, whatsa matter? You didn't think it was funny, huh?"

Joe got to his feet, pushing himself out of the booth.

"No, it wasn't funny," he said, his voice hard and tight. "You tell lousy stories."

He walked away from the booth.

"What the fuck's the matter with him?" Vito was puzzled.

"He's sore," said Ruthie. "Mary didn't come back."

Balzarini walked out of Rosario's and stood on the sidewalk looking around. There was only one sidewalk. Across the street were the piers. He tried to see where Mary might have gone. There were two lumpers lounging against the brick wall that was the front of Rosario's. He'd seen them around but he didn't know them.

"You lookin' for Mary?"

Balzarini didn't say anything.

"She went off with another guy."

"Fuck off," said Balzarini angrily.

"You losin' your touch, Joe?" said the other lumper. He laughed and pounded his hand on his friend's arm. "Maybe you too young for her? Maybe she found herself a man, huh?"

Balzarini turned around and swung at him. His right fist smashed into the man's face, slamming him back against the brick wall. The other lumper hit Joe a backhanded blow across the bridge of his nose, blinding him for a moment, and then the first lumper came off the wall, shaking his head to clear it. He hit Joe behind the ear. Joe staggered backward, the two of them on top of him, hitting him with short, wild punches in the chest, in the ribs, in the gut, in his face. They hit him as hard as they could. He went down.

They moved away, thinking the fight was over. Joe struggled to his knees, then his feet, pure black anger filling his mind, not caring if there were twenty of them. All he wanted to do was to hurt. As he got up, he reached into his back pocket.

"Son of a bitch got a knife!"

"Hit him!" yelled the second lumper. He swung a heavy, booted foot. The toe of the workshoe caught Joe in the chest, knocking him back.

Joe slashed upward with the knife. The fishknife blade slid easily through the workpants into the man's calf and slashed out again in a long, gutting stroke.

"He's crazy! Kill the son of a bitch!"

The first lumper picked up a broken brick lying in the gutter and swung it at Balzarini's head. The brick landed just above Joe's ear, making a heavy, ugly sound, and he fell. His eyes closed, his knees folded, the knife fell out of his hand. He fell without making any attempt to break the fall, his head striking the concrete of the sidewalk solidly.

Panting, the two lumpers stood over him, breathing in short, deep breaths. The one who hit him with the brick looked down at his slashed leg. He felt the wetness of blood running down his calf.

"The prick stuck his knife in me," he said in surprise.

The other lumper knelt down. He hadn't liked the way Balzarini fell. He touched Joe's face. Joe's head flopped from one side to the other when he put his hand on it.

"I think you killed him," he said.

"He deserved it!"

"I ain't kiddin'. I think you really killed him."

The first lumper looked down on Balzarini's body. He's just a kid, he thought. He ain't no more'n nineteen, twenty. What the fuck's he doin' gettin' in a fight with the two of us?

"Holy Mother of God," he said in fright. He shook his head to clear it. "He ain't dead. No way!"

His friend put his fingers into the wound on the side of Balzarini's head, just above his left temple. His fingers went deeply into the blood.

"Shit!" he said. "You smashed his head in!"

He got to his feet.

He looked down at Joe Balzarini's body. He shook his head.

"The dumb fuck," he said, "what'd he want to start a fight for?"

2.

She'd never made love in a cemetery before. They had stopped at a liquor store and he'd bought a couple of pints of whiskey. She liked the bite of the hard liquor. It burned going down, but God, the warmth spread all the way through her!

She'd known from the beginning that they weren't going to go to another bar for a drink. She didn't want to anyhow. What she wanted was to get into bed with him. He'd told her his name was Michael. She liked that. She liked the sound of the name—*Michael*. She'd said it over a few times to herself to try it out. Once she'd said it aloud: "Michael," and he'd looked at her, but he hadn't answered her.

She thought he was going to take her to his apartment. He looked like he had his own place. She was surprised when they headed out into the country after he'd gotten the liquor and gotten back into the Toyota. She really thought he was going to take her to his place, and then she figured that he must be married. That didn't bother her. It just meant that he couldn't take her home, but she didn't care.

What she wanted was to feel him inside her, to feel his naked body against hers, his naked loins pressing hard against hers and him pounding into her so that she was helpless against his thrust, spread apart and hurting with that sweet, hot, painful pleasure that she loved so much.

When they turned in at the drive of the West Harbortown Cemetery, she giggled and said, "You sure we ain't gonna bother them?"

"We won't bother them."

"You sure as hell talk a lot, don't you?"

He hadn't answered her.

She didn't like that. She liked a man who talked. But at the same time, she liked his silence. It kind of put her in her place, and none of the boys she'd ever gone with had ever been able to do that. None of them. Not even Joe Balzarini, and he was the toughest one of them all.

She giggled when she thought about Joe. He must have been madder than hell once he realized she wasn't coming back. Serves him right! He didn't own her. He acted like he did. Screw him! She'd finally found herself a man. Eighteen and he . . .

Michael, she said his name again in her mind . . . he must be in his thirties at least. Christ! He acted like a man, too! He didn't take any lip from her the way the others did. She wondered if he'd hit her. Somehow the idea excited her. Without having to touch herself, she knew how wet she was between her legs. Her panties were damp and when she moved her legs, they chafed slightly.

If he hit her, she hoped he wouldn't mark her up too much. She didn't want to have to explain to her father why she had bruises on her face. But if he slapped her a couple of times—he could do that easy without marking her up or hurting her too much. She thought she'd like that. The thought made her feel weak and helpless. It was a feeling she hardly ever got, and it turned her on so much that she could hardly wait until they got deep into the cemetery so she could get out of the car and take her damn clothes off.

She wanted to be naked, to lie on the grass without any clothes on and have him lower his weight onto her, to feel the whole length of his naked body on top of hers in the darkness.

Michael stopped the car. Mary Palumbo looked around. They were at the far end of the cemetery. All around were headstones and grave markers. Some of them were over eight feet tall and some were only a foot or two high.

"Here?" she asked.

Michael nodded. Mary got out of the car, swaying, leaning against the roof of the coupe for a moment. She hoped she hadn't had too much to drink. Goddamnit! She wanted to enjoy this. It was going to be the best lay she'd ever had. She knew that. She'd known it from the minute she'd seen him looking at her in Rosario's.

Michael got out of the car on the far side and walked around to her.

She turned her face up so that he could kiss it. He put one arm around her waist and the feel of the muscles in his forearm and biceps was like warm steel holding her in unbreakable bonds. His other hand came up and found her throat. It closed around her slender neck.

For a moment a stab of fear went through her. His hand was big enough and strong enough to snap her neck or to choke her just by closing his fingers so that she wouldn't be able to breathe.

"Hey," she said, startled.

Then his lips touched hers. His hand on her throat was still firm and domineering, but it didn't frighten her any longer. It was just that she knew what it could do to her. The thought frightened her just enough to excite her even more.

She pressed her body against him hard, feeling her breasts flatten and knowing that he could feel her breasts and her pubic arch pressing into him. She opened her mouth as wide as she could. It was wet and warm and open; she waited for his tongue to come into it, but he moved his head away from her.

"Take your clothes off," he whispered, his voice coming gently to her.

He'd moved away, just far enough away so that she could undress.

"I want you to help me," she said. She was breathing quickly now.

"No. Do it yourself."

He stood a pace away from her, his hands on his hips, his legs apart.

God! The look on his face! It was incredible! His eyes were burning her. He owned her! There was no other way to put it. She belonged to him totally and completely right then. And looking at his face, at the arrogance in it, at the strength in it, at the power and knowledge of her in it, she felt weak and helpless and she loved the feeling and loved him and wanted him— wanted to do anything that would please him. She'd never felt like this ever before in her life.

She no longer felt the effects of the liquor. It had been burned off in the intensity of the passion she was feeling.

She reached behind her neck with one hand and found the zipper tab and pulled it partway down and then reached up her back with her other hand and caught the tab and pulled it all the way down past her waist. She took her arms out of the short sleeves and pulled the top of the dress down over her hips and stepped out of it.

She unhooked her bra and let it fall from her arms. She hooked her thumbs into the sheer fabric of her bikini panties and pushed them down past her hips and down her thighs and let them fall to the ground and stepped out of them.

Now she was naked. The moonlight shone on her olive body, and she knew it was exciting to look at because she had large breasts, but they were still firm because she was young, and her waist was still narrow and her hips hadn't put on the bulging fat of middle age. Now she looked ripe and pretty and tight, and she knew her legs were long and shapely.

She wanted to pose for him, to get him excited, but before she could do anything, he said, "Lie down."

"What?"

"Lie down," he said again quietly, but that look was still on his face and it frightened her now. Yet she still wanted to do what he ordered her to do, so she lay down on the grass.

It was damp and cold and strange.

He knelt beside her.

"Aren't . . . aren't you going to take off your clothes?"

"Be quiet," he said. And she was afraid to speak. "Close your eyes."

She closed her lids, and then as the excited feeling began to ebb out of her, she felt him place one hand on her forehead and the other hand on her groin.

The pleasure came then. The pleasure came from the hand on her groin, from the finger touching her in the softest of her places, feeling the wetness. She squirmed, trying to move herself onto the finger, but his hand held her flat.

For a brief moment she opened her eyes to see him kneeling beside her, one hand on her forehead, the other on her pubic mound, his head bent as if in prayer, and his eyes closed.

She was about to ask what the hell he thought he was doing, when the blackness came.

There had never been such blackness in her life. It surrounded them both. The moon and the stars and the dim light of the night went out. She could no longer see Michael.

She knew her eyes were open. The blackness frightened her. She felt a wild maddening lurch of panic and opened her mouth to scream, but the blackness absorbed the sound of the scream. She could feel the muscles of her throat tense into solid cords with the effort of her screaming, and there was a wild, incoherent cry in her mouth, but there was no sound: The blackness poured into her mouth like a flood of ink. It absorbed the sound of her screaming, and then the blackness moved into her brain.

There was nothing.

There was dark and there was nothing.

There was only the end.

She stopped trying to scream and gave in, yielding to the lovely, lovely blackness of nothing.

God! How she loved the blackness!

3.

He could still do it! He still had the power!

That was his first thought.

If Aaron could put his hands on a corpse and bring

it to life, then he could put his hands on a live human being and will her to death.

Still on his knees, he leaned his torso away from the body of Mary Palumbo and lifted his hands from her. He held his hands up in front of him and stared at them.

Life.

Death.

His power was stronger than Aaron's.

Michael Hietala . . . Michael Hietala . . . his name spoken in sadness.

Now he recognized the voice in his mind; it was the voice that had awakened him in his dream just before daybreak, the voice he'd thought was his own. It had been Aaron's voice. Now hearing it again in his mind, he was aware of the import of the day and what had been revealed to him.

He was stronger than Aaron.

He stood up, not bothering to brush the grass from his jeans, and looked down at the nude, pale olive flesh that had been Mary Palumbo.

All afternoon he had been in a state of limbo, his thoughts inchoate, his mind churning with the images of the accident and the dead girl and hearing Aaron's voice come to him and letting Aaron use their body to bring the girl back to life again.

When he'd left the house that was The Church of the Second Life, he'd felt that he had to get away from it, away from its security, away from its warmth, away from its lightness and openness into the dark, to speed through the night, driven by some dark, unnameable force with a strength stronger than any he knew. And he also was aware that he welcomed that force; it was part of him. He was not afraid of his power; he was afraid of Aaron. Aaron was strong.

He told himself again that he was stronger than Aaron, as if to reassure himself. He needed the reassurance.

Why he'd stopped on Atlantic Avenue in Harbortown, he didn't know. Or why he'd selected Rosario's. Or why he'd gone into it only as far as the entranceway, to stand almost unseen in its dimness.

When he'd looked across the barroom and had seen the girl's face lift up to meet his eyes, he knew that he'd been looking for her. He knew, when she didn't take her eyes from his, that she'd come with him.

When he'd seen her face lifted to him and felt the stirring between his legs, he had recognized that she was responding to the dark force flowing out of him across the dark space between them.

When she'd gotten out of her seat and came across the room to him, he'd been waiting for her. When she'd spoken to him, it was the look in her eyes and not what she'd said he'd listened to.

Her eyes offered her body to him.

They said, *Please take me.*

I'll hurt you.

I know. It's what I want. It's what I've been looking for. I want you to hurt me. I want the pain.

Do you know what you're doing?

No. But it's what I want. I'm sure of that. Don't ask me why I want it. I just do.

Are you sure?

Yes.

And so they'd left Rosario's.

He'd bought her the whiskey, not to dull her apprehension, but to sharpen her anticipation, to make her acutely aware with every fiber of every nerve ending in her body, to let the anticipation build.

Excitement emanated from her in waves. In the dark confines of the small car, even without looking directly at her, he was aware of how she squirmed in the seat, aware of how her dress had moved up on the long, smooth olive thighs, of the heat that she radiated; of how she pressed thighs together and relaxed them and pressed them together again.

In the cemetery, in the moonlight, beside the still, parked car, she'd stripped herself and offered herself to him, offering more than her body, more than the slick, sweet juices of her vagina, the tumescence of her heavy breasts.

And when the blackness came, it came to him first. It swept over him as the white light had swept over him in the afternoon to herald the coming of Aaron.

He welcomed the blackness. He felt comfortable in it. He was part of it. It flowed in through his mind, through his limbs, flowing from him into the ground and then up out of the ground, surrounding them, filling him and making him stronger than he'd ever felt.

He shivered with the intensity of the excitement within him. Kneeling, his hand on her pubic arch, feeling her thrusting upward to press her labia around his fingers, he made his decision.

Knowing that through Aaron he could give life did not excite him or give him the sense of power he wanted.

To know he could give death meant nothing unless he gave death.

He gave death, jeering at Aaron.

They were coupled in the blackness; his mind entered hers like his tongue would have entered her wet, open mouth. She lay on her back in the grass. He knelt beside her, and he violated her in the foulest and most unspeakable way of all to bring her the most intense joy she had ever known.

When the blackness had gone, he was aware that his jeans were wet where he'd ejaculated into them. He got to his feet. He looked down for one last time at the body of Mary Palumbo lying on the grass of the gravesite. Then he went to the car and drove off, following the narrow roadways that circled through the cemetery until they brought him back to the gates and to the highway.

CHAPTER FIVE

Lisa Fialho said, "Mrs. Flint is here."

She stood over him, blocking the sun.

"*You* talk to her."

"She came to see you."

"I don't want to see her. Not today."

She lost her temper. "For Christ's sake, Mike! What the hell's the matter with you? You trying to blow this one? You forget how hard we worked to get to where we are? You hooked her. Now let's make it pay off!"

Hietala didn't open his eyes. He lay on a webbed nylon lounge chair, naked except for a pair of denim shorts, his eyes closed to the sun.

"She'll come back."

"She's come back every day for three days! She's going to get fed up and not come back at all!"

"She won't do that."

"She might."

He said, "Tell her to come back tomorrow. Tell her I'll see her tomorrow."

Lisa knew it was no use trying to speak to him anymore. She went back inside.

Mrs. Flint was waiting in the Bentley. Lisa went out the front door and over to the car.

"He's meditating, Mrs. Flint." She smiled ingratiatingly at the old lady.

"I trust you didn't disturb him."

"No. He said you can come tomorrow. He'll see you tomorrow afternoon."

"He really did? Tomorrow afternoon? At what time?"

"Three o'clock," Lisa said, hoping that Michael would have gotten out of his mood by then.

"I'll be here." Mrs. Flint smiled at Lisa Fialho, her small, monkey face furrowing. "Thank you," she said. "You're a good girl."

Then she realized what she'd said, and hesitated and said, "I hope I didn't say anything wrong. It's difficult for me to realize that you're actually older than I am. Or to remember that you've already been transformed."

"I don't mind," said Lisa.

Mrs. Flint turned her head away from the car window and said sharply, "Arnold, I would like a moment of privacy with Miss Fialho. Please take a short walk."

He got out of the car and walked to the end of the drive.

Mrs. Flint leaned closer to the open window of the Bentley. She motioned Lisa to come nearer.

"I wanted to ask you. Did you make much of a contribution to The Church?"

Lisa said nothing. Her face was expressionless. Inside she was furious. *God damn him, this is the part he should handle,* she thought, angrily. She didn't know how much to ask for. She was afraid she might ask for too much and blow the whole deal. Or ask for too little and find out later that she could have gotten more.

"I—I just can't bring myself to talk about money with Michael," Mrs. Flint said hesitantly. "Then I realized that you've gone through the—the—"

"Yes," said Lisa. "I have."

"So you'd probably know," Mrs. Flint said anxiously. She waited for Lisa's answer.

Lisa said gently, "We each give what we feel it's worth, Mrs. Flint. How much is it worth to you?"

"Everything," said the old lady. "What good is money if you're not young enough to enjoy it?"

"That's how I felt," Lisa said.

"Will I—can I choose the age I'd like to be?"

"Yes."

"And the person?"

"Yes, of course," said Lisa. "That's what's so wonderful about it. But you must have faith. Do you have enough faith?" she asked, remembering what Michael had said to Mrs. Flint on her first visit.

"Yes," said Sarah Flint. "I have faith."

"And courage?" She remembered that it was *courage* Michael had said, not *faith*.

The old woman nodded determinedly. "Yes. I think so."

"Michael said he would talk to you tomorrow," Lisa said, trying to end the conversation.

"I think . . . I think I should make a contribution before then, don't you think so?"

"If you think you should," Lisa said evasively. "Why, yes, that would be all right."

"I think I should," Sarah Flint said. She snapped open the clasp of her handbag and took out her checkbook. Lisa noticed that the old woman's fingers trembled as she opened the flap of the checkbook and carefully tore off the top check. She wondered whether the tremor was from nervousness or from old age.

Mrs. Flint held the check out the car window to Lisa.

"Here," she said. "I hope it's large enough to show my sincerity."

Lisa took the check.

"Do you think it's large enough?" Mrs. Flint asked, and Lisa understood the reason for her nervousness. The old lady was buying life for herself.

"I don't know," Lisa said boldly. "What's large enough for one person may be too little for another."

"Yes," said Mrs. Flint, nodding her small head. "That's what I thought, too." Hurriedly she added, "This is only the first of my contributions. Will you tell him that?"

Lisa said, "I don't talk to Michael about money. He doesn't care about money. But, The Church is expensive to run."

"Of course," said Mrs. Flint. She waited for Lisa to look at the check.

"Please look at the amount. Do you think it's enough?"

Lisa saw the concern on the old woman's face. Pretending a disinterest she didn't feel, she looked down at the check and read the amount. For a second, while her face was turned away from the old woman, she closed her eyes in disbelief. Then she opened them and lifted her head.

"For an initial contribution," she said coolly, "yes, I think it's adequate."

Relief showed on Sarah Flint's face. "I was afraid it might not be enough."

Lisa smiled gently at her, but not too warmly.

"One can always give more," she said.

"Yes, of course," said Mrs. Flint. "Did you?"

"Do you really want to know?"

"Certainly. It's important to me. I don't want to make a mistake."

"I put aside enough to live on comfortably in my second life," Lisa said. "The rest I contributed to The Church."

"All of it?" asked Mrs. Flint.

"All of it," said Lisa.

"Was—was it much?"

"Yes."

There was a slight pause. Lisa knew what Mrs. Flint was thinking.

"Of course, if you don't have enough faith—" she said, and gambled. She held out the check to Mrs. Flint.

"If you don't have enough faith," she repeated, "then you shouldn't give at all."

"Oh, no!" Mrs. Flint protested, suddenly afraid. "Here, wait."

Nervously, she opened her handbag again and took out a pen. She crouched over her lap, scribbling furiously in her checkbook for a moment before she tore out a second rectangle of blue paper. She held it out to Lisa.

"It's all I have in my checking account at the moment," Mrs. Flint said, her voice trembling with anxiety. "When I get home, I'll call my accountant and arrange for a considerably larger sum to be sent."

Her eyes searched Lisa's face for reassurance.

"Shall I have it addressed to you?"

"Make it out to The Church," said Lisa, "but yes, send it to my attention."

"And you'll let Michael know?"

Lisa felt the slickness of the two pieces of blue paper in her hand. She smiled reassuringly at Mrs. Flint.

"I told you that I don't talk about money with Michael," she said, "but I will tell him that you've seen to it that his work can continue."

Mrs. Flint said, "Thank you," and extended her hand out the window. Lisa took it. The old woman's grip was tight even though her bones were fragile and her skin as delicate as fine rice paper. It wasn't a handshake. It was a grasping for help. The old woman held Lisa's hand for a long time.

"Thank you," she said again before she settled back into her seat. "Thank you so very much, my dear."

2.

Excerpt from a telephone conversation, June 28.
Detective Sergeant Charles Daggett, Harbortown Police Department.
Dr. Amory Pierce, state pathologist, Cambridge, Massachusetts.

PIERCE: . . . uh . . . well, as I said before . . . there were no . . . that is . . . uh . . . I couldn't find any signs . . . bruises or contusions . . . you know . . . any indication that there had been violence.

DAGGETT: None at all?

PIERCE: Not that I could find.

DAGGETT: Then you'd say that death was due to natural causes?

PIERCE: . . . I . . . I don't know if I could say that either.

DAGGETT: I don't understand.

PIERCE: Uh . . . well, it's puzzling. I'll admit that. It has us puzzled, all right. There isn't much more that I can tell you.

DAGGETT: What *can* you tell me? You performed the autopsy, didn't you?

PIERCE: Yes . . . yes, I did. As I told you, there

were no indications of violence. That was the first thing I looked for, considering . . . considering the circumstances in which she was found. I . . . uh . . . have my notes right here . . . in case . . . that is . . . would you like me to read them to you?

DAGGETT: It's easier if you just tell me what you found.

PIERCE: We . . . that is, I . . . didn't find anything. There was nothing the matter with the girl. That's what's so strange. No signs of an embolism, for example. Heart, brain, lungs . . . we checked all the internal organs. There should have been no reason for the girl to die. . . . Uh, from your question, sergeant . . . did you expect us to find something?

DAGGETT: You tell me. The girl was found nude in a cemetery.

PIERCE: Yes, well . . .

DAGGETT: Was she raped?

PIERCE: Raped? . . . Oh, no. There were no signs of rape. No sperm. However, her labia, vagina and the pubic hairs directly around the labia all showed signs of a previous . . . uh, copious . . . uh, discharge from the Bartholin glands. . . .

DAGGETT: You mean she'd been sexually excited before she died.

PIERCE: Yes. . . . Yes, I suppose so. Did you get a report from the crime lab?

DAGGETT: Yeah. Her panties had been soaked, too. But no eighteen-year-old girl is going to die from that. Not unless her heart gave out.

PIERCE: Her heart was okay. She was in good physical condition . . . excellent muscle tone. . . . She must have exercised a lot.

DAGGETT: So she just went out to the cemetery and
took off her clothes and played with herself until
she died—is that what you're trying to tell me?

3.

The gull cawed and curved in a sweeping parabola,
breaking out of the mangy flock circling in the harbor
air. It stooped in a flat dive toward the water,
skimmed across the surface behind the stern of an in-
coming trawler to swoop up again, honking in raucous
defiance.

Michael walked down the length of the pier, past
half a dozen draggers hawser-laced one to another
stern to stern and bow to dock; the thick, old wood
planking of the wharf was resilient under his sneaker
soles. The salt smell was in the air, the fish smell pun-
gent in his nostrils; sea breezes came in off the ocean
through the mouth of the harbor.

Birds filled the sky, demented; screaming angry,
hoarse cries, their greedy, sharp eyes voraciously
hunting for even the smallest of scraps to fight over.

Sunlight burst through their wings. Forming and
dissolving, wheeling dizzily, nebulae of feathers, the
flocks spiraled in the air, each bird in a long, silent
arc on long, curved wings—motionless except for the
smallest twists of wingtip pinions to control its flight.
And the occasional frantic, pumping burst to fight its
way aloft from the water.

Michael came to the end of the dock. He looked
down at the cluttered deck of a dragger moored there.
Two men were working on a snarl of cable twisted
partway around the thick steel cylinder of a winch
drum, wrenches clamped tightly to rusted nuts and

pipe extensions slipped over the handles of the wrenches to give extra leverage.

Oil patches lay on the still, dirty water around the ship. The harbor was foul with garbage and debris.

He heard the throb of deck engines, the clatter of worn gear teeth turning booms and the squeal of rust-strained cables winding onto winch drums. Shouts came to him. Deck crews working on the boats, their voices in Italian as often as in English. The brief, imperative scream of a portable circular saw whining its way through a plank ceased, and then burst out again as the saw attacked once more.

One of the men on the dragger straightened up, letting go of his wrench handle. His thick, muscular body, bare to the waist, ran with sweat. He drew his arm across his forehead to wipe the sweat beads from his eyes. As he looked up, he saw Michael standing on the end of the dock watching him.

"Hey, what you lookin' at? You got nothin' else to do?"

Hietala said nothing. The man lifted his hand and gestured obscenely at him. He said something to his companion that Michael couldn't hear. He took his bandanna from his pocket and wiped his face and forehead and the back of his neck. His eyes never left Hietala's face. He pushed the bandanna back into the top of his pants.

"Yah!" he said, loudly, and made the gesture again before turning away.

I can kill you, Michael thought. *Just by laying my hands on you, I can take your life.*

He felt powerful, but the thought made him sad.

4.

Charlie Daggett said, "Tell me again, Dan. From where you saw Mary Palumbo come walking out of the bar."

"I told you. I was kinda drunk. I didn't notice much, Charlie."

Even across the desk, Charlie Daggett could smell the sourness of Dan Gilbert's breath. He noticed the broken veins on the end of Dan's nose and how the purple was spreading and how a paunch lay over the top of his trousers. He remembered how slim Gilbert had been when they'd been in high school together and played football on the same team.

We're both getting old, he thought, aware of the thickening of his own waist. His wife was always after him to go on a diet. Thirty years is a damn long time. Too long, for Christ's sake. Just look at him. Gilbert looks like he's fifty-eight, and he'll be lucky if he lives to be fifty-eight the way he drinks.

"Try," said Charlie Daggett patiently.

"What's gonna happen to me an' Red?"

"I don't know. I'm not the prosecutor."

"What d'you think's gonna happen?"

Daggett shrugged. The air in the room was heavy with smoke. The ashtray on the desk was filled with cigarette butts.

"He'll probably ask for murder one."

"Oh, shit," said Dan. "That's a hell of a thing to do to a guy."

"He might settle for manslaughter."

"Jesus! You know I didn't have nothin' to do with killin' the kid."

"Accessory for you," Charlie Daggett said. He felt

tired. He didn't like having to question Dan Gilbert. "You didn't think you were goin' to get off with nothing, did you?"

"For Chrissake, Charlie! The kid comes outta the bar. He's madder'n hell. Red makes a crack about Mary Palumbo goin' off with another guy, an' the kid tries to take his head off! Red was jus' makin' a joke! The kid didn' have to take it like he did."

"So you hit him."

"Yeah. What else you expect me to do? He cold cocks Red, an' Red's so drunk he can hardly stan' up. You think that's right? I can't stan' aroun' an' let no punk kid beat up a buddy when he can't help himself."

"Red hit him with a brick," Charlie Daggett pointed out.

"The kid pulled a knife."

"There were two of you. You tellin' me the two of you couldn't take a knife away from a kid?"

"We was drunk. I tol' you that. You know how Red drinks. You pulled him in often enough when you was in uniform, Charlie. An' that Joe Balzarini ain't really no kid. He's strong like an ox. You seen him. An' he's mean. The son of a bitch used that fish knife on us."

Charlie Daggett shook another cigarette out of the package. He noticed there were only four left.

Almost a whole pack in an hour, he thought. *Jesus, I got to cut down. Bernice is right. I'm going to smoke myself to death.*

He lit the cigarette and said, "Tell me about the guy Mary Palumbo came out of the bar with."

"I didn't see him too good, Charlie. I was lookin' at Mary."

"You say anything to her?"

"Naw. I jus' looked, you know what I mean. That

kid's stacked. She's wearin' a tight dress an' showin' off her big tits like she always does."

"They just walk out of the bar and walk away, or did they stand around for a minute?"

"They didn' stan' aroun'. They come out an' turned up the street."

"Which way?"

"Left. Went up to the corner an' aroun' it."

"There's a light on the corner. You must have seen what the guy looked like."

"I tol' you I was lookin' at Mary. You ever see that kid walk down a street. Her ass wiggles like you can't believe."

Charlie Daggett let out a sigh. "Forget Mary Palumbo. Was the guy short? Tall? How tall was he, Dan?"

Gilbert thought a minute.

"I don't know," he said finally. "I jus' don't know."

"Was he taller than you?"

Gilbert rubbed his chin and looked puzzled.

Charlie Daggett said, "When he came out of the bar, he was standing right beside you for a minute. Now was he taller than you? Shorter than you? The same height? C'mon, Dan, think!"

"He was taller'n me," Dan Gilbert said.

"How tall are you?"

"Five ten."

"Okay, how much taller than you?"

"Maybe two, three inches. Somethin' like that."

"Fat? Skinny?"

"In between."

"Husky?"

"No, not what you call husky, but he had an okay build."

"You think you could take him in a fight?"

Dan Gilbert frowned.

"Maybe," he said. "But, I wouldn' wanna try."

"So he was muscular?"

"Yeah, you could say that."

"What was he wearing?"

"How the hell do I know? It was dark. There ain't no windows to Rosario's, you know that. He got 'em bricked up 'cause they kept gettin' smashed alla time. An' the street light's down at the corner."

"Was he wearing a suit?"

"Naw, he wasn't wearin' no suit. Not down at Rosario's."

"Sport shirt?"

"I don't think so. It coulda been a turtleneck."

"And it was too dark to tell the color?" Daggett let a touch of sarcasm creep into his voice.

"Yeah. Except it was a dark color. Like his pants. They was both dark. Real dark, almost black."

"Anything else you remember?"

Dan Gilbert said defensively, "I tol' you it was dark an' I was drunk. What the hell else you expect me to remember? The kinda jockstrap he was wearin'?"

"Was he young? Old? Middle-aged?"

"He wasn't no kid, if that's what you mean. They go roun' the corner, an' Red Hansen says to me if he knew Mary Palumbo was datin' older guys he was gonna ask her for a date."

"So he was as old as you or Red?"

"He wasn't no kid. He wasn't no Joe Balzarini."

"Joe was twenty-three."

"Okay, so maybe he was ten, twelve years older. It's hard to tell when a guy's wearin' a beard, an' you don't get no good look at him because it's dark."

"Shit," said Charlie Daggett in disgust.

"What'd I say now?"

"Why the hell didn't you tell me he was wearing a beard in the first place?"

"Because I didn' think of it until right now, that's why."

"Long beard, short beard? What kind of a beard, goddamnit!"

"In between," said Dan Gilbert.

"You're a lot of fuckin' help," Charlie Daggett said sourly.

"I'm tryin', so help me. I am really tryin', Charlie."

"Did he look like a hippie?"

"Naw, not him. He was too neat."

"Him or the beard?"

"The beard. It wasn't wild like them kids wear 'em. Like they don't give a shit how they look."

"Blond hair? Dark hair?"

"Dark," said Dan Gilbert. "An' he was wearin' sneakers."

"What made you remember that?"

"Because his pants was almost black an' the sneakers was light colored. Charlie, you gonna put in a good word for me because of this?"

"You'll have to talk to the prosecutor about that," Charlie Daggett said. "I'm not on your case."

"Then what the hell was we talkin' about all this time?"

"Mary Palumbo," said Daggett.

Dan Gilbert stared at Charlie Daggett. He said tentatively, "I heard she was foun' dead. You tellin' me someone killed her?"

"I don't know," said Charlie Daggett. "Maybe."

"Jesus!" said Dan Gilbert. "Who'd want to kill a good lookin' piece a tail like Mary Palumbo?"

"That's what I'm trying to find out," Charlie Daggett said wearily.

CHAPTER SIX

The lobster boat exploded because John Christy forgot to turn on the blower before he pressed the ignition button on the control panel in the pilot house.

The *Celeste* was gasoline powered. It had been moored to the dock for two days. Something during the previous months, a swaged joint in the copper fuel line had been loosened by vibration. Gasoline had dripped from the line into the bilge one drop at a time. The leak had been there for a long time, but Christy had always turned on the blower before starting his engine, and the blower had cleared the fume-laden, explosive mixture out of the confines of the small engine compartment.

It wasn't that he was tired; he simply forgot. He climbed into the pilot house of the wooden-hulled, old lobster boat, turned on the master switch and punched the starter button.

After two days, the fumes in the engine compartment had built up into a heavy concentration. The cable connection to the number three cylinder spark-plug was loose. It sparked.

It was like igniting half a dozen sticks of dynamite.

The blast knocked Michael Hietala off his feet. The *Celeste* blew up in the middle, outward and upward at the same time. Fragmented planks twisted skyward; shards of glass from the pilot house windows hurtled across the decks of the ships on either side of her.

On the dragger, Nino Giordano was blown over the side into the harbor with a foot-long splinter of plank driven into his back. Enrique Cardoza was slammed against a steel bulkhead and broke his shoulder blade. Flying glass cut his face to shreds.

On the *Serafina*, Mike Cafalo, Tony Abruzzi, and Gino Mancini were knocked down. Cafalo broke his wrist, Abruzzi had a cracked skull. Gino Mancini tore muscles in the small of his back.

Joe Cardozo saw John Christy's body blown into the air like a giant, gross, limp rag doll. It made two slow twists as it came down to hit the water, splash mightily, and sink into the murky harbor.

Cardozo was on the bow of the *Carmine J.* Without thinking, he dove into the water after Christy.

The water was foul, murk blinded him, oil stung his eyes so he had to keep them closed. It would have done no good to keep them open, even if he could have. Oily and slimy, the water of the harbor was foulest near the docks where the fishing boats pumped out their bilges and dumped their garbage and fish scraps. Below three feet, it was almost totally dark.

He couldn't find Christy on his first dive. He came to the surface, gulped air, and dived again. He hunted until his breath gave out.

On his third dive, Cardozo frog-kicked his way down until his hands slid into the thick mud and sludge of the bottom. He crawled around, his lungs aching, until he was almost ready to give up, and he knew he wouldn't be able to make another dive. Then his hands struck something large and he felt cloth and he guessed it was Christy.

He locked his hands into Christy's belt and pushed hard for the surface. When he broke water, he reached down for Christy's hair, got a handful of it and pulled his head out of the water.

Half a dozen lines were flung at him. One of them struck him across the face.

"Knock it off!" he shouted, panting for air. "Somebody come help me!"

Tony Fontana and his brother Louis jumped into the water and splashed their way to Cardozo. The three of them, kicking, stroking, fought their way to the floating dock with Christy's inert body. Hands reached down to pull Christy up onto the dock. Joe and the Fontana brothers pulled themselves over the edge of the floating dock and lay there, spitting water and gasping. Christy lay unmoving on the dock planking, covered with slime and oil and dripping sea water.

On the wharf above, Michael Hietala dazedly picked himself up; he shook his head to clear it. He looked down over the edge of the wharf at the floating dock and at the crowd of men gathering around Christy's body.

His head hurt. He had trouble focusing his eyes and there was a ringing sound in his ears. He thought he heard Aaron's voice call his name.

Hello, Michael, the voice said, distinctly now.

The men came running off the fishing boats until the crowd around Christy's body filled the narrow floating dock. Two men had gotten down and were working on Christy. One knelt astride him, his hands on Christy's ribcage pressing in rhythmic strokes against the lower ribs. The other was kneeling beside

Christy's head. Bent over, his hands holding Christy's mouth wide open and his own mouth on top of Christy's, he blew air strongly into Christy's lungs.

Michael hadn't moved.

He heard the voice again.

Go away, Aaron, he begged.

Not this time, Michael. Not after what you did the other night.

You don't know anything about the other night. Go away.

You owe the world a life. I know that.

You want my body. I won't let you have it.

Only for a while.

It was hard to resist the gentle persuasiveness of Aaron's voice.

No!

You're afraid I won't let you come back.

Yes. Why should you let me come back? I wouldn't if I were you.

If I promise?

Will you promise?

Yes.

One of the men in the crowd stepped forward and knelt down beside Christy's body. He slid his hand under Christy's neck.

Michael heard him say: "You can stop. Son of a bitch's got a broken neck. He's fuckin' well dead."

The two men paused. The one who'd been blowing air into Christy's lungs wiped his mouth on the back of his hand. The two men looked at each other and climbed awkwardly to their feet.

Hietala heard a police siren in the distance.

The two men stood beside Christy's body and looked down at it. Mud caked Christy's hair and filled his eye sockets. Greenish slime ran from his trousers. His T shirt was plastered to the outlines of his body, his paunch pushing out the center of the shirt so that his belly showed in the gap. The skin of his belly was dirty from the water. Curled, sodden hairs lay in tight spirals against the wet, white-lard skin. There was the stink of foul harbor water around him.

Well, Michael?

Aaron's soft, compelling voice pushed at him.

There was never any moment of decision. He felt a deep serenity engulf him. He walked to the ladder and made his way down to the floating dock, pressing through the men with such authority that they gave way before him.

Someone started to say, "Hey, what the hell—"

He was jabbed in the ribs and cut off. The men closest to the body began to back away from it as Aaron Hietala came up to stand beside Christy's limp form. As they moved back, they fell silent, and the men behind them backed away too, and they, in turn, stopped talking. Finally there was a circle of space around John Christy and Aaron, and there was silence—except for the screaming of the approaching police siren and the hoarse cawing of the gulls endlessly circling overhead in the blue, clear sky. The sunlight came through the white feathers of their wings.

Aaron Hietala knelt down. He placed his hands on Christy's sopping body. He put his left hand under Christy's neck and felt the sharp break in his spine just below the base of his skull. He put his right hand on the wet T shirt plastered to Christy's chest. He bent his head and closed his eyes. He took a deep breath. He let the air go easily out of his lungs. He relaxed.

He let the light come into him.

And the light came.

As it had to him leaning over the dead girl, the light now came; slowly at first, and then it grew until it flooded his mind and he felt the electric glow pulse through his body, through his head and torso and thighs and legs and arms and through his hands into the dead, broken-necked, overweight body of John Christy.

The light blinded Aaron, but he was used to it. Its glare burned his mind, but it didn't hurt. The light was like the light of a thousand suns, like the center of a hydrogen fusion explosion. And although his head was bent and his eyelids were closed, he looked into the center of the white light and he saw peacefulness and he felt goodness and power and glory.

He was Aaron Hietala. He was more than Michael Hietala; he was what Michael Hietala could be. He was all mankind. He wept for his death, and he wept because Michael did not want him to live.

And then the fingers of his left hand felt the slow joining of the break in John Christy's spine. The palm of his right hand felt the beginnings of a pulse in John Christy's chest. The movements grew stronger. There was life in him.

Christy's head turned. His mouth opened. A spew of foul, brackish water gushed from his lungs in a huge bubble. He sat up, coughing, coughing again and again, spasms racking his chest as he gasped for air. Water and vomit spilled over his T shirt.

Aaron Hietala rose to his feet, turning away from Christy.

Louis Fontana cried out and fell to his knees in front of him. His brother Tony went down on one knee, bent his head, and made the sign of the cross.

One by one, the fishermen who had formed a circle around Christy and Aaron Hietala went down on their knees. Some went down on both knees, some on just one. Each man made the sign of the cross, touching his forehead and chest, left shoulder and right. Each man bent his head in reverence. Each man knew he had seen a sign few men have ever been allowed to see.

Each saw a light, like a halo—a radiance that surrounded the tall slim figure that quietly made his way through them and away from the docks.

Aaron Hietala began to walk up the gangway to the wharf above the floating dock.

Michael said, *Aaron!*

Yes, I know, said Aaron regretfully.

You promised.

I promised.

Now! said Michael sharply.

I'll be back, Aaron told him, leaving.

Michael made no answer. He kept on walking up the gangway until he reached the top and turned away from the docks. The police cruiser was parking as he passed it.

2.

Lisa said frostily, "Mrs. Flint was here again this morning, Michael."

They lay in webbed nylon lounge chairs on the sundeck on the south side of the house. The afternoon sun shone strongly on them. Lisa wore shorts and a thin, pale blue nylon shirt, unbuttoned but with the ends tied together in a knot under her breasts.

Michael made no answer.

"She brought a friend with her. Edith Cavanaugh. She's the granddaughter of an old friend of Sarah

Flint's, and she's into the same sort of things Mrs. Flint was."

She waited for him to reply.

"She's ripe, Michael."

He lay with his eyes closed, his face turned toward the sun. Lisa moved her legs restlessly. She had long, slim legs and her shorts were very brief. She looked down at the length of her legs, admiring them.

"Where the hell were you this morning?"

"In Harbortown," he said, his face toward the sun and his eyelids closed against its brightness.

"At the docks again?"

"Yes."

"What the hell's so exciting about watching a bunch of stinking fishermen?"

He shrugged. Lisa said, "You should have been here. Edith Cavanaugh is a mark if there ever was one. She's just begging for someone to take it away from her."

He wasn't paying attention to her. For a brief second she felt a flare of anger and then it died. He had that same strange look on his face that he'd had the week before when he'd come back to the house with Mrs. Flint and had gone down to the small beach at the foot of the cliff. He was withdrawing again. She would have to catch him before he went too deeply into himself.

"What happened this morning, Michael?"

She waited for him to answer.

"Something happened," she persisted, disturbed. "Was it the same thing as last week?"

He turned toward her, opening his eyes. She saw the pain in them.

"Yes."

"Tell me about it."

He thought about the coming of Aaron and how insane it would sound if he tried to tell anyone about it.

"There's nothing to tell," he said.

"That's not what Mrs. Flint said."

He'd forgotten about her. She must have told Lisa about his bringing the dead girl back to life. He wished he knew exactly what the old lady had told her.

"What'd she tell you?"

"That you brought a dead girl back to life. What kind of con did you pull on the old lady, Michael?"

He didn't answer.

"You think I'm dumb enough to believe a story like that?"

"It happened," he said.

"How?" she challenged him. "How'd you do it?"

"I put my hands on her."

"And today?"

"The same thing. A lobsterman was blown up in his boat. He was dead. I put my hands on him."

"And brought him back to life?"

"Yes."

"You and Jesus Christ," Lisa said sarcastically. "The guy's name wasn't Lazarus, by any chance?"

He didn't want to talk to her anymore about it. He wanted to stop thinking about what was happening to him. For the first time in his life, he was living in fear. Fear of Aaron. Fearful of losing his life to Aaron. He believed the voice in his head. He had gone away from his body twice now. He was afraid that sometime soon Aaron would come and take over his body and not let him back.

He'd never been afraid of anything in his life. Not during the years he was growing up. Not when he was in the army in Vietnam. He'd prided himself on his toughness.

"Michael?"

When he didn't answer, Lisa knew that she'd lost him. He's so damn hard to live with, she thought. She loved him. At least as much as she'd ever been able to love any man. What got to her, the thing that had attracted her from the first, was that he was hard. He never let her get away with anything. Once, at the beginning of their relationship, she'd gone to bed with another man and he'd found out about it. He'd beaten her so badly that for three days she'd been sore and exhausted.

He'd said, "The next time you do anything like that, I'll kill you," and she'd known it wasn't just words, that he would kill her. She never again looked at another man.

Yet, at times in the years when they were hard up, he'd sent her off to bed with a John.

"Doesn't it bother you?" she'd asked him once.

"If it bothered me, I wouldn't send you out."

"You're making a whore out of me," she'd protested.

"What the hell do you think you were when I met you!"

"You beat me up for doing this."

"That's because you did it on your own. This is for us."

They hadn't had to do that for a long time now. She'd liked him for taking her out of the life. She wasn't sure how much she loved him, but she knew it was more than she'd ever loved any man in her life. When he retreated into himself, she felt alone. She hated feeling alone. It frightened her.

Now she said contritely, "Michael, I'm sorry."

But he was gone. She knew she wouldn't be able to

get through to him. Disturbed and angry, she got out of the lounge chair and went into the house.

Michael sat on the sundeck all the rest of the afternoon, until evening.

He was impatient for the dark to come. As long as it was light and the sun was shining, he felt that Aaron could come again, and if Aaron came, he wasn't sure of what would happen, but the thought that it could happen frightened him. He longed for the dark, knowing that when the dark came he would be safe.

3.

The street was dark. The girl was walking by herself. She was young and pretty; she had long, blond hair that shone in the light of the street lamp. He pulled over to the side of the street close to her.

When the small sports coupe pulled into the curb beside her, the girl stopped and turned her head to see who it was. She had many friends and most of them had cars.

She didn't recognize the man whose face was framed by the open car window. She noticed that he had a beard and that he was good looking even though he was a lot older than she was. She thought he was going to ask her for directions.

What he said was, "Will you come with me?" and that was kind of scary, but not very. She knew she should have turned and walked away and not answered him, but the streetlight was shining on his face and she could see his eyes and there was something in them that held her.

He waited for the girl to answer, knowing what she would say, knowing she had no choice.

She looked at his face and at his eyes for a long time. Surprisingly, she felt no fear.

After a moment she said, "Sure," and walked around to the other side of the car and got in.

He started off.

"I'm Dana DeCoste," the girl said. She turned her face toward him, tossing her long hair to one side of her head. She smiled at him. "What's your name?"

"Michael."

She laughed. "Just Michael?"

"Yes."

She noticed again that he was much older than she was. He must be in his middle thirties, she thought. She knew she shouldn't be with him, but the thought excited her because what she was doing was bold and she'd never been bold before. She'd never been with a man as old as him before, either. And he was masculine. He really radiated that, she thought. She could feel it all the way inside of her and feel herself responding to it. Sometimes, when she'd been with a boy she'd had a crush on, she'd felt sexually stimulated when they were making out, and she'd wanted him to touch her everywhere, but she'd never gone the whole way, and she knew she could always make them stop when she wanted to. She wasn't sure she could do that now if he touched her. She'd never felt so excited sexually as she was beginning to feel right now. She was trembling slightly. She tried to hide it.

"Where are we going?"

"Where would you like to go?"

"For a ride," she said, because she didn't know what else to say. She didn't want to take him anyplace they might meet her friends. He was too old for them. They'd say things to her afterward.

He drove through the back streets of Harbortown until he came out onto the road to Turtle Neck.

"I've never seen you around town before," she said, not liking the silence, even though it excited her. She kept looking at his face in profile. She wondered what it would be like to be kissed by a man with a beard.

"I've only been in town a few weeks," he said.

"You live in Harbortown?"

"Adam's Cove," he said.

He reached over and put his right hand on her thigh. She felt the heat of his palm. The heat spread through her. She felt it mostly in her belly and between her legs. It wasn't like any other time a boy had touched her. It was hard to breathe. She could feel how hard her breasts had gotten and how her bra seemed to restrain her. She felt hot all over.

She put her hand on top of his and began to rub the back of his hand with her fingers.

"Are—are we going to make love?"

She said it in a whisper, surprised at her temerity at saying the words aloud, even though she'd been thinking them.

"Would you like to make love?"

There was no urgency in his voice. It was just a simple question.

"Y-yes."

Again she was surprised at her boldness. "Y-yes. I—I think I would."

He turned the car off the road to Turtle Neck, down a narrow lane that led to Benton's Beach. He had to put the car in low gear and drive slowly because of the deep ruts and the sand in the lane. After a while, he stopped the car in a turnout close to one of the sand dunes that hid the beach from the road. He turned off the lights.

Dana waited for him to kiss her. The tension in her had built so that the waiting was painful. She thought he was going to kiss her, but after a while she saw that he wasn't. She thought he might at least smile at her, but he didn't do that either.

There was something about his face that looked as if there was a struggle going on inside of him. She remembered his eyes when she'd looked at him under the streetlights. There'd been something in his eyes then that she'd never before seen in a man's face, and suddenly she knew what it was.

He was evil. He could hurt her. She wasn't afraid of being raped. Ellen Fahey had been raped and had told her about it. She was mad at the boy who'd done it to her but she hadn't been hurt. The idea of being raped sort of excited her. She just didn't want him to hurt her. She thought: *If he wants to, I'll let him rape me. He won't have to hurt me.*

Then she wondered why she was thinking about being raped when she'd already told him she wanted to make love with him.

She said, "Are—are you going to kiss me?"

"In a while."

"On the beach?"

"Sugar Island."

Sugar Island was an island only part of the time. It was connected to the beach by a narrow strip of land no more than ten feet wide and the strip was exposed only at low tide. At high tide Sugar Island was separated from the shore by two hundred feet of water. It was low tide now.

They got out of the car. She came around to stand beside him.

"Please hold me," she asked timidly and moved up against him. She felt him put his arms around her, and the excited, tense feeling she had grew so strong it hurt. She suddenly wanted to feel him push into her, to bury himself between her thighs. She wanted the heat and the thick, solid, rodlike pressure of him thrusting into the softness and wetness inside her.

She pressed hard with her pubic bone against him, arching her back and tightening both her arms around his neck. She held him tighter, feeling her breasts flatten out against the solid muscles of his chest. His beard scratched her soft cheeks. She breathed in quick, excited gasps.

Her mouth against his neck, she said hesitantly, "I—I've got something to tell you."

She couldn't look at him while she was saying this.

"I—I never let anyone go the whole way with me before. I—I'm a virgin," she said.

Then she said, "I'm only sixteen," her voice a whisper, trailing off into silence.

He moved out of her embrace. For a moment she thought she'd said the wrong thing, but he took her by the hand and started walking toward the sand dunes and Sugar Island. She went along with him, stumbling through the soft, fine sand, still keyed up, dazed, expectant.

They made their way across the thin neck of land exposed by the low tide and climbed up the low, rocky hillside of Sugar Island, following a faint trail. She stumbled often, and he had to put his arm around her to hold her and to keep her from falling down.

When they came to a small glen, he let go of her. They faced each other, the moon shining down on them, shining on her long, blond hair that came down almost to her waist and on his dark, bearded face. It was his face that excited her. The moon made it easy for her to see the look in his eyes that she thought was evil and frightening and that attracted her so intensely because it threatened her in a way that she'd never before been threatened. She felt fear, and it was the fear that excited her.

Fear made her want to yield to him, to give her body to him to use any way he wanted, to offer herself so totally to him that she would cease to exist. She felt herself sinking deeper and deeper into the fear that was flooding her body.

"Take off your clothes," he said.

She was wearing a blouse and jeans. Her fingers were awkward and stiff as she unbuttoned her blouse. She turned her head away from him, embarrassed. She took off the blouse and then her jeans and stepped out of her sneakers. Standing there in her bra and panties, her head still turned away from him, she asked plaintively, "Will you—will you take off the rest?"

"I want *you* to do it."

She reached her hands behind her back and unhooked her bra and slid it off. She slipped off her panties. Then she stood motionless—slim and white in the pale glowing moonlight, her small breasts firm, her nipples tightening into hard, puckered ovals, the light hair of her crotch dark against the white of her thighs.

She thought he would touch her then, that he'd put his hands on her. She wanted his hands on her. She felt herself aching for the touch of his hands, surprised at how wet she was between her legs and how swollen and how warm. She'd never been that excited.

"Lie down," he said.

Obediently she lay down on the sand, on her back. She looked up at him. He seemed so tall to her. He was standing with his legs apart and his hands on his hips and he was staring down at the length of her slender body at his feet. She knew he was looking at her body and she was aware of her nakedness and that he was still clothed. She trembled and tried to stop it, but small spasms kept racking her body uncontrollably.

"P-please," she whispered, frustrated and impatient for him to come to her and simultaneously wanting him to stand where he was.

He had to punish her. She knew that. She deserved punishment and pain. But she knew that the pain would bring her pleasure, and it was the pleasure that she wanted. She knew it would be the most intense pleasure she would ever have in her life, that she would remember it forever and ever.

"P-please . . ." she whispered again and began to cry.

He knelt beside her, and she closed her eyes against the shining evil beauty of his face.

She felt him place one hand on her forehead. His touch burned, but it was no hotter than her skin was at the moment. She felt his other hand cup her between her legs, holding her pubic arch and the cushion of fine, curly hairs, and she felt his fingers go between her legs into her slick, swollen wetness. She squirmed her legs apart so his hand would fit more easily and so he could press deeper into her with his fingers.

For a brief moment she let her eyes open to look at his face, to read the evil she had seen in it, and to reassure herself that it was still there.

She saw that his eyes were closed. She had a brief second to wonder about it before the darkness came.

It was as if the moon went out. There was blackness darker than the night. It surrounded her, closing in on her. She could actually feel the pressure of the darkness on her naked body. She tried to scream, but the blackness swallowed the sound while it was still in her throat, and the blackness went deep into her body, and around her body, swathing her in the evil she had seen in his eyes.

When the fear and the darkness and the helplessness spread totally through her, when the blackness seeped into her brain and there was no other world left—no sensation except horror, no feeling except fear, no sound except demonic laughter echoing in thunderous, savage glee inside the cavity of her skull—then she knew she was going to die.

She accepted the thought gratefully. She realized in that brief instant that the evil was in her as well as in him. She rejoiced in their sharing of it. She was his slave. He was her master.

She gave herself to him completely, and then he gave her death.

CHAPTER SEVEN

Father Vincent was sixty-two years old, with thin white strands of hair lying pale and straight across the long slope of his pate, and with pale cheeks so closely shaven that the flesh of his face seemed pink. His deeply sunken eyes were a washed, pale blue. Even after forty years in the priesthood, always in small parishes except for the few years he had served at the cathedral in St. Paul, Minnesota, he had not lost the fierce intensity he'd brought into the priesthood as a young man.

Now, lank and angular, he sat on the edge of the chair. The sun was hot on the deck. On the redwood plank table beside him was a glass of iced tea. He hadn't touched it despite the heat and his thirst.

He said, "I've come because of the stories I've heard about you from some of my parishioners." He hesitated. "They're hard to believe."

Michael Hietala stirred in his chair, waiting for the priest to come to the point.

Father Vincent said, "By the way, how do I address you? I'm told you're an ordained minister."

"Yes," said Michael. "I am." He shrugged. "Call me whatever you wish."

"Not Father," the priest said sharply.

"No."

"Reverend?" There was distaste in his voice.

"Michael will do," he said, noticing the priest's discomfort, and being pleased by it.

"I didn't know until I came out here and saw the sign on the gate. 'The Church of the Second Life.' I'm not familiar with the denomination. It's one of the minor Protestant sects, is it?"

"No," said Hietala. "We're an independent church."

"Oh," said the priest. Hietala saw the sour expression on the priest's face and was amused by it.

"It doesn't matter what we are," he said. "What brings you out here?"

Father Vincent took his time before he answered. When he'd parked his car on the road beside the wall and walked in through the gates, he'd noticed the sign. The sign was a discreet, bronze plaque with raised lettering, and the plaque itself was bolted to the wrought iron of the gates. He'd wondered then what The Church of the Second Life could be. He thought it might be Baptist. Somehow that seemed most likely to him, although he wouldn't have been able to explain why.

He'd seen the building before, but always from a distance. In all the years he'd had the parish in Harbortown, he'd come to Adam's Cove only a few times. None of his parishioners lived in Adam's Cove. There were only a few Catholics in it, mostly summer people, and they never attended masses in his church.

He'd always assumed the building was a private residence. From the outside, he saw that it was like many of the newer, modernistic glass and wood-frame churches designed by younger architects. There were many of them in the suburbs of Minneapolis; he remembered some of them vaguely from his days at the cathedral in St. Paul. Mostly they'd been Lutheran.

The young woman who opened the door to his ring had startled him with her frankly sexual good looks. She was wearing a thin summer dress with an extremely short skirt, and he could see that she wore no bra. When he learned from her that she was a deaconess in the church, he was angered.

He'd asked about the man he was looking for, and she'd said yes he was there, and his name was Michael Hietala, and he was the minister of The Church of the Second Life. She'd led him through the house onto the sundeck where Michael was lying sprawled on a chaise.

Hietala was wearing nothing but denim shorts, and on his feet were leather sandals. Father Vincent was dressed in a thin, black summer shirt; even in the heat, even with his white collar tight around his neck, he did not perspire. Was it his anger that was keeping him cool, he wondered.

He tried to hide his anger. He felt that Hietala was making a mockery of religion. He should be forbidden to set up as a man of the cloth. The priest wasn't sure that his superiors would approve of his talking to a Protestant minister about a matter like this. That he should have to talk to someone like Hietala was almost more than he could take. He was irate that Hietala was actually ordained.

By whom? he wondered, looking at the man lying in the lounge chair. He'd made no effort to dress himself, to put on the shirt that was hanging from the back of the chaise, or even to get up. It was more than bad manners. It was deliberate rudeness. He wasn't used to rudeness. People just were never rude to a priest.

Hietala had gestured to a chair and asked the young woman—*Her a deaconess!*—to bring him a glass of iced tea. When she'd brought it and placed the glass on the table beside him, the priest ignored it.

Father Vincent was disturbed that he was more aware of the young woman than he should have been, but it was hard not to be aware of her. Especially the way she flaunted her body. Deliberately, so as to arouse the carnal impulses in a man, he thought, and he was furious that she should do this to a priest.

He wondered about her. Did she live under the same roof with Hietala? He knew they weren't married. She'd introduced herself as *Miss* Fialho, and he'd caught the deliberate emphasis in her voice when she'd said the words, and then, too, there had been the slight, mocking smile on her lips. For a moment he was certain that he'd made a grievous mistake in coming out here.

Her familiarity with the man disturbed him. When she'd led him out onto the sundeck, she'd said, "Michael, this is Father Vincent, from the Church of St. Paul the Fisherman."

He'd felt uncomfortable about the propriety of a deaconess addressing a minister by his first name.

He cleared his throat and said, "Several of my parishioners have told me about the events of the other morning." He added, "Down at the docks."

Michael waited, eyes on the priest's face. The direct stare, unflinching, bothered the priest. He found it hard to go on and still control the anger he felt inside.

"What is it they told you?"

"That you brought a man back to life," Father Vincent said accusingly.

"Is that what they tell you?"

"Yes. They're convinced they've seen a miracle. It disturbs them. You're not Catholic, you see."

"No, I'm not. Would it be all right if I were Catholic?"

The priest knew the man was mocking him. He ignored the sarcasm.

"I'm here to find out what really happened."

"What did they tell you happened?"

Father Vincent described the explosion and the recovery of John Christy's body and the attempts to resuscitate him, and how one of the men swore that John Christy was dead. He'd felt the broken vertebrae of his neck. The man couldn't possibly have been alive. He'd been adamant about that. He'd seen too many dead men in Korea when he'd been a medical corpsman. Christy had been dead.

The priest went on in his thin, dry, tight voice. They'd told him how Michael Hietala had come pushing his way through them and had knelt down beside the corpse and laid his hands on it and bowed his head in prayer. How after a while the corpse had seemingly—the priest emphasized the word—*seemingly* come back to life.

What he didn't mention to Hietala was that each of his parishioners who'd been there and told him about what had happened had also mentioned the feeling of awe they'd experienced, and how each of them had felt compelled to kneel before Hietala in reverence and fear.

When he'd finished, the priest's face was stiff. He said sternly, "Of course, I don't believe them."

"Don't you? Then why are you here?"

"To hear from your own lips what really happened."

"And if I tell you the same thing?"

In shocked disbelief the priest asked, "That you brought a dead man back to life?"

"I could tell you that," Michael said easily.

"It would be a lie!"

Michael said nothing.

"Why should you lie to me? You're a man of God, Mr. Hietala"—Father Vincent noticed that he couldn't bring himself to address this almost naked, bearded man as Reverend—"men of the cloth don't tell lies."

"Why do you assume it would be a lie?"

Eyes blazing, his thin, ascetic face tight with anger, the elderly priest said, "If you tell me that you laid hands on a corpse and brought it back to life, it would be a lie!"

"Then suppose I say nothing to you?"

"You would be contributing to the false belief of my parishioners. To their sin."

"To say nothing would be a sin?"

"A sin of omission."

"So I must talk, and I must tell you the truth?"

"Yes!"

"Suppose I tell you that the truth is that your parishioners have told you the truth?"

"It would be blasphemy!"

Michael smiled at the priest. The older man was quivering with suppressed rage. Under the thin flesh of his gaunt cheeks, the muscles of his jaw stood out in ridges.

Hietala said calmly, "Blasphemy is merely my voicing that which is contrary to *your* beliefs, wouldn't you say?"

"Not mine," said the priest. "The church. I believe as the church believes."

"Yes," said Michael, getting to his feet.

Michael walked to the railing, and looked out toward the horizon, across the great expanse of blue-green ocean. The sun was hot on his back. Father Vincent could see tiny beads of perspiration oiling the tanned brown skin of the man's back. He saw how the hair on the nape of his neck curled under. A rivulet of sweat rolled down along the runnel of his spine to the waistband of his denim shorts.

Father Vincent took off his narrow framed glasses and took out his handkerchief and cleaned each lens thoroughly. He put the handkerchief back into his pocket and the glasses back on his face.

Michael's hands were clenched on the railing. The urge to tell the priest everything that had happened to him since the first morning was strong inside him. He knew that was why he was being deliberately antagonistic to the old man. He wanted to share his feelings and his knowledge with someone beside Lisa. Lisa couldn't understand. Lisa could never understand a thing like this. The priest would.

He wished, for a moment, that he were still a Catholic. He wished he could confess. He wished he could let the church take the burden from him. They were good at that. Sometimes the burden was so heavy on his mind he thought he couldn't bear it another instant. He could tell the priest about Mary Palumbo and Dana DeCoste, and about Aaron. The church could understand.

If he gave his burden to the church, it would be their burden then, wouldn't it? He would know relief. It would be their fight, not his. He longed to be free of the fear he felt inside of him.

But he was no longer a Catholic. Not since his adolescence. He thought of the nun. The image of her face came into his mind. Sister Maria Theresa. After all these years he still hated her. He hated the church because of her. The years with the evangelical, fundamentalist television preacher had given him a secret pleasure. He'd often thought of the nun during those years, wishing that she could know what he was doing, preaching Christ and mocking, in his mind, those he brought to Him.

Now, maliciously, he felt an overwhelming desire to hurt the old priest. St. Peter the Fisherman's was a small church in a small town. The priest was a small man, small minded, intolerant, in his way as much a fanatic as any grand inquisitor of Isabella's Spain. Michael wanted to outrage the man, to offend him, to shake his beliefs to their very foundation.

He turned around to face the priest and mock him.

The sun struck him full in the face with its heat and its brilliant, white light, and the light went into his mind and fought with the dense blackness clouding it. He closed his eyes against the sudden pain in his mind.

The light was more intense than he'd ever felt it before. The light struck again and again into the darkness in his mind and the light conquered the darkness, and he heard Aaron's voice.

—*Go away, Michael!*

In his mind, he shouted an outraged, despairing *No!* even as he went into the cold, formless, primal darkness, and he knew what it was like before the Lord said, *Let there be light!*

Father Vincent saw the man Hietala turn toward him. He saw the man's eyes close as the sun struck him on the face, his eyelids clenching shut against the glare.

He saw the man open his mouth to speak, and then a paralysis seemed to come over him. He'd been standing in a loose, easy slouch. Now his body straightened up in a quick, spastic jerk. He was standing erect, straining, the sunlight glaring on his limbs.

The priest noticed that despite his muscularity, the man was really slender.

Hietala's face turned up toward the sun, his neck arching, his whole head moving back slowly. Just as slowly, his arms came out from his sides, stretching, his palms out, facing toward the priest. His legs moved until they were together, so that finally his body formed a cross.

Fear came coldly into the priest's chest; a heavy, pounding chill that froze him solidly. He clutched at the crucifix dangling from his neck.

Now it was as if all the sounds of the world had stopped. The two of them were in the midst of a thick silence, the air glutinous around them. The sound of the surf, of the waves beating against the rocks at the base of the cliff, was gone. The gulls still wheeled in the sky, but the kriii-caw-caw-caw of their cries stopped. The wind still pressed against their faces, but its thin, faint whine was gone.

The two of them were suspended in a tight, invisible cocoon of soundlessness, of time that had come to a halt.

Something was about to happen. In his mind Father Vincent knew what was going to happen, yet he denied it, denied the thought, denied it could happen, that he would be present when it happened, and knew that he was wrong in his denial.

His sight sharpened. He could see clearly, as if the rays of the light now had a special, crystal radiance. He did not need his glasses any longer. He took them off, because now they were blurring his vision.

For the first time since he was a boy, he could see sharply without the lenses in front of his eyes.

He saw the drops of blood ooze slowly out of Hietala's palms. The drops were fat and grew fatter, swollen red, shining with a crimson, lovely glow. The drops swelled and burst and grew into thin rivulets that poured from the center of his palms, ran down to the edges of his hands, and then fell, red, *Oh God! so red*, to the planking of the sundeck. *Communion wine spilling red from cupped, pleading palms.*

He saw the wound open in Hietala's side. It was a thin-edged slash, just wide enough to accommodate the width of the blade of a spear; blood came from the wound in a great welling and ran down Hietala's side, ran down to his hip and over the blue cloth of his shorts and down his right leg.

The blood came from his feet, from the spike holes through his insteps.

The priest saw his body spasm in an agony of pain as each wound appeared. He saw the rapture on the bearded face held agonizingly up to the sun, and, as he stared with his new found sight, he saw the thorn wounds indent a semicircle of skin punctures along the curve of Hietala's brow.

Stigmata.

The stigmata of Christ.

He'd heard of it happening. Over the centuries of the church's existence, it had happened many times to many of the most fervent believers. But he'd never seen it himself, or known a priest who'd been present when the stigmata appeared.

Now he was witnessing it. He, Father Vincent, of the Church of St. Peter the Fisherman, the humblest of the servants of the Lord, had been given this sight.

As naked as Our Lord had been, he thought. Naked on the hill of Calvary, naked on the cross to which He'd been bound before the heavy, wooden beams had been raised high into the bright blue sky so that the multitude could see His execution. Naked, except for a loincloth, in the sun of that day of infamy and glory, naked so that the throngs—moaning, crying out—could see His suffering as the Roman mauls pounded spikes into the palms of the Jew, into the bones of His feet; the crown of thorns then placed scornfully on His brow and the final, vicious abomination of the spear thrust, hard and callous, into the soft, defenseless flesh of His side.

On that day, those who had come, who surrounded the cross, had seen the flesh of Jesus quiver and spasm with each separate, painful indignity, but it had only been His flesh they had seen suffer. On His face, raised toward the brightness and heat of that Mediterranean sun, there had been exultation and glory and humble piety.

In fear, the priest stared at the face of the man, Aaron Hietala, and saw that the look on his sunstruck features was one of exultation; of glory and humbleness and an ecstacy so great it transformed him.

The sunlight shone on the body of the man, on the tanned skin, sweating in the heat, and light rose from him and formed a nimbus around him so intense that the priest had to close his eyes against its brightness.

After a moment the brightness dimmed; he could open his eyes.

Hietala still stood where he'd been standing, but now his eyes were open. He was looking directly into the eyes of Father Vincent. His eyes were filled with pain and love. The old priest wanted to cry out.

It's a mirage! the priest forced himself to think. *It's all in my mind! It didn't happen!*

But the blood was still on Hietala's hands and on his side and leg and feet; thick red blood was on the planking, staining the wood.

The priest was aware that his glasses were in his

right hand but his sight was sharp. He realized that he did not need them. Without looking, he put the glasses on the table beside the chair.

Trembling, his limbs weak, Father Vincent got to his feet. Compulsively, knowing he shouldn't do it, he found himself taking two steps toward . . .

Michael fought his way out of the cold and the void, fighting for his life.

—*I'm back! he shouted triumphantly to Aaron.*

—*No, said Aaron. Not yet. Not yet.*

—*Yes! Now! You're not strong enough!*

—*Please . . . wait . . . please . . .*

He felt enormous, hearing Aaron beg. He'd never heard him beg before. He knew now that he was the stronger, that he'd always be the stronger.

But, even as Aaron went, Michael heard him say, I'll be back, Michael. You know I'll be back.

And he felt a flicker of fear, but only momentarily. For now, he concentrated on the priest.

. . . the man, Michael Hietala, and he found himself kneeling before him.

I am sinning, he thought as he reached up with his hands to take the wounded hand of Michael Hietala in both of his and bring it to his lips.

He felt the wetness of the blood under his fingertips, and he saw the wound and the red blood on the back of Hietala's right hand as he brought it to his lips and touched his lips to the hand.

And then he was vomiting, his body twisting to one side, racked with excruciating pain, his mind exploding, agony washing through him in bitter waves as he spewed bile from his mouth.

Evil!

Evil!

He had touched evil! He had tasted evil! He had taken evil into himself!

With a wild cry, Father Vincent thrust himself to his feet. Blindly, he turned and fled into the house, making his way in panic to the front door and toward the gate, sick and ashamed, his body wracked with fear.

For the first time in his life, he really knew what evil was.

2.

Sand had gotten into Charlie Daggett's shoes and made lumps under his toes. The wind came in strong from the ocean, ruffling his hair across his forehead. He tried to stand so that he faced the wind, but that would put his back to the lieutenant, so he didn't.

Lieutenant Bivens said, "How long do you think she's been here, Charlie?"

"Day or two at the most."

Leo Bivens stood upwind from the declivity where the wind could reach him.

"No longer than that?"

"She's not burnt enough. We've been having some real hot days for the last week, right? If she'd been here longer, she'd be all swollen up. A hell of a lot more'n she is now. Besides, someone would've found her sooner."

"Well," said the lieutenant, "the lab boys will tell us exactly."

"Sure," said Charlie Daggett. Bivens heard the caustic tone in his voice.

"You don't think much of them, do you, Charlie?"

"They haven't been much help lately."

"You mean about Mary Palumbo?"

"Yeah."

Bivens gestured at the body in the scooped out hollow, marsh grass around the rim bending and swaying in the wind.

"You think she's another Mary Palumbo?"

"Don't you?"

"I don't know. Maybe."

"Well," said Charlie Daggett, "looks like the same circumstances, don't it? Nude body, clothes off to one side. No signs of violence—"

"—we don't know that. It's hard to tell when the skin's blistered from head to foot from the sun."

"Okay, Lieutenant, but I'll bet you coffee and doughnuts for a week that's the report we're gonna get back from the pathology boys. No discernable signs of violence."

"Okay, okay—"

"I'll tell you something else they're gonna find, if you really want to know."

"What's that?"

"She was horny at the time of death."

"You sure of that?"

"Make you another bet, Lieutenant. Bet you they're gonna find evidence in her panties and on her pubic hairs that she was in a state of extreme sexual excitement just before she died."

"Rape?"

"Not unless Mary Palumbo was raped."

"You think the same guy did it?"

Charlie Daggett turned his round face toward Leo Bivens. "You're jumpin' at conclusions, Lieutenant. Mary Palumbo died of natural causes, whatever the hell they were."

Bevins snorted. "Cut the sarcasm, Charlie. You don't

believe it any more'n I do, but they got to report what they find."

"Dr. Pierce says there was no evidence of unnatural death. No violence at all. It's official."

"Is that why you're trying so hard to find the guy Mary Palumbo was last seen with?"

Charlie Daggett shrugged.

"I just like to tie up loose ends."

"Suppose you find him. What do you think he'll tell you?"

"Bunch of lies, probably," said Charlie Daggett. "But I sure would like to talk to him, anyway."

"Why?"

"Because the way it happened got me real curious about who this guy could be. According to Vito De-Luca and Ruthie Olivieri, she's sitting in the booth with them one minute. Next, she gets up to go to the bar to buy beers for herself and Joe Balzarini. That's the last they see of her. Bartender swears she never come up to the bar the whole time she was in the place. She don't come back to them, so Joe goes lookin' for her, but that ain't for another five minutes or so. Okay, now, Dan Gilbert and Red Hansen both say Mary Palumbo comes out of the bar with the guy about five minutes before Joe comes out lookin' for her and they get in that fight. So how much time does that leave her? Just about nothing. There's only one way to figure it. She sees someone she knows come in the place. She tells Joe she's gonna get the beers and leaves him sittin' in the booth while she goes off with the new guy."

"Makes sense," said the lieutenant.

"No, it don't," said Charlie Daggett.

Bevins looked at him.

"What doesn't make sense?"

"Who's the guy?" said Charlie Daggett stubbornly. "Who the hell does Mary Palumbo know that she'll dump Joe Balzarini for? Especially in a public place. You know the reputation Balzarini had. Hot-headed punk kid always in trouble from the time he was big enough to swipe his first bike. Too quick with his fish-knife. Hell, everybody knew his reputation. They knew Mary Palumbo was his girl. Nobody was gonna mess around with her. Not unless he wanted to get cut. So where'd she find a guy who don't give a shit about Balzarini? An' where'd she find time enough with him to get the hots over him? She was always with Joe."

"I see what you mean," Bivens said.

"That's why I'd kind of like to find out who the hell the son of a bitch is."

"You got any leads?"

"Bearded guy in his middle thirties."

"Big fuckin' deal," said the lieutenant. "The town's full of them now it's summer. All them goddamn vannies in town from all over the country. Looks like they make you grow a beard before they'll sell you a van, these days."

"They're not in their middle thirties," Charlie Daggett pointed out.

"Half the time you can't tell the difference," Bivens said sourly. "At least, I can't. Not when it's nighttime anyhow."

"That's true enough," Charlie Daggett admitted.

"Who described him to you?"

"Dan Gilbert."

"Dan Gilbert? Hell, Charlie, Dan was drunk when he saw the guy! You can't believe Dan."

"Not too drunk to know it was a beard he was lookin' at."

"Okay, so you got yourself a bearded man as a suspect. Sure as hell narrows it down, don't it?"

The police photographer had finished taking his pictures. The crew had wrapped the corpse in a plastic body bag. Patrolman Frank Adley came scrambling up the short slope to them,

"You get anything?" Lieutenant Bivens asked.

The police officer held out his hand. There was a wallet in it and a tiny, jewelled cross on a thin, metal necklace.

"Identification. Kid's name is Dana DeCoste. Sixteen. She went to Harbortown High."

"Shit," said Charlie Daggett in disgust. "I know her old man. He's gonna go crazy."

"Go on," said the lieutenant.

"Just the usual other stuff. Initials on the back of the cross are D.D. The wallet's filled with pictures of her an' her family an' her girl friends."

"No boys' pictures?"

"Just a couple. But they're group pictures. Four or five kids all posing for the camera."

"Nobody special?"

"Don't look like it." Adley looked at Charlie Daggett and said, "Sure looks like the Palumbo thing, don't it, Sergeant?"

"That's right," said Bevins, "you were there, too, weren't you?"

"Yeah," said Adley. "Me 'n Ray Feeney was in the first patrol car that come out to the cemetery when those kids found her."

"Who found the DeCoste kid?"

"A tourist couple. You want to talk to them? They're over on the road in my patrol car. Feeney's with them."

"What'd they tell you?"

Adley took his leather notebook out of his shirt pocket. Charlie Daggett noticed how sweat-stained his shirt was under the arms and around the collar. Adley thumbed open the cover and went through a lot of pages. He looked down at his scrawl, deciphering his notes.

"Mr. and Mrs. Thomas Webber. They're from Bloomington, Illinois. Both in their sixties. They come out here for a couple of weeks' vacation. They're staying at that motel near the Turtle Neck art colony. She paints, he likes to watch birds. That's how come they come out here onto Sugar Island. It was kinda windy, so she looked for a place that was outta the wind to set up her easel. That's when she found the body in the hollow there."

"That don't tell us much."

Adley shrugged. He said, "Mrs. Webber's real shook up, Lieutenant. Her husband wants to know is it okay if I take them over to the hospital so's she can get a doctor to give her a sedative?"

"Go ahead."

Adley turned away from them and went down the slope, slipping and sliding through the loose sand.

Daggett asked, "What d'you think we got, Lieutenant?"

Leo Bevins hesitated.

"There's no way it can be a coincidence," Charlie Daggett said.

"That's right. I'll go along with you there."

"Two young girls—one eighteen, the other sixteen—what the hell's gonna make them go out to some deserted place at night and take off their clothes because they're so horny all they want to do is get fucked?"

"A man," said the lieutenant.

"Goddamn right," said Charlie Daggett. "Only one thing."

"What's that?"

"You better not tell Pete DeCoste his kid come out here to get fucked. He thinks she was purer'n the Virgin Mary."

"Was she?"

"How the hell do I know," Charlie Daggett replied. "Far as I can see, it didn't make no difference, did it?"

CHAPTER EIGHT

Michael was very tired. After Father Vincent left, it took him a long time before he could move. The blood had stopped flowing almost immediately. Normally, the loss of so much blood would have put him into shock; now, except for a deep lassitude that enveloped his body and a dull tiredness, he felt no ill effects. What he felt mostly was fear.

Aaron had taken over his body again.

That was the thought he couldn't get out of his head. Aaron had said, *Go away, Michael,* and he had gone. He had been unable to protest, to argue, to fight against Aaron.

He was terrified that sometime Aaron might not let him come back.

His mind was tired. He found it hard to think clearly. He blinked in the sunlight, his eyes ached. He didn't like the sunlight now. It reminded him of the comings of Aaron.

Aaron!

He hated Aaron! He felt hatred welling up powerfully in him. He could admit the hatred now. From the time he knew he had killed Aaron, he'd never felt guilty about what he'd done. He'd wanted Aaron dead.

Now he knew that he hated Aaron because he feared him. He feared Aaron's power.

To bring life is a greater power than to bring death! Reluctantly, he admitted the thought; the acknowledgement coming slowly and grudgingly.

In that case, what did he have, in his power to give death, that others did not have? He answered himself, bitterly, *Nothing! Not one damn thing!* Any man can kill another. That's what men had been doing to men since Cain. What he had was the power to kill without a weapon, without violence.

He realized now that he envied Aaron. He'd always envied Aaron. *Aaron could give life!* Goddamnit! That was power! That was something no one else could do!

Was that why he hated Aaron? he wondered. Because he envied him so much? Because Aaron's power was so much greater than his own? Was that why he'd killed Aaron?

He'd killed Aaron when they were three. Christ, how much did children know at that age about life and death? Listen to them sometime, he told himself. You could hear them. Angry, pouting, screaming at their elders, at their playmates: *I hate you! I wish you were dead!*

Could it be, he wondered, that buried in the recesses of their still unformed minds was the old, prehuman knowledge that some of them had the power to give death without violence, just by wishing it—and that in every one of them lurked the desire to kill painfully?

I'm going to kill you! they shouted at each other, not knowing what death was, not knowing that it was a nothingness. Knowing only that it was the absence of the hated one. What was death to a child?

Now he knew that he'd hated Aaron. Now he knew

he'd given Aaron death because he'd envied him.
Then why wouldn't Aaron stay dead? Why had he
come back after all these years?

What right had Aaron to demand his body?

His mind ached with the effort of his thinking.

Identical twins. One ovum split in two. Two sper-
matozoa. Identical twins. Lose one. The other is the
same, isn't it? The other is identical. Right? No! Something made the two of them different.

What made them different?

One good and the other—

Grudgingly he admitted to himself that he was evil,
acknowledging Aaron's goodness.

But what if the ovum hadn't been split? What if
there had been only one body. What then?

Half good, half evil.

Christ, wasn't that what man was all about?

Then without Aaron, he was only half a man. He
denied the thought even as it came. But it came again,
forcing its way into his tired brain.

*Without Aaron, I'm not complete . . . without Aaron
. . . Aaron . . . Aaron, come back . . . I need you,
Aaron!*

Come back, so I can kill you again!

He went upstairs and showered. The water
streamed off his body, red at first, and then pale pink
and, finally, clear. He soaped himself and rinsed again
and stepped out of the shower stall to dry himself off.

When he examined his body, there were tight puck-
erings on both sides of his hands. His feet showed the
same puckered scars, but even as he looked at them,
he could see them diminish in size.

The wound in his side took the longest to disappear.
In less than ten minutes, there were only faint marks

on his body to show where the stigmata had been. Fifteen minutes later, there were no signs at all.

He put on clean shorts and loafers and a shirt and went downstairs to wash the blood off the planking of the sundeck. He filled a bucket with soapy water and took a mop from the kitchen closet, but when he went out onto the deck, there were no stains to be seen. It didn't surprise him; few things surprised him anymore. It was as if it had never happened.

2.

Father Vincent wanted to prostrate himself before the altar at the Church of St. Peter the Fisherman. That was the only thought in his panicked mind during his blind drive back from Adam's Cove. Were it not for the fact that he habitually drove slowly, he would have caused half a dozen accidents.

When he pulled his sedan up in front of the church, he left the engine running, forgetting to turn it off, forgetting to close the door when he got out of the car.

He stumbled up the brick walk to the church steps and came to a halt. The doors were open, their curved tops, which formed an arch when the doors were closed, now looked like massive, dark, oaken wings. He could see inside; he could see the dark mahogany panelling of the vestibule, and through the open, inner doors he could see the altar at the far end of the church and the crucifix. The pews were empty at this time of day, their wood dark and oiled. He could not see the confessional or the font of holy water.

In front of the altar, candles burned. Some were newly lit, others had almost guttered out. Yellow flames, soft white of wax, crimson of cloth, gold of design. From the time he had been a child, all this, in so many different churches, had warmed and comforted him. He had loved it beyond all other things. He'd felt privileged at being an acolyte; the love in him for the church had grown stronger because he served it. Even though he knew that pride was sinful, he'd felt proud, chosen, during his years at the seminary. After the ceremony of his ordination, he'd done penance for the inordinate pride he'd felt, and he tried to humble himself. He'd never had ambitions to rise in the hierarchy of the church; it was enough to give his love and live his life for it.

Now as he started up the steps, he froze. His muscles would no longer obey him.

He wasn't surprised. He knew he had sinned most grievously, had sinned beyond the sins of all but a few. He had knelt down to evil, genuflected to it. He had kissed the hand of evil.

His legs trembled and gave way beneath him. He sank to his knees on the steps of the church. His palms came together in front of him as he began to pray, but the words choked in his throat.

He could see the length of the church all the way to the tortured body of Christ, carved and painted, on the crucifix, and he realized that he could see sharply. He felt his face for his glasses. They were not there; he'd left them behind. Now he realized that he'd driven all the way back from Adam's Cove without them. He hadn't needed them. He didn't need them now. He had perfect vision.

Father Vincent began to cry. The gift of sight was a horror to him.

He knew he couldn't enter the church. He couldn't bring so great a defilement before Him. It would be an abomination beyond all else.

Slowly his eyes filled with tears until his vision blurred, and they ran down the furrows of his lined face. He bowed his head, his torso sank forward until his forehead touched the cool stones of the church steps.

In his mind, he prayed for forgiveness. *Mea culpa . . . mea culpa . . .*

Over and over and over again. *Mea culpa . . . mea culpa . . . culpa . . .*

When he was found and they tried to lift him to his feet, he was not aware of them, not when they tried to speak to him, nor when they took him away, nor in any of the days that followed.

Mea culpa!

3.

Sarah Cameron Flint came that afternoon with her young friend, Edith Cavanaugh. Michael received them in the high-vaulted living room. He was dressed in soft gray slacks and a light yellow turtleneck jersey.

"I've told Edith about the girl on the highway," she said brightly, bringing Edith close to Michael so they stood face to face.

"And," she added, "about the man on the docks the other day."

He looked at her in surprise.

"How did you know about him?"

Mrs. Flint was pleased with herself. "My housekeeper comes from Harbortown," she explained. "Mrs. Santini. Carmine Santini. Her husband was a fisherman before his death. She's been going with another one. I think they're engaged. Sal Aiello. He was one of the men on the dock. He told her about it."

Michael frowned, but inside he wasn't displeased. It

seemed as if Aaron had done him a favor, after all. It amused him greatly. That Mrs. Flint would hear about it was beyond any expectation he could have had.

Edith Cavanaugh was looking at him with wide, staring eyes.

Mrs. Flint said breathlessly, her thin, old voice almost lost in the huge room, "They're all talking about it, you know. Some of the women have lit candles to you. Did you know that?"

"Do they know who I am?"

"I don't think so. At least, not by name. I'm sure not. Mrs. Santini tells me that the priest is quite disturbed."

Michael nodded. "I'm sure he would be."

"You'll probably be hearing from him. I told Mrs. Santini who you were."

"I've already heard from him. He was here earlier today."

"I expect you saw how disturbed he was, then?"

"Yes."

"Did you have words?"

"Why should we have words?" Michael asked.

Edith Cavanaugh felt the calm and quiet radiating from him. When he turned his eyes on her, she felt love and compassion envelop her. She loved him in return and wanted to tell him so. Instead she said, "I feel grateful to Sarah for telling me about you. I only wish I could have been there to witness it with my own eyes, the way she did."

She reached out for his hand. It felt strong and large in her own small hands. It made her feel protected.

Groping for words, she said, "I—I've wronged you."

She felt the need to confess. "When Sarah first told me about you, I . . ."

She stopped, biting her lips, afraid to go on.

"Yes?"

"I—I told her you were a fraud . . . I said that what you'd done was some kind of a trick."

Michael waited. She saw him waiting for her to go on.

She blurted out, "I was wrong."

"Why?" he asked, gently. "What makes you think you were wrong?"

"I—I talked to Mrs. Santini myself. Then I went with her to meet her fiancé—"

"—the fisherman," Mrs. Flint interrupted. "Salvatore Aiello."

"Ahh."

"I talked with him for a long time. I made him describe everything he saw in detail. I made him go over it several times. And then he took me to talk with his friends. The others who'd been there, too."

"And that convinced you?"

Edith Cavanaugh shook her head. "No. But I talked with one man—the one who'd felt John Christy's broken neck. He said he could feel the broken bones grinding in his hand. He knew the man couldn't be alive."

"But he could have been," said Michael. "A broken neck doesn't always mean death."

Edith Cavanaugh shook her head stubbornly, her short hair flying. "He may not have been dead, but his neck was broken. Was it broken?"

Her eyes challenged him.

"Yes, it was broken."

She said, "Well, I went to the hospital. I have connections there. I donate a lot of money every year. It opens a lot of doors. I read the examination report. Ribs, arms, legs, and pelvis. But nothing about vertebrae. He didn't have a broken neck."

Michael waited, knowing there was more.

Edith Cavanaugh said, "I'm a very skeptical person. I asked to see the X-rays."

"And?"

"There was no sign of any injury to his neck."

She said, "You see, I have to prove it to myself. And I did. So I have to believe the rest. I believe you brought the girl back to life. I believe you brought the fisherman back to life."

She looked up at him.

"I—I believe in you," she said, her voice faltering only slightly.

Mrs. Flint had tears in her eyes. She had never known such happiness, she thought. She wanted to hug them both. She said proudly, "I told Edith about my contribution to The Church of the Second Life. She would like to do the same."

Somehow it wasn't the same as when he'd gotten Sarah Flint. He felt no sense of achievement. The old lady was pathetic in her emotions; her young friend, who prided herself so much on her cold, logical skepticism, seemed to him not very smart. Certainly not by believing that because an X-ray showed no broken vertebrae he had brought a man back to life. Christ! Maybe he never had a broken neck in the first place!

"You want to join our church?" he asked her. "Is that it?"

Edith Cavanaugh nodded.

"How old are you?" Michael asked, guessing that she couldn't be more than in her mid-forties. She was very plain.

"Thirty-one," she said.

"Then what do we have to offer you?"

"Truth," she said.

"Not a second life? Not a second body?"

She hesitated.

Plain face. Dumpy body. Probably fat thighs. He wondered if she'd ever been made love to. He doubted it.

"Someday, perhaps." She quickly added, "If I'm worthy, of course."

So they don't have to be old. They can be homely and want to be beautiful. He'd never thought of that. *They really do believe money can buy them everything, don't they?*

Lisa Fialho came into the room. Mrs. Flint saw her and smiled. Lisa came up to them.

Mrs. Flint said to Edith Cavanaugh, "You've met Miss Fialho before, Edith. Did I tell you that she's a deaconess in The Church of the Second Life?"

"Yes," Edith said. "You told me that." She turned to Michael. "Could—would it be possible—someday, that is . . . for me to become a deaconess, too?"

Michael looked at Lisa Fialho, noticing that she was dressed demurely in a white linen frock. Her long, blond hair was tied back with a simple, yellow ribbon. Her face looked scrubbed and wholesome. She wore no makeup.

Lisa answered for him. "If you believe," she said.

"Oh, yes," said Edith Cavanaugh, breathlessly. "Yes, I believe."

"Then the time will come." She looked at Michael. He understood from the expression on her face what she wanted him to do.

Withdrawing his hand from Edith Cavanaugh's, he said, "I must go now. I'm so glad you came."

She flushed, closing her eyes because they had

filled with tears and she didn't want him to see her that way. When she cried, her face got puffy and her eyes turned terribly red. She was at her worst, then.

Michael turned away, bending to kiss Mrs. Flint on the cheek and squeezing her hand briefly.

"You're always welcome," he said. "Will you come tomorrow for another private session?"

"Oh, yes! Yes!" the old lady said, her eyes sparkling with happiness. "I've been looking forward to it since the last one."

"Good," said Michael. He turned and went up the open stairwell to the second floor. The three women watched him until he was out of sight.

Mrs. Flint said, "Edith?"

"Yes?"

"When you make your contribution . . . talk with Miss Fialho. You'll only disturb Michael if you mention money to him."

Edith Cavanaugh looked at Lisa. She saw how pretty she was and wished she could be that beautiful. She'd never before liked any beautiful woman. Now, strangely, she felt no antagonism. Mrs. Flint had told her that Lisa Fialho was in her second body, living her second life. Soon, she knew, she would be, too. And she would be beautiful.

Her voice was crisp when she asked, "When can I make my donation?"

Lisa Fialho smiled softly at her. "Whenever you like."

"Now?"

"If you like."

"Yes," said Edith Cavanaugh. "I'd like to do it now."

Mrs. Flint sat in the same armchair she'd occupied on her first visit, her cane held upright by her leg, and waited while the two younger women went into the office that had once been the dining room of the house.

She could look out past Michael's chair, through the enormous glass window wall, across the sundeck and see the ocean all the way to the horizon. Sunlight sparkled on the wavetops and gulls wheeled and circled. The day was fresh and bright.

And so full of life, she thought. She felt pleased that she'd finally introduced Edith Cavanaugh to Michael. Now she also wanted to introduce Edith's sister to him.

Sandra Cavanaugh Wilkes.

She was the one who really needed Michael's grace.

CHAPTER NINE

Lieutenant Leo Bivens came into Charlie Daggett's office. The air was blue-thick with cigarette smoke.

"Don't you ever open a window?"

Charlie Daggett looked at him in surprise.

"Never mind. What'd you want me to look at?"

Daggett pointed to the four lumps of white plaster on his desk.

"Tire casts," he said. "Two sets of them."

Bivens looked at them. He pushed at one of them with his finger.

"Let me guess. You found one set at the cemetery and the other near Sugar Island. Right?"

Charlie Daggett nodded.

"Ain't that a hell of a coincidence?" Bivens remarked facetiously.

"No," said Charlie Daggett, taking him seriously, "not really."

"You just happened to find two identical sets, one at each place—and that isn't a coincidence?"

"Not if you had to have casts made of every goddamn set of tire tracks within a hundred yards," Daggett said. "It took almost three days. We made over fifty sets in each place. And then they had to be matched up."

"Who did the casting? I don't remember assigning

any of our men to the job. I also didn't know we had the equipment to do it this good." He poked at the casts again.

"I got the state police to do it."

Lieutenant Bivens lifted an eyebrow. "How'd you talk them into it? Both homicides—" He saw the expression on Charlie Daggett's face. "Okay, I agree with you they gotta be homicides. Anyhow, they both took place within our jurisdiction. How come the state police are getting involved?"

"Sugar Island is state property," Charlie Daggett informed him. Bivens looked surprised. "I always thought the same as you," Daggett went on. "But on the off chance it wasn't, I looked it up. It isn't. Along with eight or ten other islands along the coast here, Sugar Island was taken over by the Commonwealth back around 1910. Nobody's paid any attention to Sugar Island. It's too small for a state park or anything like that, but it's still state property, all right, so that puts the state police in the picture. They kinda raised a fuss when I brought it up. Told me nobody could be sure if the crime was committed on Sugar Island. It could've taken place on the beach, which'd make it pure and simple a Harbortown matter."

"So?"

"So we compromised. They agreed to do the casting and any lab work that might come up, but no manpower to investigate it. That's up to us."

"You think you could've talked to me about it before you made all these arrangements?" Lieutenant Bivens asked.

"I sent you a memo," Charlie Daggett said.

"Great. My office is right next door, and you send me a memo. When am I supposed to get it?"

Charlie Daggett said nothing. He lit another cigarette.

Bivens sighed and said, "So you came up with a pair of matching treads?"

"They did," said Charlie. "I told you they agreed to do the casting."

"What've you got?"

"Dunlops," Charlie told him. "Steel-belted radials. Made in Japan under license. Probably for a seventy-five Toyota sedan or coupe. So it's no vannie."

"Huh?"

"When I told you about the guy with the beard, you said all the damn vannies looked alike to you. Now we know it wasn't a vannie."

"All right. So you got a bearded guy in his middle thirties who drives a Toyota. Where does that get you?"

"A hell of a lot further than before."

"It still doesn't—" Lieutenant Bivens broke off. He saw the stubborn look on Charlie Daggett's face. "All right, Charlie. What do you have in mind? How're you goin' to put 'em together?"

"Registry of Motor Vehicles," Daggett said. "I've asked them for a computer printout of every seventy-four, seventy-five, seventy-six and seventy-seven Toyota registered from the Cape Mary area."

"You know how many you're going to get?" Bivens asked. "Christ, Charlie, you'll never get around to check them out in years!"

"No," said Daggett, "I won't. But Massachusetts drivers' licenses have a Polaroid color picture of the driver as well as his name, birth date and social security number. And duplicates are on file at the Registry."

Bivens held up his hand. "Okay, I get it. They go

through their list, pull all male driver's licenses registered from the Cape Mary area. They eliminate everyone over sixty and under thirty."

"Under twenty-five. But you got the idea."

"Then you match up the addresses with the Toyota addresses."

"Right," said Charlie Daggett.

"Registry going to do the work?"

"No. I thought you might assign one of our guys to the job."

"How long you estimate it'll take?"

"About a week."

"We're tight on manpower," Bivens said.

"I know."

"So it'll mean overtime."

"That's right." He waited.

"It's gonna be rough. I'll have to go to the Chief on this one. Garrity's not going to like it."

Charlie Daggett shrugged.

"You think you're gonna come up with a match?"

"Maybe."

"Why just maybe?"

"Because the car could be from out of state," Daggett said. "Or the driver."

"So you might wind up with nothing?"

"Well," said Charlie, "like you said, we don't have too much to go on right now, do we?"

2.

It was night and they turned out of Wharf Street too fast, twisting and winding along the narrow road from the heart of Barrett's Cove, their headlights ahead of them like antennae.

The tires of the Lancia squealed hard and high-pitched as they made the last turn before the triangle at the church where the road joined the county route. Route 427 was a narrow, two-lane blacktop that curved and dipped around the whole of the Cape Mary peninsula.

Sandra shouted at Doug to take the long way around, by way of Bay Cove and Gale Harbor and through Pinchon's Bay.

Mackay spun the wheel. The Lancia turned left, accelerating. They were going too fast. Sandra loved the excitement and danger of speed, of the road whipping past, of the parked cars on the side of the road only inches away from them, of the blur as they whipped past, of the rising wind sound and the press and thrust of the car seat against her body as they took the curves so fast that the shoulder belt Doug insisted she wear gripped the soft flesh across her breast and abdomen like a lover's forearm.

Mackay knew she became excited when he drove fast. He liked to excite her. Speed excited her sexually. He liked the feel of the car under his hands. He had square, strong hands and powerful forearms.

The Lancia cornered well. It was tight and precise and everything a good car should be, so that even though it wasn't anything like the Porsche Turbo Carrera he'd wanted her to buy, it would do.

At times, when he drove it fast and hard, pushing it to its limits on the back roads of Cape Mary, he liked to recall how it had been in the Lotus Ford at Monte Carlo the year he'd raced there, and what it had been like in the night, taking the corners at high speeds.

It wasn't anything at all like that, now, in the Lancia. Monte Carlo had been ten years ago. He'd made a bad showing, and he knew it was because the edge had gone. It wasn't the machine that had let him down. Monte Carlo had come too late. Even then, he'd been too old for it. Sometimes, when he could think about it without feeling the decayed anger he still felt at times, he wondered what it would have been like if he'd driven there when he was in his twenties. Or any time before the crash at Watkins Glen had put him in the hospital for almost a year.

In the daytime, Route 427 was a road well-traveled by tourists who liked to drive even slower than the posted speed limits. It was narrow and went along cliff edges with no shoulder between the road and the edge of the cliffs, and it was scenic.

The road was posted most of the way at twenty-five miles an hour. Now, in the summer darkness, Mackay had the Lancia up to sixty on the short, straight stretches, then braking hard, feeling the bite of the discs on the flat brake surfaces and the lurching dive of the front end, the speed dropping, slamming the stubby gearshift lever down a gear, down another, in a quick, double-clutching coordination of his right hand and right foot and clutch foot, taking the curve with the engine screaming and just a hair short of breaking tire traction.

He was good. He knew he was good, yet he was careful not to let the car get beyond his ability to control it, even though he let Sandra think that they were taking all kinds of chances and that they might be killed any second.

Before they came into Pinchon's Bay, he slowed down to a sedate speed. There were always patrol cars on the streets of the town, no matter what time of night it was. Pinchon's Bay lived on tourists and parking meters and traffic fines.

On the other side of the town, on the way now to Adam's Cove, the road was still as narrow and still as twisting, and, even though there was some traffic, he opened up the Lancia again, passing the few cars at high speed, hearing the wind whipping through the windows like the snapping of invisible flags in a gale. Sandra let out small, whimpering screams of pleasure as she moved against him, her hand in his crotch. She always did that when she got excited. Now she held him cupped there, hard, so that the warmth and pressure of her fingers began to excite him.

They made the circuit of the Adam's Cove shore road with its hard, sharp twists and the abrupt drop on their left, where the long swells of ocean waves curled up to smash against the rocks, Sandra seeing in her mind what would happen if they went off the road.

Half a mile before they came onto the side road that led to Michael Hietala's church, Mackay let the speed die away.

Sandra let out a long, shuddering breath and took her hand away from him and sat up, reaching up to run a hand through his hair. She kissed him on the cheek.

Breathlessly she said, "God! It's as good as a downhill run when everything's going right for you."

"Better," he said.

"Yes. Yes, it's better. You could really get wiped out totally if anything went wrong. Not just a broken leg or ankle."

He felt her give a small shudder. The Lancia turned onto the side road.

"Make a left up ahead," she said. "His place is hard to find the first time."

"When were you here before?"

"Yesterday. Sara Flint took me to see him. She and Edith."

"How long's Edith been into him?"

"I don't know. Sarah's the one who turned Edith onto him. Sarah's really hung up on the guy."

"What's his bag?"

Sandra caught the undertone of scorn in his voice. She could understand it. In the past, she'd often felt the same way about her sister. Parapsychology in New York. Duke University and ESP. Zen and Yoga and TM and est and Scientology. The most recent was Edith's series of nightly trips to Salem. She'd discovered a witches' coven that met there.

And now, Michael Hietala.

Doug Mackay asked again, "What's Hietala's bag?"

"Reincarnation."

"Reincarnation?"

"I think so," she said defensively, not wanting to be the target for his scorn. "I'm not sure. He didn't talk about it to me when we were there."

"Reincarnation." Mackay was amused.

"Maybe that's not the right word. It's like there's a life force in everyone and it never dies. Only the body gets old and dies, because the body's physical, but the life force can go from one body to another."

"That's reincarnation, all right," Mackay said.

"Not really. Sarah says there's more to it than that. She says that Hietala claims that the life force doesn't have to go into a newborn baby. It can take over a body that already exists."

"How the hell does it do that?"

"By being stronger. Something like that. Sarah wasn't too clear about it."

"Neither's Hietala, I'll bet."

She flushed. "Sarah says he's brought two people back to life after they were dead. And Edith says the same thing."

Mackay said, questioningly, "Resurrection?"

"I guess."

"Resurrection," Mackay said again. "Jesus Christ! Some people will believe the damnedest things!"

3.

"You're not listening," Lisa complained. "They'll be here in less than half an hour. You've been putting it off."

With an effort, Michael focused his attention on her. *Greedy little animal,* he thought, then wondered what the hell had happened to him, why he could no longer feel the hot stir of excitement when he smelled money. But he knew the reason.

"Are you listening?" Her voice cold, sharp.

"Go ahead."

Lisa had the looseleaf notebook in her lap. She scanned the tight scribblings on the lined pages.

She said, "We don't have as much information on her as we have on her sister."

"It doesn't matter."

"The hell it doesn't!" She flared at him. "You're the one who's always preached at me to get as much information about a mark as you could. Money in the bank, you used to say."

"Oh, Christ!" *Would she never leave him alone?* "Go ahead. I don't need a lecture."

"Sandra Cavanaugh Wilkes. Oldest of the three Cavanaugh sisters. Youngest was Elizabeth, who died at the age of—"

"Oldest? I thought Edith was older."

"No, she's older by eleven years."

"She looks ten years younger than Edith."

"She had a face lift," Lisa told him. "And I don't

know what the hell else. Silicone, probably. Edith's thirty-one. Sandra's almost forty-two."

She caught the expression on his face.

"That body's cost her a lot. Elizabeth Arden and Maine Chance. Private clinics. Annual trips to Swiss health spas. She's man-hungry, Mike."

"What about her husband?"

"Which one? She's had four of them. Carey Wilkes was the last. After him she stopped marrying them. Saves her giving them a settlement when she's tired of them."

"She living with someone now?"

"Guy named Doug Mackay. He's coming with her tonight."

"What have you got on him?"

Lisa flipped a page in the notebook. "Doug Mackay. He's in his late thirties. Came out of college into his father's brokerage firm. Made a hell of a lot of money before he was thirty. Dropped out of the firm when his father died. Spent most of the money on racing cars, the rest of it on boats. Yacht bum. Ski bum. Overage for a ski bum, but he's good looking, and a lot of the young girls go for the mature type. He met Sandra about a year ago in Vail. She got hung up on him and took him back East with her. They've been living together since then. Most of the summer they're at her place in Barrett's Cove. She bought him a motor sailer."

"In his late thirties, you said?"

"About thirty-eight, thirty-nine, yes."

"I got the idea she went for the young ones."

"She does, usually."

"Isn't he too old for her?"

"I guess not," Lisa said. "She's been with him longer than with most."

"How come?"

"I don't know. She's hung up on the guy. That's reason enough."

"Where the hell did you get all this information?"

"Sarah Flint likes to gossip. She talks to me a lot. It wasn't hard to bring the conversation around to Sandra Wilkes and her boyfriend. Sarah doesn't like him."

"And she's interested in psychic phenomena like Edith?"

"Not so you'd know it. She came to meet you yesterday only because Sarah Flint pushed her into it."

"Then why's she coming tonight?"

Lisa smiled at him, a hard, humorless twist of her lips. She shook her head, flipping her long hair back over her shoulder. "She's horny. Couldn't you tell?"

"No."

"She didn't try to hide it. Sarah Flint saw it. I saw it. She wants to go to bed with you, Mike."

Hietala studied Lisa's face. Except for the tiny, hard smile, there was nothing he could read in it.

"And you wouldn't mind?"

Lisa's expression didn't change. "Why should I mind? You used to send me out for a hundred bucks. You make this dame and she's good for a couple of hundred grand. That's what we got from her sister."

"You wouldn't give a damn? It wouldn't bother you?"

Lisa shrugged. "About as much as it bothered you, Mike."

"We don't need the money," he said.

Lisa laughed sarcastically. "Oh, get off it, Mike! You'd screw a snake for a hundred grand."

He heard the tone of her voice and recognized what its sharpness meant. He saw it in the stiff way she was sitting, and how she was holding herself tightly.

"All right," he said, "what the hell is ticking you off?"

"Not a fucking thing!"

He waited, not turning away from her glaring eyes.

"You really don't know, do you?"

"If I knew, I wouldn't have to ask."

Angrily Lisa got to her feet. She walked to the windows, staring out, but the reflection of the room lights made the glass a mirror. She could see herself, but not outside. She turned back to him, stopped, stared at him with the kind of hostility he hadn't seen in her face since their early days together.

She said bluntly, "Mike, when was the last time you made love to me?"

She held up her hand. "Don't bother trying to think back. I'll tell you. Not since the day Sarah Cameron Flint showed up here. Remember that morning? You weren't in bed and I woke up because of that. I went downstairs and found you standing out on the sundeck staring at the ocean. There was something bothering you then, Mike. I don't know what the hell it was. All I can remember is that it frightened me. We went back to bed and made love—but it wasn't like it used to be. And that's the last time we had sex. More than two weeks ago."

She was right. He hadn't thought about it. It hadn't entered his mind.

She went on, "What the hell's going on, Mike? You getting tired of me? If you are, tell me and I'll split. I won't hang on if I'm not wanted."

He shook his head, no, without sounding the word.

"Then what the hell is it?" Frustration in her voice underlying the anger.

"Is there someone else?"

"No. There's no one else. Did you think there was?"

She shrugged. "I don't know what to think. I don't see how there could be. You're always with me—except for a couple of nights when you went off by yourself. Where the hell were you, Mike?"

"Just driving around."

"I don't believe you."

"It doesn't have anything to do with you."

"Everything has to do with me. Unless you want me out of the picture. Do you want me to go, Mike?"

"No."

"That's hard to believe, the way you've been acting."

She waited for him to answer. When she saw he wasn't going to answer, she asked, "Does it have to do with this con you've been pulling on Mrs. Flint and Edith Cavanaugh? I still don't know how you got them to believe you can really bring people back to life. What's the gimmick, Mike?"

"It's no con," he said, and she saw that he was serious.

She made a sound. "Don't give me that crap. I'm not one of your marks. I know better. Remember me? Lisa Fialho? The girl you taught the game to?"

"You really don't believe me, do you?"

"About anything else, yes."

Even as she said the words, she remembered the time he'd come home with Mrs. Flint and had gone down to the beach at the foot of the cliffs to be alone, and she'd gone down to talk to him and had put her hands on him. Her hands had felt flesh so cold she'd been frightened. She hadn't thought of it again. Not until now.

For the first time, she noticed his face had changed. It was leaner and darker and there was something in his eyes that disturbed her. He was smiling at her, mockery in his eyes, maliciousness behind the mockery. And something else. She shivered, her body racked in quick, atavistic fear.

He said something to her. Now even his voice sounded different. She couldn't take her eyes away from his face. She couldn't move. She felt the fear grow and wanted to run; she felt a sweet, hot stirring in her groin.

Hietala got to his feet. She watched him come close to her, her face lifting up to his as he came within inches of her. She felt herself bathed in a damp coldness of fear, washed by waves of hot, visceral desire for him.

"Do you want to?" His voice was no louder than a whisper.

"Not with you," she forced herself to say.

He held out his hand. She looked down at it. The fingers were long, the hand sinewy.

"Come," he said.

She fought the feeling.

"No," she said. "No . . . no . . ."

"You'll come," he said, and, without touching her, he turned and went up the stairs.

She sat for a moment, hating herself, because she knew that she would follow him, that no power on earth could stop her.

When she came into the bedroom, the lights were out. Only the faint wash of moonlight coming in the window, making silhouettes of the furniture, lit the room. She didn't need light. She could see him clearly.

A pale glow of greenish light shone like an aura around his body. He was nude.

Nude and tall. He loomed enormous in the darkness of the room.

She slipped off her dress quickly. She knew he was waiting for her; saw him standing, his hands on his hips, his legs apart.

Impatiently, she tore at the rest of her clothes, not once taking her eyes from his face, sensing his body, sensing his flesh, the male skin, the hardness of muscle under the skin, the solid bones, the power of hands that would grip her painfully. She knew only the incredible need to have his body in hers.

She came to him in a rush. She touched him. His flesh was cold. So cold, it hurt. She put her hands to his face; cold skin, roughness of beard hairs under her fingertips. She ran her hands across his chest, trying to warm him. She wanted to warm him with her own heat. Christ! She had heat. She was burning. She pressed herself against him, wanting him inside her. She'd never been so wet or felt herself so open.

When she moved her hand down his stomach, across the flat, hard muscles and through the curled, coiled hairs, he filled her hand as she clutched him—larger, thicker, stronger than she'd ever felt any man. She sank to her knees, holding his length in both her hands, bringing it slowly up between her breasts, bending her head so that her hair fell over them like a veil, touching her mouth to the head of the hardness she held in her hands, wetting it, tasting it, letting it finally slide slowly, infinitely slowly, into her mouth.

And then she was on the carpeted floor, begging him to enter her, screaming at him to fulfill her, beating on him to penetrate her, to fill the insatiable emptiness inside her that was burning her with a fire she'd never known before.

And he did. It was unlike any coupling she'd ever had with Michael Hietala. Even in her feverish lust, her mind hallucinating, desiring only to be ravished brutally and agonizingly, she realized that Michael Hietala had changed.

She screamed. Pain went through her like no other pain she'd ever had. It seared. It burned with a hellish coldness and fire. It was a knifeblade along the length of her body, deep into her body.

She loved it, loved the pain that was so much a delicate pleasure.

She gave herself up to the pain. Yielded to it. Yielded to him as she'd never been able to give herself before, even to him. She was nothing; he was everything. She grovelled to him, whimpered for him, felt him enter her so completely that she had no will of her own. Was nothing. Would be nothing.

Except as he wished her to be.

When she felt that, she came. Mindlessly, blindly, screaming, she went into another world and lived there for seconds of time that were an eternity of gratification.

Oh, yes! . . . oh, yes! . . . oh, yes! . . . Yes . . . yes! . . . yes . . .

CHAPTER TEN

She looked sideways at his cold, frozen profile, a dark shadow in the dark of the car, and felt the chill inside herself. She felt soiled and used. *How could I have done it?* she thought despairingly. *What the hell ever got into me!*

They were on their way back to Barrett's Cove, driving the dark road too fast.

"Say it," she said, sharply, unable to bear the silence any longer. "Goddamnit! Say it and get it out in the open!"

"Say what? What the hell is there to say?"

"You know. I hate it when you won't talk to me. Let's get it over with. Say it!"

"What? That we're through? That I've had it? Okay. We're through. Is that what you want to hear? As soon as we get back, I'll pack my bags and get the hell out."

"No, that's not what I want to hear. You know it. It's not what I want you to say."

She waited. Stared at his frozen profile, felt despicable, felt unclean. Felt the tightness in him. *God! How he must hate me!*

"Go ahead. Call me names, if you like."

"What for? What good would it do to call you names?"

"Because you're furious. You're bottling it up. Let it out."

The windows of the Lancia were rolled up. It was dark in the car. The only light came from the glow of the dashboard instruments. He was driving the Lancia as if he could drive the anger out of himself. She felt it in the hard, sudden lurches as he rounded the corners, in the protesting scream of the transmission as he slammed through the gears, letting the clutch out too fast.

"I don't blame you," she told him. She wanted him to understand that she was sorry. "It was a dirty thing to do."

"I should have expected it from you. You've always been a horny bitch. There wasn't any reason for me to think you've changed."

She bit her lip, holding back the flow of her protest. *Let him talk it out of his system. I deserve it.*

"I'm sorry," she said. "I'm really sorry."

"Sorry!"

"I—I couldn't help myself."

Even as she said it, she knew it was no excuse.

She said, "I love you, Doug."

He laughed; a short, bitter explosion of sound.

"You love me. Fucking liar!"

"I do! Doug, I love you!"

"I see. You love me, so you go get yourself laid the first chance you get with him. Goddamnit!" He slammed the rim of the steering wheel with the heel of his right hand. "You made a goddamn fool out of me!" Mimicking: " 'Doug, I've got to talk to Michael in private. I'll be back in a few minutes.' "

"I meant it!"

"You meant it. Yes, of course. You meant it. That's why you didn't come back for almost an hour."

"Doug—"

"Shut up!"

"Please, Doug!"

Silence. Noise of the tires. Noise of the wind. Noise of the engine. *I could kill myself. What the hell have I done to us?*

"What the hell difference does it make?" he asked, his voice flat, the tiredness coming through. "You don't have to justify yourself to me. Hell, I'm just another guy you've been shacking up with and paying his bills. I was dumb enough to think I meant something to you. Okay. I was wrong. I know when to get out. The only thing—" He took a deep breath and exhaled slowly. "Damn it, you could've let me know in a different way!"

The Lancia sped forward in the darkness. There was no moon. The road seemed blacker by contrast with the bright slash of hard and blue-white light preceding the car.

"It wasn't me!" She screamed at him, unable to hold it back any longer. "Don't you understand? It wasn't me!"

"Sure. He raped you. Is that what you want me to believe? He raped you?"

"He didn't rape me. I don't know what happened. All I know is, I couldn't help it. I couldn't fight it."

"You couldn't fight it. Did you try to fight it?"

"I—"

"*Did . . . you . . . try . . . to . . . fight . . . it?*"

"N-no."

"Then *shut up!*"

She said, driven, "Doug, you've got to understand! You have to! Please! Just listen! For Christ's sake! Listen to me! Please listen!"

"Ah-h-h, shit! Go ahead. I'll listen. But don't expect me to believe you."

She began desperately, "We went upstairs. I didn't even think it was strange that we went upstairs instead of into the office. And then he shut the door and looked at me. That's all he did. He just looked at me, and . . . and I—I couldn't take my eyes away from him. I don't know what the hell happened, or how it happened, except we were on the bed . . . and I—I couldn't help myself. So help me God! I don't know what the devil got into me! I just—Christ! I just had to have him or I'd've gone crazy!"

"Yeah," he said. "I can just see it. One look from a guy and you get so horny you have to pull him into bed. Happens to girls all the time."

"Doug, I'm scared."

"You?" He laughed. "That's a good one."

"I am. He frightens me. It's going to happen again, Doug. All he has to do is look at me—touch me—and I'll crawl to him. It's like I have no will of my own. I can't help myself. Don't you understand?"

"It's your problem, baby. I'm cutting out."

"No! You can't! I need you, Doug! Doug, I want us to go away. Tonight."

"Okay," he said. "We'll pack and leave tonight. Where are you going?"

"I don't know. I think I'd—what do you mean, where am I going? You're coming with me."

"No way. I'm splitting. I know when I'm not wanted."

"It's not true! Doug!"

She reached to touch him. Her hand touched his face. He knocked it away with a swift backhand blow, catching her across the lower part of her face. Knuckle-bones split her lip. The sudden pain burnt a bright, explosive light in her head.

"Keep your fucking hands off me!"

She fumbled in her purse for her handkerchief, wadded it, pressed it to her numb lip.

She began to cry.

"Doug, I love you . . . I—I need . . . you!"

She huddled, pulling her legs up onto the seat, curling, hugging her knees, squirming into a ball. Crying. She was afraid.

The Lancia was ripping the night apart. Fast. Faster. Screaming into the curves, yet it did not frighten her because of the fear inside her. Because of what had happened. Because of what could happen again.

Out of the corner of his eye, he saw her dark huddled shape on the seat. He hated her. He wanted to hurt her, wanted to smash at her face and body until she screamed for forgiveness, and then to hurt her more.

His mind could only focus on one set of images. Of her, naked, her legs wide, her thighs apart, her head flung back, hair sprawled on the pillow, sounds coming from her throat, ugly moans of pleasure pressed out of her in a thick, persistent rhythm, bucking upwards with her hips, grunting, damp with sweat, slick on her stomach and thighs, her arms around the solid, muscular male body on top of her, pulling him into her, thick and heavy going into her, glistening, out and then in again and—

The clarity of the images, burned the pain and anger into him. With a cry of rage, he slammed his foot against the brake pedal. The Lancia nosed forward, slid, broke traction, fishtailed from one side of the road to the other.

She screamed in panic, lifted her head.

"Doug!"

He brought the car to a stop, pulling to the side of the road.

She sat up, frightened.

"What are you doing?"

He reached across her, his face twisting in a snarl. His fingers flipped the door handle. He pushed against it.

"Get out!"

Frozen, she stared at him.

His hands clawed at the release of her seat belt.

"Goddamnit! Get out!"

Pushing at her, throwing her off balance, he forced her into the road. She almost fell, caught herself at the last moment, stumbled, regained her feet, turned and screamed into the car.

"Goddamn you, Doug! It's my car! You can't do this to me!"

"I'll leave it at the house. That good enough for you?"

"Why? Why are you doing this to me?"

"Because I can't stand being with you any longer! I'm ready to kill you!"

"Doug—*please!*"

He slammed the door, threw the car into gear. It spit gravel at her, stinging her bare legs as it raced off into the darkness.

The red glow from the taillights encompassed her as she stood mute, shocked; then the light faded, the car turned with the road, and they were gone.

She listened to the last rumblings of the engine. She didn't move. She heard the crickets start up again on the hillside. There were no houses around. The crickets were louder.

She began to cry.

* * *

The images came back into his mind. He raced the Lancia along the twisting curves of the bad road, not caring, trying not to think of her, but his mind would not let go. The images came back again and again.

Angry, blind, his foot pressed savagely down on the accelerator, pressing more speed out of the car, as if speed would bleed the hot, crazy anger out of him. He knew he was going too fast. He knew the road was too narrow, the curves too tight, that even at three o'clock in the morning, there might be other cars on the road.

He knew and didn't care.

The Lancia zooming ahead, the curve coming up almost as if he knew the curve would be there and ran to meet it . . .

. . . Not just not caring, but knowingly, deliberately not hitting the brake pedal, knowing there could be time, if he wanted to, that he could react quickly enough to slow the car, deliberately, angrily, explosively mashing down on the accelerator pedal with all the muscles of his leg locked hard . . .

. . . The Lancia's drive wheels skidding, catching, hurtling the car forward . . .

. . . The front wheels not turning . . .

. . . The road bending sharply away but the car flinging itself forward in a straight line . . .

. . . The guard posts splintering . . . the guard rails breaking as the front end smashed into them . . .

. . . The car lurching free, sailing into the black void of the night. . . .

There was the free fall. Sandra's scream filled the inside of his head as if she were still in the car.

Thinking, *Now what the hell did I do that fucking*

stupid thing for? The sick frozen feeling knowing that it was done. The anger gone and wanting to tell her that he did it because he loved her. . . .

Turning in the air, turning again, the Lancia landed on its thin metal roof that crumpled as the car slammed onto the boulders forty feet below the road.

The car bounced from the high boulders to the lower ones, finally to be caught between them just short of the ocean.

And held there.

2.

The call from Patrolman Vern Melburne was logged in at 3:21 A.M. Al Goucher, dispatcher.

—This is car two . . . three . . .

—Go ahead, car two . . . three . . .

—Al, I've got a woman here in a dazed condition. Says her name's Mrs. Sandra Wilkes . . .

—What's your location, Vern?

—On 427 about a mile east of Gale Harbor.

—Okay, go ahead.

—She's in a dazed condition. She was just standing in the middle of the road when we saw her. Doesn't seem to be hurt. She wants us to drive her home.

—Get her checked out at Parker-Compton first, Vern. Could be something wrong with her. She tell you how she got there?

—She won't tell us anything except her name and where she lives and will we take her there.

—Where's she live?

—Barrett's Cove.

—Take her to the hospital, Vern.

—Ten-four, Al.

Second call from Officer Vern Melburne, logged in by Dispatcher Al Goucher at 3:26 A.M.

—This is car two . . . three . . .

—Go ahead, Vern. She giving you trouble?

—We got more'n that, Al. I'm about half a mile west of Lawton's Race. You know that sharp curve—

—I know it. Go ahead.

—Car's gone through the rail, Al. Took out one of the guard posts, too. It's down on the rocks, forty, fifty feet below us. Catalini's gone down to see there's anybody in it.

—Can you put your spotlight on it?

—We tried it, Al. Angle's too sharp. Got to lean way the hell over the rail just to see it. Hold on.

(PAUSE)

—Come in, car two . . . three . . .

(PAUSE)

—Car two . . . three . . . Come in, Vern.

(PAUSE)

—Car two . . . three . . . Call in.

—This is Car two . . . three . . . uh . . . Al, I think you better get some vehicles out here. Catalini says there's a body trapped in that car. No way to get him out. Car's upside down on its roof, an' it's jammed between two, three boulders. No way to open the doors. Over.

—He dead or alive, Vern?

—We don't know. Catalini can't get to him. We're gonna have to lift that car to get him out.

—Okay, Vern. You an' Catalini hang on. We'll get some help out to you.

—What about the woman, Al? Do we take her to the hospital? Over.

—What's her condition?

—Damned if I know. We come up to the curve and

seen the guard rail was all smashed in, so we stopped. Me 'n Catalini get out to take a look an' she pops outta the cruiser an' runs to the rail. Almost fell over. Catalini grabs her just in time. I shine my flashlight down on the wreck an' she lets out a scream an' passes out. She's in the back a' the cruiser now. What do we do about her? Over.

—Hold on a minute, Vern. Lemme go ask the sergeant.

(PAUSE)

—Car two ... three ... you read me?

—Go ahead, Al.

—Vern, Sergeant Maddox says take her on to the hospital. Put out a couple of flares and take her to Emergency.

—Ten-four.

Patrolmen Tom Babson and Art Seaver arrived at the scene of the accident at 3:42 A.M. In the darkness they climbed down the face of the cliff to the wreck, looked at it helplessly and climbed back up again. The red flares on the roadway hissed and spat small corollas of sparks into the blackness.

At 3:54, Sergeant Oliver Maddox drove up alone. He shone his flashlight down on the car. The beam of light played over the underside of the vehicle, its wheels, transmission, differential, oil pan all exposed obscenely. He climbed down to the wreck more slowly and more carefully than Babson or Seaver had. He took more time examining the wreck and the body trapped in it by the bent and twisted steel.

At 4:02 A.M. the ambulance from Parker-Compton Hospital arrived. Dr. Joseph Carr, intern, made his way down the cliff with Patrolman Tom Babson helping him. He peered into the wreck, shone Babson's flashlight onto the body. There wasn't much he could see of it. Most of it was under the curve of the dashboard.

Panting, he hunkered down beside Sergeant Maddox. Maddox said, "Well?"

Dr. Carr shrugged. "There's just no way I can tell if he's dead or alive. You're going to have to get him out first."

Maddox considered the information.

"Yeah. That's what we figured, too."

"How long will it be before you can get that car out of there?"

"It depends. It could take some time."

"You want us to hang around?"

"Unless you got something better to do. I mean, I can't tell you to stay."

"Yeah, well—"

"You do what you think best, Doc."

"Well, that's why I'd like to know how long it's going to be before you get him out."

Maddox scratched his jaw. He stood up.

"Let's get up top, Doc."

Dr. Carr followed the heavy figure of Sergeant Maddox, scrambling and slipping up the rocks, Maddox lending him a hand every now and then and Patrolman Tom Babson shining his flashlight on the rocks so he could see his way.

Patrolman Art Seaver helped him over the lip of the cliff. He saw that the wrecking crew was there and the yellow and green Fire Department Rescue Squad truck was there and a red fire truck. The Rescue Squad and some of the firemen had begun setting up emergency floodlights. They came on as he turned to find Sergeant Maddox.

Maddox was at the door of the patrol car talking

into the microphone. He finished, leaned in the window and hung up the mike.

"Wally Stowell's on his way out here with the mobile crane from his marina at Lawton's Race. He should be out here in about half an hour or so."

"And then?"

"Well, you gotta give him time to get set up. Let's say it takes him maybe fifteen to twenty minutes to level it. Figure another fifteen minutes to get swung over an' get his cables down to the wreck an' get hooked onto the harness. We can get that done while he's on his way."

"Harness?"

"Wire cables to support the car. Like a cradle."

"Okay, I got it."

"Now, that's if he don't run into trouble an' he can do it on the first try. An' if we got the harness all set up for him to hook onto."

"You've got an hour right there, at the least," said Dr. Carr.

"Easy. Then we got to winch that thing up here an' we got to cut that poor son of a bitch out of it. I don't know how the hell long that'll take us. Another forty minutes, maybe. Maybe more. We ain't gonna be able to use torches. Gas tank's sprung. The car's sopping wet. It's a wonder she didn't touch off when she hit."

Dr. Carr ran his fingers through his hair. He felt chilled. The night air was cold, coming in off the ocean. He should have worn a sweater under his jacket.

"I just don't know what the hell to do," he said.

"Call in on your radio," Maddox advised. "You ain't that far away from the hospital they can't reach you if they have to."

"Yeah," Carr said. "I'll do that."

The flares were almost burnt out. It was daylight now; gray, cold fog blanketed the ocean so there was no horizon. They were all cold from standing around waiting.

The big, twenty-ton Bay City mobile crane took up the whole roadway, like a giant insect squatting on the road. Four huge, double-tired wheels supported the hoist mechanism. The hoist's steel skeleton loomed more than forty feet into the air.

In the narrow crane cab, Wally Stowell threw in a lever. The big Diesel engine growled, broke into a roar. Wires tightened, took up slack, took up the strain; the boom quivered under the tension, vibrating along its length. The winch turned.

Metal screamed. The car wrenched loose from the boulders. Men steadied it with lead wires, keeping it from swinging or spinning. They guided the broken vehicle as it rose. Inch by inch, the grotesque carcass of the Lancia came up. When it was high enough to clear the roadway, the crane turned on its base plates, swinging the car over the roadway; then it lowered the hulk on its side until it rested on the ground.

The police and fire department crews went to work with crowbars and bolt cutters and metal shears, ripping through the sheet metal of the roof.

At 7:12 A.M. the ambulance crew wormed the bloody body of Doug Mackay through the torn rooftop, slid it onto a stretcher and brought him to the ambulance.

At 7:14 A.M., siren howling, roof spotlight flashing, the Parker-Compton ambulance raced off down Route 427 toward the hospital with a police cruiser ahead of it.

Doug Mackay was still alive.

CHAPTER ELEVEN

Sandra did not look at him. She hadn't looked directly at him since she'd come in some fifteen minutes before. Edith was with her. Edith did the talking, her plain face animated, intense. Lisa had shown them in and then left them with Michael in the living room.

"We need you, Michael. Mackay needs you. He's dying. The doctors have given up on him. You're the only one who can save him."

"You still haven't told me how it happened."

"I don't *know* how it happened. Nobody knows how it happened. He went through the railing on a curve. I don't know why he was going so fast. He just smashed through the guard rail and over the cliff. He didn't even try to put on his brakes. The police said there were no skid marks. He's damn lucky he wasn't killed outright."

"On the way back from here?"

"Yes. That's what Sandra says."

"Why wasn't she in the car with him when it happened? That's kind of odd, isn't it?"

"I suppose. She won't talk about it. All she said was they'd had an argument. He stopped the car, pushed her out, and drove off."

He looked across the room. Sandra was sitting on the couch, her knees together, her back straight, staring blankly across the room with reddened, swollen eyes. She still wore the same dress she'd had on the night before; now it was badly wrinkled.

Edith said in her strident, slightly nasal voice, "Michael, the doctors have given up on him. They've been working on him all day. He was on the operating table for six hours! They've told us he's going to die. Don't you understand? You're the only one who can save him!"

Hietala kept his eyes on Sandra. She hadn't moved. There was a smudge of dirt on one cheek and a run in her stockings.

"Please!"

He got to his feet.

"Let me talk to Sandra."

"She won't talk to you. She won't talk to anyone. She hasn't said a word since early this morning. She should be in bed and sedated. I'm afraid for her."

He went over to Sandra.

"Let's go outside," he said.

She turned her head away.

"If you don't care—"

She got up. Hietala walked through the open glass doors to the porch without looking back at her. The late afternoon sun came across the trees, warm and golden, touching the far end of the sundeck. Mutely, she followed him to the corner of the deck where he'd gone to feel the last of the sunlight on his body.

She looked at his face as she came up to him, wondering why it seemed so different now, what there could have been in it only a few hours before to have made her do what she did. *We're not the same two people,* she thought. *He's not the man and I'm not the crazy bitch in heat. Who the hell are we? Why are we here talking like this? Why aren't I with Doug?*

She heard him say, "Do you want him to live?"

"What did you say? I'm sorry, I wasn't listening."

"Do you want him to live?"

She shrugged. "He'll leave me if he lives. What's the difference?"

"Then why did you come to me?"

"I didn't. Edith did. She made me come with her. I don't give a damn if I never see you again. Edith said you could save Mackay's life. That's a bunch of bullshit, isn't it?" She challenged him to deny it.

"No."

"Can you save his life?"

"Yes."

Her eyes begged him. The sunlight was cruel to her. He could see the fine wrinkles around her eyes and at the corners of her mouth and the unnatural tautness of the skin over her cheekbones and along her jawline. Crepy skin lay at the base of her neck. The face lift was obvious now. Her makeup was a day old and blotched. Mascara had run into the corners of her eyes. She looked more than her age, a pathetic, middle-aged woman desperately trying to appear younger.

"Don't lie to me. Please."

"I'm not."

"You really can?"

Before he could answer, she said bitterly, "But what the hell good would it do. He'll leave me."

"Do you love him?"

"Who says I love him?"

"Do you?"

"All right, so I love him." She turned her head away. "It's hard to believe, isn't it? I don't know if I really believe it myself. After four husbands and God knows how many lovers and one-night stands, I finally find the right guy and don't know how much I love him until he's dying." Her lips moved in a wry smile. "I'm really fucked up, aren't I?"

"We all are."

She put her hand on his forearm, feeling the sun-warmed skin and the fine hairs.

"What the hell am I going to do, Michael?" Her voice broke. She began to cry. As she stood in front of him, her face turned back and lifted to him, tears coming from her eyes and running down the sides of her nose and she not caring how she looked.

"I can't help you. It's up to you."

"My decision," she said bitterly. "Oh, boy, that's great. But then, it was my fault, too, wasn't it?"

"What was the argument about?"

She told him. He listened without any emotion showing on his face.

At the end she said rancorously, "You son of a bitch, it was all your fault! What the hell did you do to me? And why? Why me?"

"You wanted it." As if that were enough explanation.

"Maybe I did. So what?"

"I only gave you what you wanted."

"Is that what you do, Michael? Give people what they want but are afraid to ask for? Don't you give a damn about the consequences?"

Glaring at him with hatred.

"I could kill you. So help me, I could kill you!"

"We were talking about Mackay," he pointed out.

"Yes. So we were. All right, I want him to live. Even if he leaves me. Can you do it? Edith says you can."

"I told you I could."

"But there are conditions, right? There are always conditions." Cynicism sharpened her voice. "What are they? Money? Me? What the hell do I have that you want?"

"Nothing."

"I don't believe you. How much did you get out of Edith? Or Sarah Flint?"

He started to move away from her. Her hand tightened on his forearm.

"Don't go. I'm sorry. I shouldn't have said what I did. Whatever you want, I'll give it to you."

"The price might be too high."

"Any goddamn thing I have is yours! Just tell me what the hell it is you want!"

"A substitute."

"A sub— I don't understand."

"Someone for Mackay."

She understood then.

"You're crazy!"

"Someone you love," he said. "Otherwise, it's no sacrifice. It would cost you nothing."

She stared him in the face, fear growing in her the way it had the evening before. She knew he was sane and that he meant what he said.

She shook her head.

"I—I can't."

"All right. If that's your decision."

"It would be murder."

"Shall we go back inside?"

"No," she said, desperately. "Goddamnit, no! I want Mackay to live! I'll give you every damn cent I have."

She knew he was laughing at her. The expression on his face hadn't changed, but she saw it in his eyes, in the quirk of his lips. He was playing with her. She hated him.

"You bastard! Look, I'm rich. I've got even more

than Edith. How much of it do you want? I want Doug Mackay alive!"

She pounded on his chest with both her hands clenched into fists.

"You can't let him die! I need him, Michael! He's the only thing that matters to me! Don't you understand? I love him!"

He caught her hands and held her so that she couldn't strike him. He pulled her closer. Her face was turned up to his; she felt the heat of his body against hers. It was like the night before. Cruelty narrowed his eyes, beating against her.

He said, "I told you money's no good. Someone has to die in Mackay's place. That's what it takes. Tell me who."

She stared up at him, her face inches from his, stared blindly, the world only his bearded, arrogant face seen through the blurry lens of her tears. Afraid of him. Sick with fear.

"Anyone! I don't care! Anyone at all!"

"No. Pick someone."

"All right!" She screamed at him. "Edith!"

He let of of her hands. She stepped away from him, from the terrible heat of his body. She felt cold; a thin, mean chill shot through her. She tried to laugh.

"I—I really didn't mean that, Michael."

He said nothing.

"Michael, I didn't mean it."

"It's too late," he said, and she knew that she really had meant it and that he knew she'd meant it, and that they'd struck a bargain.

The cold came back stronger than before. She shivered. She realized the sunlight had gone.

"I'm cold, Michael," she said in a small voice, desperately needing comfort. "I'm so goddamned cold. Take me inside."

2.

When they went to the hospital, Sandra refused to go with them. She wanted to go home. Lisa said she'd drive her to Barrett's Cove.

"Later," Sandra said. "I want a drink first. I want to get drunk."

They'd left her at the house. Edith drove Michael to Parker-Compton in her Mercedes.

At first they wouldn't let him into Mackay's room. Dr. Charles Newcombe was adamant about it, but Edith took Dr. Trask aside and talked bluntly to him. Matthew Trask was medical director of Parker-Compton. He knew Edith's influence with the other members of the board of directors. He knew, too, how much she donated each year to the hospital. She offset a considerable portion of the annual deficit. When she was through, he called in Dr. Newcombe and spoke to him. Then he called the head nurse and talked to her on the telephone.

Edith took Michael to the floor and then went back downstairs to Dr. Trask's office. He left her alone.

Michael went into the hospital room. The head nurse shut the door behind him.

Odor of disinfectants. Faint smell of anesthetic. Smell of freshly washed linen. Smell of death. They were all in the room with him.

He went over to Mackay's bed. He could see only part of Mackay's face. The rest of it was bandaged. The thin hospital blanket was drawn up to his chin. The plastic oxygen tent reflected the ceiling lights into Michael's eyes. Mackay's face looked rippled through the plastic.

The room was silent except for the hissing of the oxygen into the tent. I.V. bottles were racked on a stand at the head of the bed. Beige rubber tubes ran in a loop from the bottles under the lip of the oxygen tent. Colorless liquid in one bottle; the bright crimson of blood in the other. Both bottles were down to the halfway mark.

With both hands, Michael lifted the side of the oxygen tent. The plastic felt cold to his fingers. Now that he was so close to it, the hissing of the oxygen was louder.

He looked down at Mackay. A thin rubber tube came out of one nostril. The rubber was taped by an adhesive plaster strip across his upper lip.

Michael put his right hand on the blanket, feeling Mackay's chest. There were bandages under the blanket distorting the torso, but Michael could feel the slight rise and fall of each breath. He bent, placing an ear to Mackay's slightly opened mouth. Faint sounds of breathing reached his eardrum.

He straightened up. Then in a firm, deliberate motion, he grasped Mackay's nostrils with his left hand, pinching them tightly shut. His right hand, cupped under Mackay's jaw, closed over his mouth, sealing his lips shut.

Mackay's body twitched only slightly under his hands, more like a shudder than a man fighting for breath to remain alive.

Michael held his grip for a full minute. Then another. He could see the second hand of his wristwatch tick around the dial in tiny jerking motions from mark to mark. He waited until it had completed three circles before he released his grip.

On the night table at the head of Mackay's bed, he saw a stethoscope. He put it on, the earpiece pressing into his ear channels; hollow sounds, the faint throb of his own pulse, the echo of his jawbone moving gigantically in its sockets.

Carefully he pulled down the blanket until Mackay's chest was exposed. The bandages came up to Mackay's armpits, but there was enough room; he was able to slide the flat disc of the diaphragm under the bandages. He listened, moving the disc about, trying to pick up a heartbeat. He found none.

He took off the stethoscope, put it back on the table. He pulled up the covers, arranging them as they'd been before he moved them. Now he let down the side of the oxygen tent, the cold plastic slick in his hands.

He stood beside the tent, looking at the still face through the plastic. Mackay's dead features were pale and waxen through the plastic sheet.

He moved away from the bed.

He lifted his hands, staring first at his palms, then turning them so he looked at their backs. He'd never really looked at his hands before. It was almost as if they weren't his. Big hands, strong fingers. Long ridges of thin tendons raised the skin on the backs of his hands. The skin was loose. Random curls of veins snaked across, over, under the tendons of his middle and forefingers. He bent his fingers and then relaxed them.

Mackay looked so peaceful, so much at rest. *Let him have his death,* he thought. He felt confident and strong, invincible in his power.

If Aaron could do it, so could he!

If Aaron could bring them back to life, if Aaron could cure them and heal them—he, Michael, was stronger than Aaron! He would send Aaron away once and for all!

He held out his hands over Mackay. He closed his eyes, waiting for the light to fill his mind. To bring Mackay back to life again.

Nothing happened.

There was no light.

He tried again. Nervously, this time, his confidence beginning to slip away from him. He felt perspiration break out on his forehead and under his arms.

Nothing. Nothing at all.

Inside, he began to feel the familiar rage at Aaron building up in him. It took all his strength to quench the sour hatred. He needed Aaron. He needed Aaron's power.

Damn Aaron!

Once more he held out his hands.

Nothing. There was nothing. Nothing was happening.

Michael turned away from Mackay's body—the dead, pale face remaining in his mind.

He couldn't be found in the room with Mackay dead. Not after he'd smothered him. They'd find out. He fought the feeling of panic that began to invade him. He had trapped himself.

He came back to the bed and looked at Mackay again. The dead man's face mocked him. He wished Mackay were still alive so he could kill him again!

He turned from the hospital bed. He hated himself; he hated Aaron, but he gave in. In his mind, he shouted as loudly as he could:

—*Aaron!*

—*Why are you calling for me, Michael?*

—*To bring Mackay back to life.*

—*You've never called on me before.*

—*I need your help now.*

—*Why?*

—*Why do you care?* His tone was sharp, irritated that Aaron should question him. *It's a chance for you to take over our body, isn't it? I should think you'd welcome the chance!*

—*Why, Michael?* Aaron persisted.

—*All right, damn it! I need you!*

—*You've always needed me.*

—*Aaron, help me!*

The Aaron voice was silent.

Aaron Hietala looked at Mackay. Behind the thick, plastic sheeting of the oxygen tent, under the drawn, light hospital blanket, there was no movement. The face was blanched, the features beginning to tighten in death.

The glow came to him. It suffused him gradually. After a while, he stretched out his arm, his palm forward as if pushing against an invisible force. He could feel the aura fill his body, take over his mind, expand him until he filled the room, until the walls of the room felt the pressure of the life force coming from him and were all that restrained it from expanding throughout the corridors and every other room of the hospital.

But nothing happened to Mackay. Mackay didn't stir. He lay still, his chest not moving; still and quiet and dead.

Aaron felt the first flicker of concern, aware that something was wrong.

He felt Michael stirring within him, and let him come to the surface. He looked at Michael, and he knew.

It was not just Michael alone. Michael believed in a

dark force. The force the church had taught him about when he was young.

Now he wasn't sure he was strong enough to fight them both. Not when the only weapon he had was love. Love for Michael; love for his twin, flesh of his flesh, flesh he no longer had, flesh he came into as a stranger, as he came into Michael's mind.

He wept with love for his brother, loving him in spite of his evil, loving him because he was weak, forgiving him for all the harm he had done.

His eyes filled with unshed tears. He let the pure light come into him, knowing the dark force in Michael could not stand the purity of light. All was light. Bright, intense, glaring, blue-white light, pure and clean.

And the dark force in Michael went away. And Michael went away.

Light streamed from Aaron's hand, from his arm. It engulfed the oxygen tent and the bed enclosed within it. The radiance blotted out the world. The hissing of the oxygen faded away. There was only total silence— as if the world had stopped and time with it.

Pulse . . .
and again . . .
Pulse . . .
and pause . . .
Pulse . . .
. . . pulse . . . pulse . . . pulse . . .

When Michael Hietala came back into his body, he was tired to the marrow of his bones. The glow had dissipated. The sound of the oxygen hissing into the tent was in his ears. The hospital smells were in his nose. Under the light blanket Mackay's chest moved.

It was strong. Mackay was breathing deeply. The fluid in the I.V. bottles was way down.

Mackay would live!

Mackay would live because Aaron had taken over.

He felt shame for his weakness; shame that Aaron had succeeded where he had failed. A huge sob of despair burst from his throat, and once again he felt hatred for his brother.

3.

Edith drove Michael home. She saw how tired he was when he came downstairs to the medical director's office. Someone brought him a cup of coffee. He drank it slowly, his eyes staring at the wall.

On the drive home, Edith said nothing. She let him rest. He sat slouched, his hands together in his lap.

She turned into the gravelled drive of the house that served as The Church of the Second Life.

When she stopped the car in front of the door, he sat for a moment, letting his eyes come open. After a while, he opened the door but didn't get out of the car.

Edith said, "Thank you, Michael." She hesitated and then, timorously, asked, "Will he live?"

"Yes. He'll live."

"It was a miracle, wasn't it, Michael?"

He made no answer.

"And I was there. I was actually there!"

Her plain face was radiant. Tenderly she placed her hand on top of his.

"You look very tired. Isn't there something I can do for you?"

"Lisa Fialho's home."

Edith saw the girl's car in front of the garage.

"Yes," she said enviously, "so she is," and took her hand away. He put his hand on her arm, surprising her. When she looked up into his eyes, she wondered at the strange expression on his face.

"Good-bye, Edith," he said, and got out of the car.

At first, on her way home, she didn't think about it, and then she did, and it puzzled her. Not that he'd said good-bye, but the finality of it, and the surprising warm response she'd felt inside when he'd said it. As if he'd said *hello* instead. It had made her so happy to hear him say it.

4.

Bernice said something to Charlie Daggett and he looked blankly at her.

She said, "You didn't hear a word I said, Charlie."

"I heard."

"What'd I say, then?"

"Okay, so I wasn't listening. What'd you just say?"

"That you weren't listening."

"That's not what you were talking about. What'd you say before that that I missed?"

"What's the difference? You haven't paid attention to me the whole meal. What's the matter with you, Charlie?"

"I was thinking."

"About those two girls?"

He nodded.

"It really bothers you, don't it?"

"Yeah."

"You think you'll catch him?"

"Probably not."

"Is that what bothers you? That you won't catch him?"

"I guess. I don't know. I sure as hell would like to catch the son of a bitch."

She said, "Why can't you be like Ollie Maddox? It wouldn't bother Ollie the way it's bothering you. Cathy tells me Ollie leaves police business at headquarters. He says they don't pay him enough to take it home with him."

"I'm not like Ollie Maddox. You know that. So why talk about him?"

"Because I wish you wouldn't spend all your time thinking about your work, is why. Look at tonight. I spend all afternoon makin' you a pot roast. You eat it, but you don't know what it tastes like."

"It was good," he said. "I really enjoyed it."

"You enjoyed it, huh? Did you like the lima beans?"

"Yeah. They were pretty good."

"You didn't have lima beans. You had peas. That's how much attention you paid to what you were eating."

"Okay," he said, "you made your point."

"You been like that from the first time we dated. You got another few years before you retire. Ain't it time you stopped?"

"I can't help the way I am. Complaining ain't gonna change me."

"Oh, I'm not complaining. It's just sometimes I get tired of it, especially when there's things I'd like us to enjoy together, and your mind is somewheres else."

"You mean you'd like to go see a movie tonight?"

"That's what I had in mind. But now I don't know."

"Okay, we'll go to a movie. You got one in mind?"

"Yes, I do," she said, and told him about it as she took the supper dishes off the kitchen table and stacked them in the sink. She ran hot water over them and began to scrub them.

"You heard anything about what's goin' on down at St. Peter's lately?" she asked, her back to him and talking over the noise of the running water.

"You mean some kind of social event? I haven't heard anything."

"No," she said, "it's them fishermen's wives. You heard about what happened to John Christy, didn't you?"

"Everybody in town's heard about what happened to John Christy. What's that got to do with what's going on at St. Peter's?"

"Well, a lot of them fishermen are from the old country. Some of 'em been here only a few years, you know. And their wives are almost old country. I mean, they were born here, but their folks was old country and they married guys who just come over so they're almost old country themselves."

"What are you tryin' to tell me?"

"They're superstitious," she said.

"And what the hell's that got to do with John Christy?"

"Don't yell at me. What it's got to do is that they heard about what happened to him from their husbands. Some of the men were there when it happened. They seen it with their own eyes. They swear Christy was dead and that man brought him back to life again."

"You believe that?"

"No, I don't believe it. But they believe it, and that's what counts. They been setting up a shrine to him, is how much they believe it."

"Jesus Christ," he said, shaking his head. "The Father is going to blow his top when he hears about this. Not in the church?"

"No, not in the church. They rented Paoli's old fruit

store, you remember it, over on Cumberland Place."

"I remember it."

"Well, they fixed it up. They cleaned and scrubbed that little store, you wouldn't believe how it looks. You should see it, Charlie. It's really somethin' to look at. They painted it all in light blue. Everything—walls, ceiling, beams. Everything but the floor. And they put in red velvet curtains and drapes. They even sanded down the floor and varnished it so it looks like new. And they put in a big statue of Christ. I don't know where they got it. Somewheres in Boston. It's almost bigger'n life size. Musta been from some Italian church because it's painted, you know? Like them statuettes they got. The cross is painted brown so it looks like real wood instead of plaster, and the Christ is flesh colored, and His eyes are painted brown and so's His hair and His beard. And His lips are painted red. It even looks like there's real blood coming out've His hands and feet and side. How do you like that?"

"That's really something," he said.

"That ain't all," Bernice said, and began to wipe the dishes. "Everyone of them women comes in at least once a day and lights a candle. There must be fifty, sixty candles burnin' all the time."

Charlie said, "That don't sound any different from the shrine they put up a couple of years back to the Virgin over on East Dock Street."

Bernice turned around, drying her hands on the dishtowel.

"You ask me, there's a lot of difference between the Virgin Mary and some guy who's walking around right here in Harbortown!"

Charlie shrugged.

"Furthermore, when they go to that shrine, they ain't praying to the Virgin Mary. They're praying to whoever it is they think brought John Christy back to life."

"Okay," said Charlie.

"You know what they call that shrine?" she demanded.

"How'd I know? This is the first I heard of it."

"The Shrine of the Second Life," Bernice said. "That's what they call it. I call it blasphemy!"

"I can see why they'd call it that," he mused.

"Well, it's wrong! That's what I think. Charlie, how'd you feel about us switchin' to St. Aloysius?"

"We've always gone to St. Peter's the Fisherman," he said.

"Only because my folks went there," she said. "But my father stopped being a fisherman when he was in his twenties and you never been one. Most of our friends go to St. Aloysius, anyhow. What do you think, Charlie?"

"If you really want to," he said.

"Well, Father Vincent ain't there anymore. And I'm not so sure I like the new priest. Maybe we'll switch."

"Look," he said, "we just got barely enough time to get to the movie. You want to talk, we can talk on the way."

"Let me change my shoes."

Bernice went into the bedroom and changed her shoes. She stopped in the bathroom to powder her face and put on lipstick. She brushed her hair quickly. When she came back into the kitchen, she saw her husband hadn't moved from his seat at the kitchen table, and then she saw the expression on his face.

She let out a sigh of exasperation.

"Charlie? For God's sake, will you get your mind off them two girls? Huh?"

5.

"You son of a bitch! I could kill you!" She screamed hysterically at him, her face distorted and discolored in fury. Her hands tried to rake at his face with sharp, pointed fingernails. She wanted to get her nails into his eye sockets, to rip his eyeballs out of his skull. She wanted to lay his cheeks open. She wanted to kill him.

He held her slender wrists together, easily pushing her away from him. She tried to knee him. He twisted his body to one side, avoiding her without effort. Her hair was disheveled and snarled, flying messily about her face as she struggled to get out of his grasp. Her makeup was smeared so that her lips looked raw. Her eyes glared her hatred at him.

"You knew! You knew all the time, didn't you, you fucking son of a bitch!"

He held both her wrists in one powerful hand and brought his other hand around, palm open, to slap across her face without anger. Just hard enough to shock her out of her hysteria.

The blow stung. She felt her cheek smart and then swell into pain. The pain got through to her. She began to cry.

"Why? Why'd you do this? Christ, haven't you done enough to me?"

The fight went out of her. She stood limp in front of him, her hands slack, her body slack, her shoulders slumping. He let go of her hands. They dropped to her sides.

For a moment she just looked at him pleadingly, and then tears filled her eyes and broke and spilled down her cheeks. Her head bent as if the weight of the burden in her mind was too great for her to carry; she slid to the floor, her legs spraddled and awkward, her head going down into the cup of her palms and her hair falling slovenly around her hands to hide herself from him.

"Why?" she cried out. "Why?"

When he'd opened the front door to her insistent ringing, he had time only to recognize that it was Sandra Wilkes before she lunged at him with a letter opener in her hand, trying to blind him. Barely in time, only because his reflexes were fast, he twisted aside. The sharp point missed his eye, sliding along his temple and cutting a thin gouge through the skin along his cheekbone and over the top of his ear. He struck at her hand, knocking the blade out of her grasp.

She went for him with hooked fingers, her long fingernails raking at his cheeks with a fury he could barely control. He knocked her away. She tripped headlong over the edge of the hall rug, crashing to the floor, sprawling, her skirt flounced high around her midsection, her pantyhose ripped along one leg, the other in ladderback runs.

She'd scrambled to her feet, small mewings of blind anger coming catlike out of her throat, lunging for him again, wanting only to tear him bloody, to inflict terrible pain on him.

Now her legs were bent under her as if they no longer had the strength to support her, and she held her face in her hands, closing out the world, shutting herself away from Michael Hietala, feeling completely helpless and weak, knowing the sourness of total defeat. She cried in deep, convulsive sobs.

Hietala stepped away from her, watching her carefully but with no expression on his face.

Only the overhead hall light was on. The living room behind them was dark.

Lisa Fialho came down the stairs. She saw Michael standing over Sandra Wilkes. She stopped before she got to the bottom of the stairway.

She could feel it. It emanated from him in slow waves that spread implacably. They reached her. She could feel the evil. The flesh on her arms chilled. She felt the rising of hairs hackling the nape of her neck and her own chills of fear rippling along the length of her spine like ghostly satanic fingertips. She had never felt such fright. Michael looked taller than she'd ever seen him. Taller even than the time in the bedroom just before he came into her and she knew that something had changed in him, something powerful and dangerous.

The recessed ceiling light of the hallway threw a beam downward, making sharp shadows. The walls seemed to expand and contract with her breathing. Sandra was in the center of the overhead beam. Michael was at its edge, the light striking him on the top of his head, his face, his shoulders, leaving the rest of him in darkness.

Shadows shouldn't be that dark. Nor light so bright. It was as if the light on Sandra Wilkes was more intense because it had drawn the light from the shadows, making them blacker than they should be. And the shadows were cold. She felt the coldness seep outward from Michael and come and touch her. It drew the heat from her body. She shivered.

Without turning his head Michael said, "Get out of here, Lisa."

She began a protest. "Michael—"

"Get . . . the . . . hell . . . out . . . of . . . here!"

Lisa Fialho turned and went back up the stairs, away from the darkness around Michael and the glare surrounding Sandra Wilkes. Away from the spreading pool of chilling cold. She was glad to get away from them both. She went into the big bedroom and locked the door behind her and turned on the lights and the record player. She turned up the volume.

Sandra tried to push herself erect. She stopped weeping. She lifted her head, turning to look for Michael, surprised at the dark, her swollen, reddened eyes finally finding him.

"It . . . it must . . . it must have been a real . . . joke . . . to you. . . . Very . . . very funny . . ."

His voice came out of the shadows to her.

"I promised only to bring him back to life."

"He'll be a cripple," she said bitterly. "You knew that, didn't you? The doctors told me less than an hour ago. He'll live, they said. They were surprised that he didn't die. Oh, yes, he'll live. And then they told me he's paralyzed. From the waist down. He'll always be like that. Forever. The rest of his life."

"I can't help that."

"But you knew! Goddamn you—*you knew*!"

"Yes, I knew."

"Then why didn't you tell me?"

"You wanted him alive. He's alive."

"Alive? In his condition. You call that living?"

"You're the one who chose."

"I didn't want to come to see you. It was Edith who made me come. She drove me here."

"You made the choice."

Sandra struggled to her feet. Trembling, she brushed at her skirt. She pushed her hair away from her face.

"Well," she said, fighting to catch her breath. "I just want to tell you the deal's off."

"Is that why you came at me with a knife?"

"It was a letter opener."

"You tried to blind me."

"I wanted to hurt you, yes. Haven't you done enough to me?"

"I've done nothing you haven't wanted."

"I didn't want to go to bed with you!"

"Didn't you?"

"No! I didn't want to hurt Doug. I didn't want to feel like a slut. I didn't want to feel dirty and guilty about what I did to Doug. The way you made me feel. I didn't want him to try to kill himself. I didn't want him smashed up—or dead!"

"You really believe that?"

"Yes!"

He came out of the shadows then, coming the two steps to her, standing inches away from her. He held out his hand. Frozen, she saw his hand come close to her, touch her on the arm; then the coldness around him was replaced with the heat she felt surging upwards from her loins, spreading through her body. She tried to tear her eyes away from his, but it was impossible. She had never felt so weak or so vulnerable.

What was most degrading was the knowledge that she wanted him to degrade her even more, to subject her to the vilest things she could imagine. Hatred of him burnt through her at the same time she ached to rip off her clothes, to lie down right then on the floor and to feel the hard wood against her spine, to open her legs, to be open for him and to feel him plunging within her as he had just the night before.

She looked into his eyes, seeing the evil, the black, bottomless evil in them, and she felt again the implacable cold. She wanted to let go, to swim down into their depths, to lose herself totally in them. The excitement in her mounted. She heard her mind screaming at him: *"Take me! I want it! Now! Now! I don't care what happens to me as long as I can have you in me!"*

Hietala let go of her arm and stepped back. The feelings began to die in her. The emotion drained away. Exhausted, she closed her eyes. Shame and disgust swept over her for what she had felt.

"Now what do you believe?"

"Oh, God!" She began to cry.

"You wanted all the dirty feelings."

She nodded her head.

"You wanted to hurt Mackay."

She nodded her head again, pressing her knuckles into her mouth until her teeth cut through the skin. Numb. Cold. Her mind paralyzed. Her body paralyzed. Unable to speak. She knew he was right. She *had* wanted it. To feel guilty. To hurt Mackay with what she'd done. To hurt herself because of what she'd done to Mackay. To push him as far as she could to find out if he really loved her. To punish him for loving her.

Only not so much!

"Do you believe it now?"

Why doesn't he let up? Why is he so relentless? . . . Leave me alone!

"Do you?"

She forced herself to speak. "Yes. *Yes.* I believe it!"

"You can go now," he said.

She made one last effort.

"Leave . . . leave Edith . . . alone!" The words convulsed out of her throat. "Leave her alone! If anything happens to her—"

"Yes?"

She shook her head, aware only of the foulness of

her mind, the filth of her carnal desires, ashamed of what she had done and knowing she would do it again and again to quench the need for him that overwhelmed her. She felt like throwing up.

Instead she said in a helpless, desperate voice, "Please?"

"There's nothing I can do."

"Take me instead of Edith."

"No."

Her shoulders sagged. Blindly she turned away from him, wanting nothing more than to get out of the house, to get away from him, to be free of his presence and the pressures that locked around her whenever she was near him.

Hietala watched her stumble slack-legged to the door. He heard the sound of her car starting and the crunching of the gravel as she turned in the driveway and went out the gate to the road.

From the HARBORTOWN DAILY NEWS, July 12, page 14, column 8

EDITH MARY CAVANAUGH

Services for Edith Mary Cavanaugh, 31, of 2134 Eastern Highland Avenue, were held yesterday morning in the Arlington Funeral Home.

The Reverend James Squires, of the First Congregationalist Church, officiated.

Burial followed at the Chestnut Grove Cemetery, with committal services conducted by the Reverend Squires.

Pallbearers were James Riggs, of Boston; Eric Clarke, of Hamilton; Edward Gilbert and Daniel Warren, of New York City; Victor Frye, of Quogue, Long Island; and Michael Hietala, of Adam's Cove.

Miss Cavanaugh is survived by her sister, Mrs.

Sandra Cavanaugh Wilkes, of Sarasota, Florida, and Barrett's Cove.

Mrs. Wilkes was hospitalized two days before her sister's demise. She was unable to attend the funeral.

CHAPTER TWELVE

For three days after Edith Cavanaugh's funeral, Michael saw no one. Sarah Flint called worriedly several times. Lisa told her that Michael was in seclusion, that he would certainly see her as soon as possible. She didn't tell Michael about the calls. Her fear of him had grown. She kept remembering the dark, looming figure standing menacingly in the shadows of the hallway with Sandra Wilkes crouched at his feet, and she could recall the fury in his voice as he shouted at her to leave. She slept in another bedroom now, afraid to be with him at night.

She no longer asked him where he went at night or what he did during the hours he was gone from the house. She was afraid he might tell her.

On the third night, Michael returned to the house just before dawn. He let himself in and walked through the hallway to the living room and out onto the wide expanse of deck. The deck was damp with the night dew. When he put his hands on the redwood railing to brace himself against the wind that had begun to arise, his hands were chilled by the moisture; he shivered slightly.

For a long time, he watched the small lights on the boats of the fishing fleet moving through the darkness, moving out of the harbor, past the breakwater, toward the slow, long swells of the ocean.

He was tired; his eyeballs were dry and gritty against the underside of his lids; he needed sleep. Thoughts of Aaron filled his mind. Aaron had shown him up, had shown how weak he was. He should never have challenged Aaron at the hospital. His power was not Aaron's power. His power was stronger. All he had to do was prove it and he would prove himself better than Aaron. Aaron would have to leave him alone then.

But how?

Michael found himself watching the masthead lights of the fishing fleet across a mile of darkness. The lights were almost hypnotic. After a while, the idea came floating into his mind. He thought about it briefly. The thought pleased him. His lips split the dark beard around his mouth in a grin.

He began to laugh.

Now that he had the idea, he knew that finally he could best Aaron. He would conquer Aaron for good. He would teach Aaron that death is stronger than life!

And Aaron would never come back again.

2.

By afternoon of that day, dark and heavy, clouds began forming in the northeast, a thick, gray overcast with smaller, denser, black rain clouds scudding below the overcast, and the wind rose, sweeping in a giant circle counterclockwise around a deep, barometric low whose center was the North Atlantic south of Nova Scotia.

Small craft warnings were issued for the entire area off the coast of New England. Winds gusted up to thirty-five knots. Almost immediately afterward, the meteorological reports were updated to gale warnings. Winds began rising to forty and forty-five knots. The barometer plunged.

The ocean became a mass of green movement, churning, angry roiling. The sky was gray-green, the water was dark green and massive. Rain came down in great lashings, beating the surface of the water, lost against the white spume of the wave tops. There was no horizon. Sky and water blended together. A hundred thousand tons of green water lifted itself into a wave five hundred miles long and raced southwestward toward the granite cliffs of the New England coast. Winds howled in, faster than the waves, lifting tons of water from the curling tops of the swells, blowing the spray along with it. Like a great, sad, moaning dirge, the wind screamed across the ocean and over the coast.

When the waves raced in, roaring toward the rock cliffs of Adam's Cove, and met the solid granite, they smashed green water into white water, spume flung eighty feet into the air, and the air was filled with booming, echoing crashes, one after another without end.

The storm grew all evening and throughout the night. By the next morning the storm was at its height. By noontime the sky was as dark as late evening, and the rain still kept on, lashing out of the darkness, driven by the winds, coming in great sheets of water, beating against the ocean and against the land and against all the things that were on the ocean and on the land.

On the Georges Bank, which is east of Cape Cod and some one hundred miles southeast of Harbortown, almost all the fishing fleet from New Bedford, Boston, Gloucester and Harbortown had turned back to their home ports the night before, the stubby boats ploughing heavily through the mounting seas. Lifelines had been rigged on their decks, but no one ventured out. Long before they reached port, the lifelines had been swept away.

All around the Georges Bank, the Atlantic is deep. Even close to the northern and eastern edges, the ocean bottom lies well over 150 fathoms, but the Georges Bank itself is shallow; it varies from twenty to forty-five fathoms, and the bottom feeding fish— haddock, cod, yellow tail flounder, hake—swarm in great numbers because of the shallow depth and the rich feeding.

Because of the shallowness of the Georges Bank, the wind effect is heightened and the waves mount to towering proportions. The vessels of the fishing fleet are lost in troughs whose waves are sometimes twice as high as their stubby masts.

Less than eight hours after the first small craft warnings were issued, gale winds of more than sixty knots were battering at the helpless ships fighting to return to port. The waves pounded at them, first from the quarter, then from astern, smashing at the hulls, lifting the boats from the troughs and the wind whipped their decks clean.

In the deckhouse two men were needed at the wheel. The wipers were useless against the wind and the sea; the men steered by compass and depended upon their small radar sets to keep them from colliding. And when the radar masts were carried away, they continued to steer by compass and by prayer. Long before they got to port, the seas carried away masts, booms, lifeboats, and rigging. On ship after ship, the decks were swept clear.

The rusty, dented hulls pushed their way through the storm, single propellers thrashing against the water, sometimes whipping in a burst of mad, uncontrolled energy when the stern of the vessel was lifted clear of the water; mostly throbbing in thick, strained beatings to push the craft forward, quartering against the gale.

Outside the 200-mile limit, east of Georges Bank, the foreign registry fishing vessels—the huge Russian factory ships and their broods of beam trawlers, and the Danish, Norwegian, and Polish vessels—had long turned to steam southeastward, crashing through heavy seas, but in this area, the Atlantic is deep and the wave effect less. All but one of these ships cleared the storm area without loss of life.

For some reason, three of the fishing vessels from Harbortown tried to ride out the gale. Two were steel-hulled draggers; the third was the old, wooden-hulled *Carmine J.*, once named the *William F. Burke*, and before that, *The Neptune*. More than forty years old, patched and repaired, her timbers no longer sturdy, badly in need of caulking, the *Carmine J.* sank during the first three hours of the storm.

The *Santa Serafina* and the *Evangeline* were steel-hulled draggers. The *Evangeline* was eighty-five feet long and the *Santa Serafina* was sixty-five feet in length, and both ships were broad beamed and under-powered.

Each of the vessels carried the smallest crews they could get away with. The crews were on shares and the insurance was high. There was more for each man if the crews were small. Aboard each ship, there was only the captain, an engineer, a cook and two or three crewmen.

The *Santa Serafina* went down during the first night of the storm, sliding into a trough and broaching. The *Evangeline* capsized and sunk before dawn.

There had been no radio calls for help. In the first hour, long before they knew they were in trouble, the waves and the wind had carried away their ship-to-shore radio antennae, the radar, and finally the masts themselves.

There were six men aboard the *Santa Serafina* and six aboard the *Evangeline*. Five men made up the crew of the trawler, the *Carmine J*.

All but one of the men were married. All of them lived in Harbortown.

As soon as the winds died down, Coast Guard search planes were over the Georges Bank, buffeting in the still bumpy air. The planes reported sightings of more than twenty vessels in distress. By late afternoon of the day after the storm, all vessels reported in need of aid were under tow toward their home ports. All the others were accounted for, except the three ships from Harbortown. There was no sign of either the ships or any survivors.

Long after the wreckage of two vessels from New Bedford had been found and survivors from their crews had been rescued by amphibious aircraft, the air search continued. It was finally called off long after night had fallen.

Four vessels out of Boston had foundered. Almost

all of their crews were saved by Coast Guard cutters.

Gloucester lost one ship. Two of the crewmen were rescued, but there was no trace of the three fishing boats from Harbortown or of their crews.

For the next two days, Coast Guard planes continued the search over the entire Georges Bank and then expanded the search area for a hundred miles in each direction. They found nothing. No wreckage. No lifeboats. No men.

In Harbortown, the wives of the fishermen waited for word.

3.

The women began gathering in The Shrine of the Second Life in the early afternoon of the day after the storm, when word was passed that all three ships had been lost at sea. Not one woman called another. They just came. Within the hour, the small, newly painted shrine that had been Paoli's fruit store was crowded. Some of the women were accompanied by their closest friends who came to pray with them.

There had been seventeen men aboard the three ships. Sixteen of them had been married. Sal Aiello's fiancée, Carmine Santini, Mrs. Flint's housekeeper, was the seventeenth.

At the front of the shrine, just at the feet of the Christ statue, a row of candles burned, their flames flickering in a slight draft. Behind this row of candles, in irregular groups, another fifty or more candles burned, each lit by a fisherman's wife or mother or sister, giving thanks that their men had returned safely. It was not the first time the women had lit candles.

All the women wore black. The dresses were black,

the stockings were black. The shoes were black. On their heads they wore small black head scarves, and each had a crucifix hanging from her neck.

All afternoon women came and lit their candles. By evening the small area in front of the Christ statue was filled with tiny lights. More women came, lit their candles, and retreated to kneel with the others and pray.

Later some of them went home to cook for their husbands, and then returned, so there was a constant, silent stream of black-clothed women coming from the small store that was now a shrine and returning to it.

The vigil continued throughout the night and the next morning. Some of the women did not go home at all. They had no one to go home to. The neighbors fed and bedded down the children in their own cramped homes.

Inside the shrine, hour after hour, there was only the sound of whispered prayer and of subdued sobbing. The sound was like the rising and falling of rolling surf on a sandy beach.

In the early afternoon of the fourth day, Carmine Santini got to her feet. She was a big woman. Middleaged. Her husband had died at sea five years earlier. She had been engaged to Sal Aiello for the past six months. Determinedly she made her way through the mass of women and turned to confront them. Her eyes were swollen and red with weeping. There were dark pouches under them from lack of sleep. Her doughy features were twisted with suffering.

She blew her nose in her small handkerchief and cleared her throat. In a loud voice she said, "We gotta do more than pray here."

The women stopped. Heads lifted. Silence fell on

them. This wasn't the Carmine they knew, the quiet woman, the one who hardly spoke above a whisper.

She said, "This John Christy. Alla you know about him. You know he got blown up an' his neck broken an' he was dead. My own Sal Aiello seen it with his own eyes. Some a' you husbands was there, too. They seen the same like my Sal seen. With their own eyes. Christy was dead. The man came and brung him back to life again. Christy, now he's inna hospital still, but he's alive. Sal tells me what he seen was a miracle an' he don't care what the new Father says. It was a real miracle. I believe him. You believe what you husbands tol' you. That's why we got together an' we build this shrine an' why we light the candles, so if anything happens—"

She broke off, wiping hard at her eyes with her sodden handkerchief.

"Well—it's happened. But, we gotta do more than jus' pray here. What good's it do to pray here when the man who saved John Christy lives somewhere else. You think he can hear us?"

She let the question sink in. There were nods, a few at first, then a wave of whispering that swept through the crowd of women, and then all of them were nodding.

"Mrs. Flint, the woman I work for, she tol' me who he is an' where he lives."

Carmine said, "He lives in Adam's Cove. That ain't so far from here."

Mary Cafallo spoke up from the back.

"Then let's go pray to him!"

"Yes," said Carmine Santini.

"All of us together!" Rosalie Mondelo cried out.

"Yes!" Carmine Santini nodded her head.

"An' our friends! Alla the women we know!"

"Yes!"

They began scrambling to their feet.

"Wait! Wait!"

They paused.

"This is a holy thing," Carmine Santini said hoarsely. She wiped her eyes again.

"Yes," said Angela Ciamentaro. "We can't go like we gonna jus' pay him a visit. We gotta show him it means somethin' to us. We gotta show respect."

Gina Abruzzi spoke up. "I think we should get candles. Tall ones. I don't think we should go in cars. I think we should walk. An' we gotta do penance. I think we should walk in bare feet. No shoes. No stockings. In bare feet."

There were cries of agreement. The voices broke out in English and Italian and in Portuguese.

Teresa Cardoza, the wife of Joe Cardoza from the *Carmine J.*, spoke up. "My husband seen this man when he saved John Christy's life. My husband's on the *Carmine J.*"

The room fell silent.

Teresa said, "I think we should take the Christ with us."

Someone said, "It's too big."

"It's not too big," said Teresa stubbornly.

Gina Abruzzi called out, "My brother Pasquale, he's strong. He can carry it."

"Two miles? He can carry it two miles?"

Isabel Cardoza, Teresa's sister-in-law, spoke up. "Enrique's brother, Luis. He's strong, too. He can help Pasquale. They can take turns."

The voices began shouting, each of the women volunteering a brother, a brother-in-law, a son. There were more than enough men to carry the statue the two miles to Adam's Cove.

And so the procession was organized. The women left The Shrine of the Second Life to call their friends and their relatives and their sons and brothers and brothers-in-law.

By mid-afternoon, what would have been a thin line of women straggling toward Adam's Cove had become a full-scale march.

4.

In the bright sunlight, now that the storm had gone and the skies were without a cloud and intensely blue, the wives of the men lost at sea marched in the first group. There were seventeen of them, including Carmine Santini.

Behind them in a mass came the mothers and sisters and sisters-in-law. Then came the relatives, the cousins, the aunts, the cousins by marriage, the nieces and mothers-in-law. And their women friends.

The men walked behind the relatives, taking turns carrying the statue of the crucified, painted Christ figure. Pasquale Abruzzi carried it for the first few hundred yards before he handed it over to Tony Abruzzi who, after a while, gave it to Guiseppe Gallo. It was heavy and only the strongest among the fishermen could carry it far, but each was honored to march among the men carrying the statue. They carried it proudly.

Behind the men who carried the statue came the wives of the fishermen who had survived the storm. And then came their relatives along with the fishermen themselves.

There were more than three hundred people in the procession. All of them walked in bare feet.

Black dresses, black head coverings, bare legs, and

bare feet falling on the black tar pavement, taking secret joy in the pain of the sharp pebbles, the quick hurts that proved to them they were doing penance.

The men wore dark suits and white shirts and dark neckties. Their trousers were baggy and the cuffs rolled up to mid-shin to show they wore no socks or shoes.

After a while, by the time they had walked the first mile, most of them were limping and many of them had blisters on the soles of their feet. The pain was real and constant and some of them cried from the pain and others cried from sorrow and anguish and loss. Some of them held each other, comforting each other, the younger women holding the older women, sons holding mothers, supporting them as they limped.

Lucy Scali was seventy-one years old and small and frail. After the first half mile, she could walk no longer. Now she was being carried in the arms of her son, Dominic, who cradled her like a child. His daughter, Nella, who was eight, walked beside him holding onto his sleeve. Lucy Scali had her eyes closed, her crucifix clutched in both of her small hands, her lips muttering the prayers of her rosary. Dominic's cheeks were wet with tears for his brother, Umberto. Umberto had been on the *Evangeline*.

The procession came along Atlantic Avenue and then turned and moved onto the narrow road that led to Adam's Cove.

In front of the procession, a Harbortown police cruiser rolled slowly along, its roof lights flashing to clear the road for the people behind it.

Because the procession moved slowly, it took almost three hours to get to Adam's Cove and the house of Michael Hietala.

5.

As the procession turned the curve of the road, the marchers caught sight of the house. It was the only house in a half-mile section of this stretch of roadway, sitting between the road and the cliffs and the ocean on the far side of the cliffs. The house was set back from the road, and a gravel drive angled through a lawn and around an oak tree, and then it circled back on itself in a great curve that fronted the steps to the house before sweeping on toward the triple garage. Along the front of the house, stretching for more than a hundred feet on either side of the gates of the driveway, was a high, granite block wall.

The procession came to the wall, hobbling now, tired, almost at the point of exhaustion. Some of the women were crying now more from the pain of their swollen, burning feet than from the anguish inside them. Those in the front of the procession slowed down, and those in the rear hastened to catch up so the mass of women and men began to walk in a tighter and more compact mass. Unconsciously they straightened up and walked more erect and with more dignity.

Guiseppe Agrusso, who was now carrying the Christ statue, held it higher and tried to walk so that it would not bob up and down.

Angela Ciamentaro clutched her daughter's hand tighter. The girl brought her mother's hand up to her mouth and kissed it.

They came to the gates of the house. The police cruiser drew up beyond the gates. The women in the procession stopped at the wide, wrought iron, double gates. One of them was open. Carmine Santini was the first to notice the bronze plaque.

THE CHURCH OF THE SECOND LIFE

She flung out her arm, her finger pointing. "Look," she cried out. "Look at what it says!"

Faces turned toward the plaque.

"It's an omen!" Gina Abruzzi burst out. She fell to her knees in front of the gate, bowing her head.

One by one, the other women knelt in the roadway, the younger ones quickly and easily, the older ones slowly, their old joints protesting, first with one knee, then with both, grunting with the effort, until finally the road in front of the gate was blocked with black-clad figures, solid, shapeless bodies; gigantic, headless ravens rocking.

The men with the Christ statue brought it up to the front of the group and set it on the macadam road. The statue had a wide base. It stood by itself. The men retreated behind the mass of women, kneeling to blend with them.

In unison, the voices chanted in subdued desperation.

"Hail, Mary, full of grace . . ."

In the bedroom overlooking the courtyard, Lisa Fialho heard the voices drifting in through the opened window. She went to it and looked out. Because of the wall on either side of the gate, she could see only the women in front of the wrought iron gates—so many of them that they blocked the road from one side to the other. She saw they were kneeling and there was a statue of Christ in front of them. The face of the Christ was turned toward the house.

Frightened, she ran downstairs to Michael.

She found him on the sundeck, lying in the shadows, his eyes closed, his long body relaxing on the aluminum and webbing lounge chair.

"Michael, there's a crowd here."

He opened his eyes and looked at her. His eyes had the deliberate, feline look of a hunting cat. Even in her excitement she noticed that his face was different. It was the face he had when he had taken her in the dark.

"What are you talking about?"

"Outside the front gate. God knows who they are. There must be a couple of hundred of them. Women. Men. Children. I've never seen anything like it. They're just kneeling in the road."

Michael got to his feet.

"There's nothing to worry about," he said, "I've been expecting them."

Lisa followed him as he walked through the house to the front door, the feeling of fright still permeating her body.

Carmine Santini lifted her head when the front door opened and Michael Hietala came out. He walked down the drive toward them.

"Look," she whispered. "Look! Look!"

One by one the heads came up. They looked at him.

The sunlight shone on his head, making his brown hair glow with richness. He wore only faded denim shorts and leather sandals. The sunlight glistened on his tanned skin, emphasizing the tight muscles of his thighs and arms and torso. They saw his beard and his high cheekbones and his dark, deep-set eyes.

"Look," they said to one another. "Look! Look!" The voices whispered and the whispers ran among them, from one to another, like the rustling of a gentle wind in a field of wheat, a great sigh sweeping from one end of the throng to the other.

But they were frightened of him. No one could explain it. They were afraid to turn their heads away once they had looked at him and afraid to keep on looking at him. A great fear moved among them. Some of the children began to cry.

Michael Hietala came up to the front of the throng and stopped. He saw the faces lifted toward him. He saw the tired lines on the faces and the reddened wrinkled eyes. He saw exhaustion, pain, deep anguish, and hope in the eyes staring at him. And he saw fear. The fear pleased him. The fear in their eyes made him feel powerful and confident.

He came up in front of the statue of the crucified Christ; plaster painted in flesh tones accentuated the agony on the tortured face. It was the same agony he saw in the faces of the women kneeling in front of him, their faces upturned in hope and fear. For a long time, he stood looking into the face of the Christ statue.

In his mind, he said calmly, *"Hello, Aaron."*

"Why, Michael? Why did you do it?"

"To prove something to you. To prove that death is stronger than life."

"And you think that makes you stronger than me?"

"Doesn't it?" Michael challenged. He stared boldly into Aaron's eyes.

Compassion for him flowed out of Aaron's gentle gaze. Michael felt it seep into him and he fought against it. He wanted to fight Aaron. He wanted to feel Aaron's anger, not his love. He wanted to grapple with Aaron, to wrestle with him, to defeat him by force. He knew that Aaron hated him. How could he not hate him for what he'd done. But Aaron gave him understanding and warmth and kindness. He hated the strength in Aaron.

In a furious frustration, he cried out, *"Fight me! Damn you, Aaron. Fight me! I can beat you now!"*

There was only love in Aaron's face, and he felt himself becoming weaker. He tried once more.

"I hate you! I will kill you again! Fight me!"

Yet as he cried out the words, he knew he had lost, that he was slipping away, that even as he was leaving the flesh of his body and the consciousness of his mind, Aaron was taking his place.

One last time, desperately, he cried out, *"Aaron! Fi . . . ght . . . me . . . e . . . e . . ."*

Then he was gone, the echoes of his cry diminishing in the recesses of his mind as he went into limbo.

"Look!" The whispers moved among the women like little feet scurrying, silent almost and without bodies.

"Look! Look!"

They saw his face, and the fear left them.

Aaron Hietala turned his face away from the polychromed features of the statue. He moved among the women and men as they knelt in the road. Heads turned as he walked past. Hands reached out tentatively, shyly, to touch his legs, his sandles.

No one spoke.

He came into the middle of the roadway and looked searchingly at the massed, supplicating, silent faces of the kneeling men and women. He wondered how they could stand the heat of the sun dressed in their heavy, dark clothing. He saw that their feet were bare, and he saw that the soles of the feet of the kneeling women were raw and bloodied, skin hanging from burst blisters.

Palm touching palm, fingers aligned, hands pressed together in silent humility, silently begging him to bless them. Brown faces above the hands, wrinkles on the faces, lines around the eyes and the mouths, slack skin along the jowls, wrinkled, sagging skin on necks. Above the palms pressed together in supplication, the silent faces begged him.

He turned away from the faces and walked back to the front of the throng.

Charlie Daggett lolled against the side of the police cruiser parked some thirty feet up the road from the gate. Patrolman Anthony Catalini got out of the car to stand beside him.

"He don't look so special," Catalini said sourly.

Charlie Daggett grunted.

"You really think he brought Christy back to life?" Catalini asked.

"What do you think?"

"I think it's a bunch of bullshit," Catalini said in disgust. "They ought to know better."

"Suppose you were there and seen it?" Daggett asked.

"Seen what? Seen a guy start breathin' again? Hell, that ain't nothin' new. Half the guys that get saved from drownin' stopped breathin' before they been resuscitated. What's so different?"

"Christy's supposed to have broken his neck."

"Who says?"

Daggett shrugged. He was watching Hietala, taking in the height of the man, his physique, the way he moved, the way he walked. He noticed that Hietala had a beard. These days, he paid careful attention to every man he saw who wore a beard. He wondered what kind of a car Hietala had, and he made a note to find out before they drove back to Harbortown.

Catalini made a snorting sound and opened the door to get back into the car.

"I can't take no more," he said, irritated. "You mind if I have a cigarette?"

"Go ahead," said Daggett.

Catalini got into the car on the driver's side. He took out a cigarette and lit it. Daggett knew Catalini was angry because everyone in the crowd, except for a few Portuguese, was Italian. Catalini was sensitive about that.

Catalini said something that Daggett didn't hear.

"What'd you say, Tony?"

"I said they should ask him to walk on water. Let's see if he can do that, huh?"

Aaron came back to the front of the throng and walked through them. He saw that Lisa Fialho had come out of the house and was standing on the far side of the gates. He turned to face the women.

Carmine Santini got to her feet, awkwardly and painfully pulling her heavy body erect. Her long hair had come loose and had fallen down onto her shoulders and across her breast. It was snarled and uncombed.

She held out her palms to him beseechingly. Almost in a whisper, she said, "Please!"

She took a small step, hesitatingly, toward him.

"You . . . you gotta . . ."

Her voice failed. She stood mute, her eyes pleading with him, begging for him to understand.

Gina Abruzzi stood up beside Carmine Santini.

"My husband . . . Tony Abruzzi . . . he's onna *Santa Serafina* . . . pray for him."

Aaron looked at the two women standing in front of him.

Another woman stood up. She did not move to the other two. She said, "My husband . . . Nick Baldasino . . . pray for him."

Gussi Scali stood up.

"Umberto Scali . . . pray for him."

And then the others, one at a time, each waiting until the other had finished, waiting their turn, in turn spoke out.

"Sam Gaspar . . . pray for him."

"Nino Giordano . . . pray for him."

"Enrique Cardozo . . . pray for him."

"Joe Ribiero . . . pray for him."

"Mike Cafalo . . . pray for him."

"Benito Mondelo . . . pray for him."

"Tony Fontana . . . pray for him."

"Louis Fontana . . . pray for him."

"Guiseppe Gallo . . . pray for him."

"Salvatore Agrusso . . . pray for him."

". . . pray for him."

". . . pray for him."

". . . pray for him."

". . . pray for my son . . ."

". . . pray for my husband . . ."

". . . pray for my brother . . ."

". . . pray for them . . ."

The words washed over him. One phrase at a time. One voice at a time. Harsh voices. Soft voices. Voices begging. Voices imploring. Voices sanctifying him.

The sun beat down into his face; he closed his eyes against its brightness, but the heat and the brightness went through the soft membrane of his eyelids. In his ears there was only the persistent litany of the soft, harsh voices begging, imploring, demanding, touching him gently. And there was, finally and above all, the ferocious impact of the white light smashing down on him from the furious white eye of the sun, blocking everything else from his mind. He waited for the pain to come.

When the women saw his body twitch, they did not understand what was happening. Then they saw his head fall helplessly onto his right shoulder. The voices stopped. There was silence.

His hands rose slowly, drifting in the air, moving upward from his sides until they were finally stretched out to their full length, and his body lifted slightly so that he seemed to be standing on his toes.

". . . pray . . . for . . . him . . ."

One last voice came drifting through the still, hot air.

Agatha Gaspar saw the blood come out onto his right palm in a quick gush and spill down the side of his hand onto his wrist. She screamed and closed her eyes against the sight and sank down onto the gravel on her knees.

The blood came out on the palm of his left hand; his body winced.

They felt the pain. All of them felt the pain. The women lowered themselves to their knees and bent their heads. Only a few of them dared to look.

Blood spouted from the insteps of his feet.

"*Holy Mary, Mother of God . . .*"

When the wound in his side appeared and the blood spurted from it, his body jerked as if a blade had been thrust into his ribcage.

Now there was a red haze in the air. The redness of blood, the bright, bold redness of life; it seemed to cover them all in a cloud so that even behind their closed eyes they could see it.

Isabel Cardoza was to the side of the group nearest the gate. She could see both faces: the face of Aaron Hietala and the polychromed, anguished face of the crucified Christ. They were the same. The bodies were the same. The same tortured musculature, the same suffering on each gaunt face.

It was if the man were posing for the statue and the statue was an imitation, crudely done, of the flesh and the blood of the man.

She saw the wound marks of thorns pressed deeply into the skin of Hietala's forehead. She could not see the thorns, or the nails, or the spear in his side, but she knew they were there.

She tore her eyes away from the wracked, suffering face of the man and closed her eyes and bent her head and wept for him. And for Him.

She prayed to the man for the life of Enrique Cardoza.

Rosalie Mondelo came and flung herself at the feet of the bleeding man. Prostrate, lying full length on the sharp pebbles of the gravelled drive, she rubbed her face against the stones, cutting herself with them, bleeding so that she could bleed with him, so that she could share the same, purifying agony, and she cried aloud the name of her husband.

"Benito Mondelo . . . pray for him!"

Anna Baldasano tore at her dress, ripping it, and then she raked her long fingernails down each cheek.

Blood welled into the shallow furrows. She screamed the name of her husband aloud again and again.

Estelle Ribiero held her small son in her thin arms, rocking him back and forth, her face buried in the boy's neck, pulling him into her, feeling his warmth and the delicacy of his child's bones, frightening him so that he burst into tears.

"*. . . pray for him . . .*"

He had expanded. He was no longer Aaron Hietala. He was enormous, filling the space around him, permeating everything with his being. Light shone from him, a soft glow that was brighter even than the daylight, brighter than the sun falling on him, so that those of the men and women in the crowd who tried to look at him could no longer do so and had to turn their faces away.

And then they knew.

It was the brightness that let them know.

The voices died away. There was no sound. Not even of weeping.

Sorrow and pain left them. Each of them felt the lifting of anguish. A gentle peace came drifting into each one of them so that their minds were at rest. Those whose feet had been torn by the pavement on the march from Harbortown to Adam's Cove no longer felt the sharp sting of raw, blistered skin. The flesh where the blisters had burst and the blood had come out was healed. There was only the strong, hard callus on the soles of their feet.

The scratches Anna Baldasano had clawed in her cheeks were gone. Her skin was smooth once more.

Rosalie Mondelo's forehead, torn and gashed by the sharp gravel, as she sought to mortify her flesh, was unmarred; the scratches were gone and the blood was gone.

Then they heard the music. Faint at first, growing louder until it overwhelmed them, the singing of high, sweet voices. It lasted for an eternity. Then the singing began to die away. The light began to fade.

When they no longer heard even the faintest of sounds, and the light no longer hurt their eyes and they could open them, they saw Aaron Hietala standing in front of them as he had in the beginning.

He held up his hands, palms toward them in a silent benediction, and they could see, every one of them, that the blood still dripped from the wounds in his palms, and from the wide, ugly slash in his right side and from the puckered holes in each of his insteps. It was as if he did not know that he had bled.

They moaned—a long, sorrowful, soulful wail that swept among them. Now they knew what he had done. Now they could see that he had taken their suffering into himself, and their agony and their pain and their sorrow and their grief.

Slowly, one by one, the women rose to their feet, some awkwardly, some easily, some having to be helped by those next to them.

Aaron Hietala lowered his hands and turned away from them. He walked past Lisa Fialho, not noticing her disturbed, contorted face. She followed him back up the drive to the open door of the house, went in behind him and closed the door.

Pasquale Abruzzi came up to the statue of Christ and lifted it carefully in his powerful arms. He was not a tall man, so the statue was not lifted very high off the ground, but it was enough. The women gathered around him. He made his way through the throng, walking back down the road that led to Harbortown, the women closing in around him as he went.

Anna Baldasano walked next to him.

She had a strong voice.

"*Hail, Mary . . . full of grace . . .*"

The others began to chant with her.

They intoned the prayer all the way back into town. Each time they finished, they began again, chanting the prayer to the Virgin, for they had seen her Son and had been blessed by Him and had been part of Him.

No one, not even the new priest, could ever convince them otherwise.

6.

Charlie Daggett watched the throng straggle back toward Harbortown.

"You think they're gonna need us on the way back?" Catalini asked him.

"I don't think so."

Catalini cleared his throat nervously.

"Charlie?"

"Yeah?"

"What . . . what the hell was going on?"

Daggett heard the fear in Catalini's voice.

"You saw as much as I did," he said.

"I saw it, but I don't believe it," Catalini said. "Things like that . . . they just don't happen."

"Then it didn't happen."

"But I saw it."

"Okay. You saw it, but it didn't happen."

"For Christ's sake, Charlie, you know what I mean!"

"I know," said Daggett. "I'm as good a Catholic as you are, Tony."

"You gonna tell the Father what you seen?"

"I dunno. I haven't thought about it."

"I don't think I could," Catalini said. "First of all, he wouldn't believe me."

"So don't tell him."

"Is it . . . is it a sin not to?"

"How the hell do I know? I'm not a priest."

He pushed himself away from the police car. The throng of men and women had moved well down the road by this time. What he wanted to do was to walk in through the gate and see if there was a garage behind the wall fronting the road. And if there was a garage, he wanted to see what kind of cars were parked in it. He especially wanted to see if a Toyota was one of the cars.

He started walking toward the gates.

CHAPTER THIRTEEN

Lisa helped him up the stairs to the bathroom, closing off the repugnance she felt at the blood which was smearing her arm and staining her white linen dress. While he stood trembling, she turned on the shower and adjusted the temperature of the water. When she turned back to him, she saw that his eyes were still closed and that his body jerked and twitched in small throes. She bent and loosened his belt and peeled off his bloodsoaked shorts and took off his sandals.

He was naked in front of her. She was shocked to see how gaunt and thin his body was. She tried to remember if it had been so fleshless when he'd been lying on the sundeck. She decided that she just hadn't noticed, but even as she thought that, she knew it wasn't so. He hadn't been so gaunt. The skin was now drawn tight over his ribcage. His hipbones jutted out.

Gently she helped him to step over the rim of the tub and she turned on the shower. The water sluiced over his head, over his face, onto his shoulders, splashing on the hollows formed by his collarbones and running in streams down his chest, turning red and then pink as it washed away the blood on his right side. His hip and right leg were bathed in a stream of redness that cleared under the cleansing water.

She took off her dress and her underclothes and

stepped into the tub behind him. She began to soap him down with gentle, soothing motions of her hands. His skin was soft. She could feel the wiriness of his long ropy muscles under the smoothness of his skin.

The blood was gone now, even from his feet. The water ran pure and clean on their bodies. The soap lathered into white foam. She covered him with lather, hiding the thinness of his body with it. Her hands felt slick with the soap and the smoothness of his skin; a gentle, peaceful sensuality stole over her as she ran her hands along his arms and chest and over his hips and down his thighs. When she turned him so that she could soap down his back, she felt as if she were washing a child. She cleansed him with the same gentleness she would have used in washing an infant only weeks old and found herself murmuring a tuneless, gentle croon that came from her throat without her being aware of it.

When she finished, she washed herself. Now they were both naked and innocent and wet under the waterfall of the showerhead, encased by the white tiles of the bath. She had never felt so much at peace before.

After she helped him out of the shower and began wiping the length of his body with the big, soft towel, she noticed that the wound in his side had closed. Even as she watched, the puckered skin smoothed itself out, and in a moment there was no sign at all of where the skin had been slashed through. It didn't seem strange to her. Even when she lifted each of his hands in turn and saw no sign of a wound, she was not surprised.

Bending, staring at the skin of his side, she felt moved to place her lips on his skin where the wound had been and she kissed him there. Straightening, she lifted each of his hands to her mouth and kissed the palm of each one in turn.

Then she led him gently into the bedroom and helped him into bed.

2.

Even before the storm was over, the big, four-engined HC-130B had been flown up from the Coast Guard station at Elizabeth City, North Carolina, to assist in the search-and-rescue mission when the storm lifted. It came in to Otis Field on Cape Cod bucking a headwind and the driving rain on the tag end of the gale. When the gale began to abate, the HC-130B took off on the first of its search missions.

From Otis Air Base to the Georges Bank is about one hundred miles. Twenty minutes after takeoff, Lieutenant Commander Thomas Webber throttled back on the engines and let the aircraft descend to search-pattern altitude. The airspeed slowed from 305 knots to just over 130 knots. He shut down the outboard engines, pulling back on the throttle and mixture controls and punching the feathering buttons. The props windmilled to a halt.

At search cruise, with two of its four engines shut down, and at an airspeed of just over 130 knots, the huge HC-130B cargo plane could stay in the air for approximately twelve hours. There was a crew of eight aboard. In the cavernous hold were seven- and fifteen-man inflatable life rafts and the cargo parachutes to drop them.

As the aircraft began the first leg of a creeping search pattern, the navigator, Lieutenant j.g. Henry Chase, made the first marks on his charts of the

Georges Bank. In the seat next to the pilot, Lieutenant Patrick Magill held a pair of Navy binoculars to his eyes, sweeping the turbulent, gray-green waves. At other stations throughout the aircraft, five more men were stationed, each with binoculars, each searching his quadrant.

Twice on that first run they spotted wreckage and the pilot banked the aircraft in a tight turn, circling until they were sure that there was no one clinging to it. Then the plane levelled off and the search pattern continued.

They found nothing the first day or the second. The morning of the third day brought clear weather. The Coast Guard plane picked up its search from where it had left off the day before.

Almost all of the third day was spent as the two days before it had been spent: long, monotonous hours, flying at a low altitude out to the end of a leg, then turning and flying back again parallel to its original path, almost as if the aircraft were a needle trying to sew up an invisible rent in the sky. Hour after hour with two crewmen resting while the others searched the choppy waves, the pilot and the co-pilot taking turns flying the aircraft, they continued to search.

That afternoon in Harbortown, the women began their march of penance to Adam's Cove. . . .

In the late afternoon the aircraft turned and began heading back to Otis. It was then at the farthest end of its search pattern.

For some reason he couldn't define, Lieutant Commander Webber didn't immediately restart his outboard engines and climb to flight altitude as he turned the plane on a heading for Cape Cod and the airbase at Bourne. He remained at his search altitude, cutting a diagonal across the area the plane had already covered before. Because he didn't restart his two idle engines, the plane remained at search cruise speed.

Aviation Machinist's Mate Dwight Bradley was one of the two scanners in the waist of the aircraft. Binoculars to his eyes, he continued to sweep the aft starboard quadrant. He saw nothing. Aviation Electronics Technician Lionel Tracy, one of the two radiomen aboard, came up to stand beside him. Tracy punched him easily on the biceps to get his attention.

Bradley turned his head toward Tracy.

"Got a cigarette, Brad?"

He nodded and began to dig out a pack from a zippered pocket.

"How long we gonna keep this up?" Tracy shouted over the engine noise.

"Ask the old man," Bradley yelled back.

"Three days," Tracy said. "You think anyone coulda lasted three days in that gale?"

Bradley shrugged. "Maybe," he said. "I dunno." He took the glasses from his eyes and wiped the back of his hand against his lids.

"You can stand down now," Tracy said to him. "We covered this area. We're on our way home. I just got through radioing the base our ETA."

"Okay," said Bradley, but he put the glasses back up to his eyes again.

"You find something, you let me know," Tracy said laughing.

After Tracy left him, Bradley continued to search the gray, cold waves. Even now, even with the sun on them, they looked threatening. He wondered what kind of a man it was who could go out on those seas in a small fishing vessel and remain to fight against the force of the wind and the waves.

They must be crazy, he thought, remembering how small and tawdry the vessels he'd seen tied up in Gloucester were when he'd been at the Coast Guard station there. Sixty, eighty, a hundred feet long. Not too many over a hundred feet. He remembered one time going out on the Coast Guard cutter *Hamilton* out of Boston. The *Hamilton* was 378 feet long and it looked big as hell sitting there tied up at the pier, but when they were out at sea on the North Atlantic and wind came up, the cutter didn't seem so big anymore.

The *Hamilton* was somewhere on the Georges Bank right now. Its skipper was the on-scene commander for this search-and-rescue mission. Bradley looked down at the high waves and was damn glad he was plane crew.

. . . in Adam's Cove, the women knelt and saw the stigmata and bent their heads in awe and timidity and fearfulness. They felt the great, white light encompass them and the sorrow and pain leave them. . . .

Bradley saw the outboard engine unfeather and the blades begin to turn slowly as the wind caught them. A moment later, they were spinning rapidly and then the engine caught as Lieutenant Commander Webber restarted the engine. The port engine was already running. Bradley could feel the increased power as the aircraft began to pick up speed and then the nose went up and they began to climb, and that's when Bradley saw the first of the orange, dayglo life jackets come up over the crest of a wave.

He jammed the binoculars tighter to his eyes, his thumb spinning the focussing wheel to bring the ob-

ject in sharply. He saw the man in the life jacket, limp
and motionless. He could see the beard on the man's
face and his sea-matted hair. Almost immediately he
saw the second and third life jackets come into view,
and then there were a score of them in an area less
than a hundred yards square. . . .

Bradley thumbed the button on his intercom to report to the pilot.

Aboard the Coast Guard cutter *Hamilton,* the
search commander received word from the HC-130B.
The *Hamilton* was thirty miles from where the HC-
130B spotted the survivors. The cutter heeled in a
sharp turn, picking up speed, its bow beginning to
lift, a white wake streaming back behind it as it raced
at flank speed toward the men in the water. . . .

On the HC-130B Lieutenant Commander Webber
circled the area in a slow, gentle turn. All four engines
were throttled back. In the cavernous maw of the aircraft, the crewmen were unlashing a deflated, fifteen-
man rubberized life raft and attaching it to a cargo
parachute harness.

Aviation Machinist's Mate Stanley Carr was the
dropmaster. The big plane straightened out of its
curving path about five miles from the men in the water. The gigantic clamshell doors in the rear of the
hull opened slowly. Bradley and Carr, with Tracy and
Randall Peavey helping them, pushed the bundle to
the edge of the cargo hold.

As the plane roared over the heads of the survivors,
they shoved the life raft out of the aircraft. The static
line jerked the ripcord out of the cargo chute. The pilot chute popped and then the main chute came drag-
ging out and the air caught its folds and opened them

and then the orange and white panels filled and the bulk of the life raft swung below it as it drifted the last few hundred feet to the water.

Bradley saw that the life raft would land less than fifty yards from the nearest life jacket. He couldn't tell, even with his binoculars, if the man was still alive. He hoped so.

The *Hamilton* picked up the first of the survivors at 4:55 that afternoon. There were seventeen fishermen altogether. None of them were conscious when they were rescued. The last survivor was brought aboard at 5:18 P.M. and then the *Hamilton* turned and raced for its home port. Except for exposure, none of the men were in bad shape. But none of them could remember anything from the time their ships had capsized to the time, almost three days later, when they were rescued.

As the *Hamilton* ran for Boston, it radioed ahead for ambulances to meet the ship. After that the radio operator set up a ship-to-shore link with land connections to Harbortown, and those of the fishermen, like Joe Cardozo and Tony Fontana and Umberto Mondelo and Nino Giordano and Sam Gaspar, who were able to make their way to the radio room, talked to their wives.

Just before the cutter turned into Boston harbor, Sal Aiello took his friend Benito Ciamentaro to one side. They stood by the bow rail, the breeze fresh and sharp in their faces.

Aiello was troubled. He said, "Benny, your wife tell you about this . . . this thing that happened up there in Adam's Cove?"

Ciamentaro said, "Yeah. Whadda you think?"

Aiello rubbed his jaw. "I don' know what to think. I

woulda thought it's women's talk. You know how they are. Everythin's the church. The church this. The church that. Okay. But this thing. I dunno. I dunno what to think."

Ciamentaro pulled the borrowed jacket closer around his shoulders. He said, "You remember where you been since the *Evangeline* went down?"

"No. Not a fuckin' thing. That's what's makin' me think."

"You feel okay?"

"Sure. A little cold, but I been colder. I feel okay."

"After three days inna water, you feel okay. You think that ain't a miracle?"

Grudgingly, Aiello admitted, "It's a miracle. But it scares me to think about it."

Ciamentaro was a big man and older than Sal Aiello. He put one arm around Aiello's shoulders.

"Let me ask you a couple more questions, all right? How close to the *Carmine J.* and the *Santa Serafina* were we?"

"How the hell should I know? Tony's the skipper. Ask him."

"I did," said Ciamentaro. "We was nowheres near them. They musta been thirty, forty miles from us when we went down. He don't know for sure. Not in that storm. I talked to Guiseppe Gallo. He's skipper of the *Santa Serafina*. They didn't go down the same time we did. Same thing for the *Carmine J.*"

"What're you sayin'?" Aiello asked him.

"Look. We didn't go down the same time. We was nowhere near each other. But alla us, they foun' us floatin' no more'n a hundred yards apart. After three days. An' you don' think that's a miracle?"

Aiello felt a trickle of fear in his stomach.

Heavily, Ciamentaro went on as if he couldn't stop.

"You remember John Christy, Sal? I was a one who put my han' on the back of his neck. He had a broken neck. I'll swear to it to my dyin' day. He was dead. That guy brought him back to life again. Tony Fontana was there. Ask Tony."

"What're you tryin' to tell me?" Aiello asked in a whisper, afraid to hear the answer.

"I think that Jesus—"

Aiello spun, his hand flashing through the air to clap itself tightly across Ciamentaro's mouth, shutting off the words.

"Shut up! Don't say it! It's blasphemy!"

Ciamentaro pulled Aiello's hands away from his mouth. He looked down at the smaller man. His large, swarthy, unshaven face was tired.

"I ain't afraid to say it, Sal," he said, his voice trembling. "Not if it's true."

"No! Not aroun' me!" Aiello shouted at him. "I don' wanna have a curse on me!" He turned and ran down the deck of the cutter as if the devil himself were after him.

3.

The sun set and night fell. There was no moon so the night was very dark and the room in which Aaron lay with the shades tightly drawn and the drapes closed over them was even darker than the dark night.

It was not yet time for Aaron to stay in Michael's body. He lay in the great bed and sadly let the thought wash through his mind. He wished it were otherwise. He wished that he were stronger than he was. So far, he had defeated Michael, but Michael was strong and the struggle had exhausted him.

Michael knew what Aaron was thinking; the

thought gave him confidence. He could feel Aaron's great tiredness and his own strength. He came back from wherever he'd been since Aaron had driven him from their body that afternoon.

Michael slid into the darkness of the room. Aaron lay exhausted on the bed, the covers stripped back. He felt Michael flow into the room and slip into their body. There wasn't room enough in it for both of them.

Michael felt Aaron go. He sensed the great sorrow in Aaron as he left; the feeling pleased him. Neither of them said anything to the other. There were no words sounding inside Michael's head. No confrontation. No challenge. It was as if Aaron knew that he was weak and knew how strong Michael had become.

In the dark, after Aaron had gone, Michael began to laugh. The laughter was soft at first, and then it grew louder, filling the room; sardonic, evil, unclean, demonic, until it became an inhuman peal that rang against his skull.

4.

Smoke from Charlie Daggett's cigarette drifted out the open window of his car into the night. The ocean breeze came in the other window, cooling him. His car was a 1972 Rambler sedan, the blue paint sunfaded and marred by patches of rust, and the fenders were dented. The front seat had a broken spring and the upholstery was torn, and he'd taped down a square of foam rubber and covered it with a patch of oilcloth and taped that down and then put a seat cover over the front seat to hold it all in place, but it hadn't worked too well. He could still feel pressure from the broken spring, so every once in a while, he'd shift his buttocks to get more comfortable.

The Rambler was parked off the side of the road that ran past The Church of the Second Life. Charlie Daggett was watching the driveway and the gates. It was after two o'clock in the morning, and there was no moon, and it was very dark on that stretch of the road. Charlie Daggett was tired. His eyes felt scratchy. His mouth was dry from smoking too much. He'd been sitting there since eleven thirty. The dashboard ashtray was filled with cigarette stubs. There were two empty plastic coffee containers on the floormat at his feet.

To his left, on the far side of the road, a low wall of rock boulders and brush separated the roadway from the edge of the cliff. The ground on the other side of the wall dropped sharply to the water. Daggett could hear the waves lapping against the boulders at the base of the cliff and he knew that the tide had come in.

He'd had a long time to think about why he was sitting there. It made no sense. He knew he had no business being there, yet before he went off duty at ten thirty, he'd called Bernice to tell her that he didn't know when he'd be coming home. Bernice knew what he meant. She'd sighed and taken his dinner out of the oven and put it into the refrigerator.

When he left headquarters, he'd stopped to get two containers of coffee and a couple of hamburgers and had driven out to Adam's Cove where he parked and began his vigil.

Now the coffee was gone and the hamburgers sat heavily in his stomach and the greasy smell was still in the car from the waxpaper they'd been wrapped in, and he was tired.

Most of the time since he'd parked, he'd tried not to think about what he was doing or why he was doing it. It hadn't worked. The thoughts came anyway. He hadn't tried to order them. He knew he didn't have enough facts to put together to make a pattern, but there was a pattern—he kept telling himself—if you could find it. Daggett was a logical man. He dealt in facts. Something happened because something else caused it to happen. It was all very logical. Cause and effect. Nothing happened by itself. There were all sorts of little things. Details. You looked for the details and you added them up and they made a pattern. Then you knew what you had, and you knew what to look for because it could be only one thing and when you found that, the pattern was complete.

It was like a giant jigsaw puzzle. He liked the feeling he got when he put all the details down and they were all exact and correct and no one could challenge them because they were true. Then the pattern was complete and made sense and he could write it down on paper in a report. It was a good feeling to be able to do that.

But this thing. It bothered him. He knew he was sitting there in his old Rambler waiting for the man, Hietala, to come out of the house and get into the Toyota and drive off. Then he would follow the Toyota and see where it went to and what Hietala would do. That part was logical and made sense. What bothered him was the compulsion he had to do it himself. There was no reason for him to be sitting out here at two o'clock in the morning after putting in a full shift, and on his own time at that. He could have assigned the job to one of the men in his department. Not that they had so many men that he could do it without Lieutenant Bivens getting onto him about it, but he could have done it, and Bivens would have okayed it finally. There was no reason for Charlie Daggett to be there himself. It was a simple surveillance assignment that any man in his department could do. And he wasn't so young anymore. He got tired easily. What the hell was he doing going without sleep at his age?

Then why was he doing it?

He was angry with himself because he couldn't put his finger on what was pushing him so hard. He was angry because he knew that he'd stay up night after night, no matter how tired he got, sitting in the Rambler watching the gateway for the Toyota to come out.

What did he have to go on? he asked himself. Not very damn much. Two girls who were dead, with no apparent cause of death. Two identical sets of tire casts, one found at each scene of death. That was the only thing that tied the whole thing together, and it sure as hell wasn't very much. Oh, yes, he thought, and a bearded man who'd gone off with Mary Palumbo.

Well, there was a bearded man who lived in that place down the road, and there was a Toyota parked in the garage and he'd bet himself a year's salary that the tires on the Toyota would match up with the casts he had sitting in his office. He knew he was going to get a set of casts from that Toyota, but he really didn't need them. The feeling in his gut was too strong.

The events of the afternoon came into his mind. The slow, penitential march of the black-clad women and the stocky, dark-suited men, all of them barefooted, all of them chanting, the tears on the weathered faces. The heat of the afternoon. Tony Catalini driving the squad car at the head of the procession at a snail's pace along the road that led from Harbortown to Adam's Cove. The massing of the women in front of the gates of The Church of the Second Life. Kneeling on the gravel road. The prayers. The appearance of the man, Hietala, and the crazy thing he saw with his own eyes and refused to believe and believed deeply at the same time.

It made no sense, he told himself.

That was another thing that bothered him. Nothing made sense. What happened this afternoon didn't fit the pattern that should have been building up.

Nothing about this whole thing made any sense. People just didn't die without a reason. Not healthy young girls, anyhow. They just didn't go out into some lonely place' at night and masturbate and die. So somebody killed them. It was his job to find out who killed them, wasn't it? Well, that's what he was going to do. He'd find out who it was and how they'd been killed. That's all he was doing.

John Christy.

Now why the hell did he think of John Christy all of a sudden. That was another thing that bothered him. Hietala had been there. The talk was that Hietala had brought John Christy back to life. He'd heard it since the afternoon it happened. Bullshit! That's what it was! Nobody could do what Hietala was supposed to have done. Once a man's dead, he's dead. Except Hietala had been there and guys like Tony Fontana and Sal Aiello and Benny Ciamentaro had seen what happened with Christy and they swore that John Christy had been dead and that Hietala had brought him back to life. That's why the women had built their shrine and that's why they'd made their march this afternoon. To pray to him.

And later—after they'd gotten back to Harbortown and the telephone calls came in from the Coast Guard, the way the women went wild. He'd never seen anything like it in his life.

Seventeen men lost at sea for three days in one of the worst gales New England had known in more than fifty years, and they came through it alive! What do you call that?

Jesus! He didn't know what to think anymore. It was another thought that didn't fit the pattern. He pushed it out of his mind.

Why should he think of John Christy or the fishermen?

What did they have to do with the case he was trying to build?

Hietala.

Hietala was the link.

Okay. So let's think about it, he told himself. Hietala's there when John Christy gets blown up and is supposed to be dead of a broken neck. And Christy comes through it alive.

And the women who believe he saved Christy go out to pray to him and their men are found alive.

What does it prove?

Not one damn thing. Hietala's a minister. Did you forget that? he asked himself. Ministers are supposed to try to help. In a way, they're just like priests.

He didn't understand about this Church of the Second Life. When he'd come back with Patrolman Catalini, he'd checked on Hietala and The Church of the Second Life. The church had been registered at City Hall as a tax-free, religious organization some two months previously when the property was purchased. Hietala was listed as head of the organization. The Reverend Michael Hietala. Minister.

He didn't know what The Church of the Second

Life stood for. It didn't matter. Hietala was a minister. Ministers don't kill.

But the son of a bitch killed those girls!

The thought came leaping back into his mind.

Minister or no minister, he killed them. I know it!

His anger dispelled the feeling of tiredness, but he knew he was tired all the same. He could feel the tiredness in his eyes and in his body. Christ! It was bad not to be young anymore.

He lit another cigarette and looked at his watch. Twenty-five minutes after two. He should be at home in bed, sound asleep with the warm, round body of Bernice at his side. He had to be crazy to do this. He ought to start up the car and drive home and forget the whole, insane mess.

But he knew he wouldn't. He'd wait until it got light before he went home. He'd have something to eat and then he'd sleep until it was time to go on duty in the early afternoon. He knew he'd be back again, night after night, as long as he had the stamina to do it. He just wished he were younger, that's all.

5.

Lisa had been sleeping apart from Michael since she first felt afraid of him. Tonight the fear had abated; washing him in the shower, sudsing his gaunt body, feeling his smooth, male skin under her hands, she had lost the fright that had been with her constantly. Tonight, for the first time in a week, she had been able to slip easily into sleep.

She awoke with a start leaping out of the abyss of unconsciousness into awareness. Her pulse was pounding erratically; she found it hard to breathe. She got out of bed and flung the drape away from the window to let in the coolness of the night air. For a while she stood there, taking deep breaths as if she couldn't get enough air into her lungs, trying to calm herself.

She knew it hadn't been a nightmare that awakened her. She could still hear the voice in her head calling her name.

"Lisa . . ."

She knew the voice; it was Michael's. It was compelling her to come to him. She knew what he wanted. Standing in front of the window, breathing in the coolness of the moist sea air, she fought against him.

She could hear the voice in her head again, now whispering, now cajoling, now tempting her, putting fragments of images into her mind, scraps of remembrances, making her recall the intensity of their last meeting together and her total, servile surrender to him and how she had loved it. She grew aroused in spite of herself. After a while her resolve slipped away into the darkness of the room, and she found herself wanting desperately to go to him as quickly as she could.

Trembling, she turned away from the window. Her cigarettes were on the night table beside her bed. Without turning on a light, she found the cigarettes and a packet of matches.

The brief, explosive flare caught at the end of the match. In that small, yellow light, she saw herself in the mirror: tall, nude, her long blond hair falling down over one shoulder and over her right breast so that it was hidden and only the left one showed. She lit the cigarette, still staring at herself in the mirror, and blew out the match, but the brief glimpse of herself was enough to stimulate her arousal. She loved the shape of her body and the long slope of her torso curving into her hips and of her hips tapering into her smooth thighs. She often stood in front of her mirror, brushing her hair, standing tall and naked, taking an erotic, sensual pleasure in the sight of her slim body. She liked the faint, narcissistic excitement it aroused in her. The thought would always come of how men would look at her with longing and desire and how easy it was to excite them and to frustrate them. The thought of their arousal and frustration would excite her and pleasure her.

Now the thought came again, but this time it was not of showing herself and leaving. This time she wanted to give herself totally, and it was the thought of giving herself so completely that excited her now; that, and the remembrance of Michael's body and the violence with which he'd mounted her and the feeling of what it had been like with him the night that Sandra Wilkes and Doug Mackay had come to visit them.

She knew he had taken Sandra Wilkes that same night. She'd never mentioned it to him. She was afraid to ask. She could still see him in the dark hallway, towering over Sandra Wilkes; could sense the evil that had hung malevolently in the air and her own fright as she'd run up the stairs away from the two of them.

She didn't feel fright now. What she felt was the urge to go to Michael in his room and to get into bed with him and to have him put his hands on her. She wanted him to possess her.

"*Lisa . . .*"

In her head the cajoling voice called her name again. She knew he was waiting for her.

Deliberately she forced herself to finish the cigarette. When she crushed the stub in the ashtray, she reached for a perfume bottle. Taking her time, she dabbed the scent behind her earlobes and between her breasts and put a drop on the small triangle of pubic hair at her groin.

When she put the flacon down and moved away from her dressing table, she still hadn't turned on a light. Or even when she walked quickly down the hallway between the room she now slept in and Michael's bedroom. She didn't need light. She felt comfortable in the darkness and could see easily.

When she opened the door to Michael's bedroom, she knew that he was waiting for her. She could feel his presence in the room. Even as she got into bed with him, she felt more aroused than she'd ever felt in her life before.

Primitive, raw, animal like, she flung herself onto his powerful male body and drew him into her with all her strength. What she wanted now was what she'd avoided all her life.

More than anything, she wanted him to make her pregnant.

CHAPTER FOURTEEN

Charlie Daggett drove home just after five o'clock in the morning when the sun came up high enough to make it light outside. He made himself two hard-boiled eggs and toast and coffee and sat down at the kitchen table to eat it. Then he washed the dishes and put them away and went upstairs to the bedroom. Bernice was asleep in their double bed, curled into a ball as she always was when she had to sleep alone. He set the alarm clock for eleven o'clock and got undressed as quietly as he could. He slid into bed and fell asleep almost immediately against Bernice's soft bulk. Just before he lost consciousness, he felt her straighten her body against his and burrow her head against his shoulder.

At eleven, when the alarm went off, he got up and showered and shaved and came into the kitchen where Bernice had made him a cup of coffee. He rarely had more than that for breakfast. This morning, because he was so tired, the coffee soured his stomach.

At headquarters he shut the door of his office, which meant that he didn't want to be bothered by anyone. They all knew what Daggett's closed door meant, and while they were surprised that he came in so much earlier than he was supposed to on his duty shift, they knew better than to ask him about it or to walk in on him.

He called John Higgins at Harbortown Bank and Trust. Higgins checked his records. The Church of the Second Life had a checking account with his bank. It was a four figure balance. That didn't sound like very much, but Higgins said that if they had anything larger, it was probably with a Boston bank. Daggett asked him to find out which bank, and Higgins said he'd try but it might take a few days to get the information. There was no record of an account in Michael Hietala's name.

Harry Benson at the Atlantic Savings Bank told him the same thing. Michael Hietala had no account with them.

Over at the Cape Mary Trust Company, Oscar Tremaine came up with the information Charlie Daggett was looking for. Hietala had a personal checking account with the Cape Mary Trust Company with a six figure balance. Daggett didn't care about the amount.

"What's his social security number?" he asked Tremaine.

Tremaine gave it to him.

"That's all the information I'm allowed to give you, Charlie," he said. "You know that. You want any more, you can probably get it from the Cape Mary Credit Bureau. Call Jerry Martinson."

"I don't need any more," Daggett said. He thanked Oscar and hung up.

He waited until the morning teletype traffic died down. It was busiest in the morning between nine o'clock and noon. In the afternoon, it was still fairly busy, but in the morning it was hard to squeeze in on the teleprinter.

Peter Bachman was communications officer, but Daggett said he'd like to handle his own requests this morning, and Bachman took one look at him and knew Charlie Daggett wanted to be alone so he went out and had a cup of coffee down the street. He left Daggett alone in the small room with the worn, gray teleprinter machine.

Using one finger, and slowly, Daggett punched out his query on the keys, the thin, yellow tape inching out of the machine symbol by symbol.

Q-HARB/0508   13:512595   28:PC   22:5   #

The query came in directly to the computer at the Massachusetts Registry of Motor Vehicles, 100 Nashua Street, Boston.

Query from the Harbortown Police Department, file number 0508. Line 13. Massachusetts license plate number 512-595. Query on ownership.

Daggett fed the strip of perforated tape into the holder, snapped down the cover, the small, cogged wheel catching the tape. He pressed the send button; the red light lit up; the tape began ratcheting through.

A few minutes later, the keys on the teleprinter began to chatter.

A 2RMV   4820   1   0/09/77   1212   EDT
   HARB/0508
STATUS ACTIVE   EXP 05/79
REG 512595   HIETALA MICHAEL
CHURCH OF SECOND LIFE   ADAMS COVE
   EFF 06/01/77
TITLE E216554   INS   514   FEE   3 00   WGT
TOYOT 1975   COROLL SEDAN NO   2DR 4CYL
BROWN   TRANS   1   4 PASS   VIN TE31072318

The Toyota sedan was registered in the name of Michael Hietala.

Daggett began his laborious punching of the keys again, slowly hunting for the symbols and striking them with his stubby middle finger.

On the teleprinter, after a short time, the type began to punch itself, letter by letter, onto the yellow roll of paper. This time, he had fed in Hietala's social security number. In Massachusetts, a driver's social security number is the same as his license number.

On the yellow paper, the symbols spelled out:

Q HARB/0508.01 HIETALA/MICHAEL

11:014143503
22:1.
#

A 2RMV 4981 4 08/09/77 1225 EDT
   HARB/0508
STATUS ACTIVE FILE NO
LIC 014143503 EXP 79
HIETALA, MICHAEL
CHURCH OF SECOND LIFE, ADAMS COVE
TYPE 2 CLASS # HEIGHT 72 REST 1
   DOB 07/08/41

The description tallied with that of the man Daggett had seen standing in front of the church gates confronting the polychromed statue and the horde of kneeling, praying women.

Now Daggett knew that Hietala was thirty-six years old. He had been born on July 8, 1941.

Once more Daggett began his steady, methodical punching of the keyboard.

The answer came back:

Q HARB/0508
1: HIETALA, MICHAEL
2: W.M.
7: 07/08/41

A LEAPS 5293 10 08/09/77 1248 EDT
  HARB/0508
NILS LEAPS FILE   HIETALA/MICHAEL//
  07/08/41

Massachusetts had no Law Enforcement Agency Procedures file in its computer on Michael Hietala. The machine continued to chatter.

A 2RMV 5293 11 08/09/77 1249 EDT
  HARB/0508
NO SUSPENSION OR REVOCATION
  INDICATED
HIETALA, MICHAEL
07/08/41

The machine paused and then began its mindless clattering. This time the information came from the National Crime Information Center in FBI headquarters, Washington, D.C., whose computer was tied in to computers at state police headquarters, motor vehicle registries, and major city crime information centers. Any query to any of these computers would automatically draw an answer from the NCIC computer about the subject in question.

A 1NCIC 5293 12 08/09/77 1249 EDT
  HARB/0508
MA   0050800

NO NCIC WANT DOB/070841
NAM/HIETALA, MICHAEL SEX/M
RAC/W

Daggett tore off the long yellow paper sheet just below the last line of the teleprinter's message and went back to his office. He hadn't learned much. Hietala wasn't wanted by police anywhere in the country, but that didn't mean he didn't have a previous record. He wasn't looking for that information anyhow. Not right now. There was still a lot of information he wanted on the man.

He called the main office of the Registry in Boston on the special line.

"I'd like everything you've got on Hietala, Michael," he said. He spelled out the name carefully. "Date of birth: July 8, 1941. Driver's license number: 014-14-3503. Code word: Snow."

The code word to identify official police calls changed every month.

Daggett gave his name and telephone number and hung up. He knew that sometime that afternoon he'd get more scraps of information. That's what you build up a file on: scraps. A word here, a note there, a notation somewhere else. It was amazing how much you could learn about someone these days. The goddamn computers knew everyone's history and their secrets, too. All you had to do was to put them together—that, and know where to look.

When the call came back to him, he was interested in only one piece of information.

Michael Hietala had been born in Boston.

He called City Hall, got the Registry of Births and arranged to have a copy of Michael Hietala's birth certificate mailed to him.

2.

In the early afternoon, while Charlie Daggett was making his inquiries, Sarah Cameron Flint called Lisa Fialho.

"I would like to see you very much." The old woman's voice on the telephone was weak, but Lisa could still hear the imperative tone underlying it. "It's important. Very important."

"When would you like to come out here, Mrs. Flint? I'll set an appointment with you to talk to Michael."

"I can't come to you. I'm ill. I haven't been feeling very well for the past few days. And I don't want to talk to Michael about this. I'd rather talk to you. Can you make it right away? I'll send my chauffeur for you."

"It'll be quicker if I drive," Lisa said. "In about an hour? Is that soon enough?"

"Yes. Do you know the way?"

"I can find it. Just give me the directions."

She jotted them down, wondering what had upset the old woman so much that she had to see her immediately.

"In about an hour," she said.

"I'll be in my bedroom. If there's no one here, just come in. Mrs. Santini won't be in today. Arnold may be busy in the garage and won't see you. I'll have him leave the front door unlocked for you."

"I'll see you soon," Lisa said.

She wondered if she should tell Michael about Mrs. Flint's call. She decided not to. She didn't want to see Michael. Not after last night. Not for a while anyhow.

On the drive from Adam's Cove to Hamilton, Lisa wondered why Mrs. Flint had been so insistent about seeing *her*. The old woman had sounded worried and angry. What could have disturbed her?

The stone pillars at the entrance of the estate held up a wrought iron archway. The letters in the arch spelled out "Flint Rock" in ornate, ironwork scroll. From the gateway at the road, the drive wound in a long, double-S curve through elms and maples and uncut brush for almost a quarter of a mile. Then the grounds began. The house was built of granite blocks, three stories high, with a wing on each side of the main house. The wing on the left was a four-car garage with servants' quarters above it. On the right, the wing was glass walled and glass roofed for a hothouse.

Lisa left the car in front of the shallow, three-tiered flight of steps that led up to the broad piazza. The front door was ajar.

Mrs. Flint, tiny and frail, lay in the huge carved mahogany fourposter, her back propped against oversized pillows that made her look even smaller than she was. There was a tray on the table beside her and papers spread out over the covers of the bed.

When Lisa Fialho came into the bedroom, Mrs. Flint said abruptly, "I think I've been taken advantage of. I hope not. I hope you can explain it satisfactorily."

Her small, pinched eyes stared at the younger woman, cold and hard and angry.

"What makes you think you've been taken advantage of?"

"Because of Edith."

"Edith?"

"Edith Cavanaugh."

"Edith Cavanaugh is dead."

"Exactly," snapped Mrs. Flint sharply. Her thin lips

tightened in a line, the word snapped out at Lisa
Fialho, as if it were impaling her.

"She shouldn't be—should she?"

Now Lisa knew what the old woman meant.

"Edith was one of us. She was one of the elect. I
brought her to Michael myself. He accepted her."

Her small eyes were bright with anger. In spite of
her frailty, there was a core of mean, hard resilience
at her center, and her mind was sharp, and she was
burning with anger.

"Where is Edith?"

"I don't know."

"You just said she was dead," Sarah Flint pointed
out. "Does that mean she was never brought back to
life? That she was never given another body? She was
promised that. You lied to her. You and Michael. Did
you lie to me, too?"

"Michael doesn't lie," Lisa Fialho said, staring back
into the old woman's face.

"Then where is Edith?"

An edge of hysteria began to creep into Sarah
Flint's voice.

"I can't answer that. I don't know."

"You should know!"

"Would it be possible," Lisa said, trying to placate
the old woman, "that having come back to life again,
Edith has gone elsewhere?"

"No. That's not possible. Not possible at all. We had
an agreement. Whichever one of us was resurrected
first would come to the other."

"As proof?"

"Yes. In a way."

"As a test of Michael?"

The old woman was silent.

"You doubted him," Lisa accused her. "You didn't believe."

"That's not true! I was the one who saw him bring the girl in the accident back to life! How can you say that I don't believe!"

"You're questioning him. You doubted him. That was the purpose of your agreement with Edith. You wanted more proof."

"No."

"And if you get more proof, it still won't be enough. You'll want even more. There'll never be an end to it! How can you say you believe?"

"I do!" The old woman was frightened now. Without belief, she was doomed. Worriedly she burst out, "You can't blame me for worrying. Or thinking. Where is Edith Cavanaugh? Tell me that! That's all I want to know!"

Lisa knew how much she could frighten the old woman. She knew that the old woman's fear of death overrode every other concern she had, and that the old woman was helpless in the face of her fear. "You're questioning Michael," Lisa said calmly. "You're saying that he lied to you. That he cheated you out of your money. You're more concerned about your money than anything else."

"It's not true! I don't give a damn about my money!" the old woman cried out at her. Her tough facade cracked; panic and fright were in her voice. Her small eyes were black and beady and her narrow mouth was no more than a puckered line above her chin. Her eyes were wet with tears of fright. Imploringly she held out her hand to Lisa.

"Please," she said.

Lisa took the thin, dry hand in her own. Sarah

Flint's bony fingers clasped her hand tightly. She was surprised at how strong the old woman was.

"You've been resurrected," the old woman said in her thin, faint voice. "You know. What's it like? How will I know when it's going to happen? I've asked Michael again and again. How much longer do I have to wait? All Michael tells me is that I must be patient."

"Then be patient."

"I haven't got time to be patient!" the old woman cried out. "Don't you know how old I am? Don't you know how weak I am? Every time I get ill—even with just a cold . . . I—I'm afraid!"

"It will happen soon," Lisa said, pacifying her. It was incredible how strong she felt. She could feel the fear flooding the old woman's decrepit, wizened body. She reveled in the old woman's fright. The fear of death. They all feared it. They feared the eternity of nothingness that stretched blackly ahead of them. The old woman's fear made a stench in the room that was different from the stench of sickness or even of death itself. This was the smell of fear oozing out of her pores.

"Will it really happen soon?" The old woman reached over to grasp Lisa's hand with her other fleshless, dry palm so that both of her hands were clasping Lisa's.

"Yes."

The hands tightened on Lisa's fingers. The small, black eyes pushed at her, brightening as the idea came into her mind and surprised her and frightened her at the same time.

"Can—can you—" She could not finish the sentence. Her small tongue came out and wet the thin lips on the old face.

"Can I—what?" Knowing somehow what the old woman wanted to ask and not surprised by it.

"—make it happen?" Sarah Flint burst out, her eyes begging the younger woman for an answer that would make her happy. That would take away her fear.

"Yes," said Lisa, and felt no surprise that the word came out of her mouth. And, as she said the word, she knew she could make it happen.

From the time she'd come into Sarah Flint's bedroom, she had begun to feel different. She was no longer the Lisa Fialho who was Michael Hietala's mistress. Since the night before, she'd felt no fear of Michael Hietala. When she'd awakened in the morning, she was in her own bed, stretching to appreciate the sweet surfeit that permeated her, to feel the deep fulfillment inside her. She had given herself to him totally. He was a Michael she'd never known before and she wondered why she'd ever been afraid of him. She had matched him violence for violence; she had fought him with her body, making him exert himself to dominate her, exulting in his domination, drawing into herself what there had been in him that had frightened her. And when it was over, he'd been as exhausted as she. It was then that she slipped away to her own bed so that she could be alone and examine her feelings alone. It was as if she had been transformed into another being. She had placed her hands on the still damp skin of her abdomen, feeling the smoothness of the taut skin and the hard muscles underneath the skin and had smiled catlike and secretively to herself in the dark of her own room, lying in her bed, knowing that she had been impregnated, knowing that a life had been implanted in her, knowing that she would nurture it to full growth and give birth to it and that it would be a male child like no other male child in the world.

"Yes," she said again to Sarah Flint, "I can make it happen."

"Will you? Please? I haven't much time left to me."

"When?" Lisa asked, knowing the answer even as she asked the question.

"Now? Would it be possible now?"

"Yes. I can do it now."

The old woman had been holding her breath. It escaped from her slowly in a long exhalation. She let go of Lisa's hand and relaxed, sinking back onto the pillows.

"Is—is there anything I have to do?"

"You've already done what has to be done. You've already given your soul. You want eternal life. One lifetime after another. Forever."

The old woman closed her eyes. "Yes," she said. "Yes, that's what I want."

"Then that's what you'll have," Lisa said, placing one hand on Sarah Flint's forehead.

"That feels good," the old woman murmured. "Your hand is so warm."

Even though it was the first time for her, Lisa felt no surprise. Nothing would ever surprise her again, she knew, not after her night with Michael, not after the way he'd possessed her.

Now she was filled with him, filled with his strength and craftiness and power and ferocity and evil. His seed had spewed into her like a great flood. She was now as much a part of Michael, she felt, as one human being could be of another.

The darkness began to close in on the room. It came into her, and it was like the darkness of the night before. Even when the darkness turned to complete

blackness, she wasn't afraid. It was a warm and familiar blackness. The blackness began to fill her.

Sarah Flint said in a small, weak voice, "It's getting
dark, Lisa."

"I know," she replied soothingly. "It's nothing to be
afraid of, Sarah."

"I like that," the old woman whispered. "You called
me Sarah. No one's called me that in years."

"Sarah," Lisa Fialho said again, her voice comforting the old woman.

"Oh, yes. That's so nice."

Now the darkness began to seep out of her and fill
the space around her. It moved out to cover the bed
and the old woman lying in it. It spread through the
room like a dank, malignant effluvium.

After a long time the old woman spoke.

"Am I dying, Lisa? Is this what dying is like?"

"No," she answered, not speaking for herself or out
of her own experience, knowing as she spoke that the
words that came out of her mouth were the words of
Michael, and as she spoke them, she knew what it was
about Michael and herself that was alike.

They were evil. Deep down, down beneath the
deepest surface, she and Michael were alike, had always been alike, would always be alike. They were
like twins. They were evil and different from all other
people. And she rejoiced in the knowledge.

"No," she said a second time. "You are becoming
eternal. Life after life. You will live each one of them.
All through eternity."

"On this earth?"

"Yes," said Lisa. "On this earth. Forever. Until time
comes to an end."

It was a while before the old woman understood
what that meant, before comprehension came to her.

She began to shriek in horror at the sentence that had just been passed on her, but the sound of her screams was absorbed into the blackness that lay around her and the noise was not heard anywhere.

All that remained was the sound of Lisa Fialho's soft laughter and her voice saying, over and over again, Michael's name.

Michael . . . Michael . . . Michael . . . Michael . . .

After a while, the blackness went away. Light returned to the room. Blinking, her eyes not used to the light, Lisa Fialho stared around her as if coming out of sleep. The walls were light and the sunlight streamed in through the window. The brightness of the room hurt her eyes. She looked down at the bed.

There was hardly a bulge in the comforter that was pulled up neatly over Sarah Flint's scrawny chest, the old woman's body was so thin. She lay half erect against several pillows that had been piled up to support her back and her head. The top pillow was soft; Sarah Flint's head indented it deeply. Her eyes were closed and her head was held by the pillow so that it did not slump to one side or the other. Her short white hair was sparse; her pink scalp showed through the hairs. She looked as if she'd fallen asleep. Her mouth was open; a thin dribble of saliva had trickled down one corner of her mouth onto her chin.

There was a great feeling of pleasure inside Lisa Fialho as she looked at the old woman.

It looked, for a moment, as if the comforter moved slightly. She frowned. It was as if Sarah Flint had breathed in a shallow, tentative breath.

It couldn't be. She knew that. The old woman was dead.

The comforter moved again. This time, there was

no mistake. Disturbed, Lisa Fialho reached down and took Sarah Flint's limp, left wrist in her hand. Under the delicate ancient skin, the tendons of her wrist stood out in high relief. The hand and wrist were fragile; skin and veins and tendon and bones, but no flesh. The pads of Lisa's young fingertips felt the softness of the old skin and the ropiness of the old wrist vein. She pressed her fingertips down on the vein.

She felt the slow beating of the pulse. It throbbed steadily against her fingers.

Life . . . it said. *Life* . . . *life* . . . *life* . . .

. . . laughing at her, scorning her as the old lady had.

Sarah Flint opened her eyes. Lisa Fialho saw them focus slowly on her; bluish-white rheum over the eyeballs clouding the retinas.

"Are you still here, my dear?"

The old voice was faint and extremely tired. "I'm sorry. I often do that these days. Drop off to sleep when I'm talking to someone. I haven't been feeling well all week, you know."

Lisa made no answer. Her face was tight; inside her, rage burned; she strove to hide it.

The old face tried to smile at her.

"What were we talking about?" The eyelids began to drift down. "I haven't been feeling well lately. I get tired easily. Sometimes my mind wanders. Did I ask you to come?"

"Yes," said Lisa.

"I don't know why," said Sarah Flint. "I can't remember. It probably wasn't important."

Lisa took her hand away from the old woman's wrist.

"I think I'd like to go to sleep again," Sarah Flint murmured, her eyes completely closed.

Lisa Fialho saw the thin blue veins in the old woman's eyelids; the skin was so thin that it was almost translucent. Old flesh, old skin, wrinkled, crepelike. Hard bone of shoulderblade and collarbone jutting out under the thin silk of her nightdress.

She should be dead! Why is she alive!

Anger flared up inside her, consuming her. Old bitch!

She noticed how frail the old woman's neck was. She wanted to put her hands around it and squeeze them together.

Even in her sleep, the old woman's face was arrogant. Her thin nose jutted up, haughty, glacially distant, her features still carrying an expression of disdain and superiority.

At the foot of the bed, there was a small lap pillow. She picked it up, holding it in both hands, feeling the texture of it and the firmness, staring all the while at the aged, aristocratic face and the closed, helpless eyes.

There was no hurry. She felt as if she had all the time in the world. Her anger had gone. She felt no emotion. It was something she had promised the old lady. Carefully she put the small pillow over the small face and pressed down hard on it with both her hands and all her strength.

She wasn't prepared for so violent a reaction, she didn't expect that small body of bones to thrash so strongly under the comforter. But she was strong herself. She ignored the desperate clawing of the old, brittle fingers at her wrists. It didn't last long. The body soon stilled.

She held on for a long time before she took the pillow away.

Now the old face was no longer so aristocratic. It held a different kind of stillness. Pitiful. Lost.

The old woman's body was sprawled disjointedly on the bed. The bedding was disarranged. Lisa pulled down the comforter to straighten the old woman's legs. For the first time, she was able to see what Sarah Flint looked like. Her knee joints and ankles were swollen bone; her feet were distorted; gnarled, twisted toes curled under one another. Under her silk nightgown her small stomach was bloated, swollen to distention by age and frailty, the muscles of her abdomen no longer able to hold in the mass of intestines and the gases in them.

She pulled down the nightgown to cover the woman's legs, arranged the comforter neatly over the old lady's body and moved each arm down so that it lay on top of the comforter on either side of the body. The old woman's jaw had fallen open, gaping at her, showing orange gums and a few, yellow teeth. She didn't know what to do about that.

Now she stepped away from the bed. It seemed to her that there was still something out of place.

The pillow. The small lap pillow belonged at the foot of the bed.

She replaced it where she'd found it.

Now everything looked as it had when she'd first walked into the room.

She was in no hurry. She felt no fear of discovery. There was no sense of urgency. She felt calm.

The large gilt mirror over the dressing table at the side of the room caught her eye. She walked over to it to look at herself.

She was pleased with the way she looked. She liked her slenderness and the graceful way she stood. She liked the length of her blond hair. She shook her head, cascading her hair, making it ripple and fall neatly. She noticed that her face had a slight flush to it. The color made her look good. She did not notice that she was absently rubbing first one wrist and then the other where the old woman had clawed at her. The scratches weren't deep. Certainly not deep enough to draw blood. Just enough to have abraded the skin and to itch slightly.

She thought of calling Arnold to tell him that Mrs. Flint was dead. Had died in her sleep? Was dead when she arrived? What would she tell him? She thought about it for a moment, and then decided not to call him, or to tell him about Mrs. Flint's being dead—unless he saw her coming out of the house. Even then she could tell him that she'd left the old woman asleep. Arnold wouldn't come into the house. It would be hours before the old woman's death was discovered. Hadn't she said her housekeeper—whatever her name was— wouldn't be in today?

She tried to see if there was something different about herself; she couldn't see it.

She left the bedroom and walked downstairs.

When she drove off, Arnold was still nowhere in sight.

CHAPTER FIFTEEN

"Tell me again," he demanded, his voice implacable and insistent. "Start from the time you began to black out."

"I didn't black out," she said angrily. "It was like a darkness came over me."

"Start from there. What happened?"

"I've already told you."

"Tell me again. I want to know everything that happened."

"She said it was getting dark for her, too."

"Then what'd you say to her?"

"I tried to reassure her. I said that it was all right. I called her Sarah."

"Why'd you do that?"

"I don't know! I just did. I don't know why I did anything!"

"You're getting hysterical. Calm down."

"I don't like being questioned like this! I told you what happened. Why don't you believe me?"

"I do believe you. That's the problem. What'd she say when you called her Sarah?"

"She liked it. So I said it again."

"Then what?"

"Then it got darker. Then she asked me if she was dying."

"What'd you tell her?"

"I said she wasn't. I said she was going to have eternal life."

"What'd you mean by that? What made you say that?"

"I don't know. I just did."

Lisa felt trapped by his questions, pinned down and helpless. She hated him for doing this to her. She'd thought he'd be pleased with her. Sarah Flint could have made trouble for them. She'd prevented the trouble, that's all.

"How did she react to that?"

"She tried to scream, I think. It seemed like that, anyhow. Her eyes kind of bulged out and her throat got all tight and then she passed out."

"You just said, 'You're going to have eternal life.' Is that how you said it?"

"No. I told her she was going to live forever. I knew it was a lie, but it didn't make any difference. I was bleeding the life out of her body. That's what it felt like, if you want to know. Like I was soaking up her life, draining it right out of her. And you want to know something else? It felt good!"

He ignored the fury in her voice.

"Are you saying that's how she died?"

She let out her breath helplessly. She wanted to strike at him. She hated him. She'd driven home from Sarah Flint's, not remembering the details of the drive or the road or the signposts or even going through the downtown streets of Harbortown. She'd been conscious only of the euphoria and strength she felt. She felt strong enough to cope with Michael now. It was more than just not being afraid of him. She felt that she was now his equal.

She hadn't said anything to him about her afternoon

when she'd gotten back. She had waited until after dinner when they were in the dining room having coffee. Then, seated in the long couch across the coffee table from him, she'd told him about Sarah Flint's urgent telephone call to her and how she'd gone out to the estate and how the old woman had shouted at her and about her fears. And then she'd told him what she'd done. That's when the questions began.

She thought he would be pleased with her. That he'd be proud of her. Instead he turned cold and quiet and began to question her, pinning her down on every detail, making her repeat it over and over.

"No," she said sharply. "I told you that. She didn't die then. I don't know where I got the crazy idea I could make her die just by willing it. I really thought I could do it. It made me angry that I couldn't."

"Don't tell me how you felt. That doesn't mean a damn thing. I want to know what you did."

"I smothered her," she said, resentfully, thinking even as she spoke that they both must be insane to carry on a conversation like this.

"How?"

"I've already told you!" she burst out.

"Tell me again."

"There was a pillow at the foot of the bed. I picked it up in both hands and put it over her face and pressed down on it. That's how I did it."

"Did she struggle?"

"Yes, but she's so damn frail I could hardly feel it. I leaned on the pillow with all my weight. It only took a few moments."

"And then?"

"Then I took the pillow away and she was dead. I straightened out her legs and arranged the comforter and made sure that everything looked like she died in her sleep."

She saw the expression of doubt on his face.

"I *did*! I checked and checked again. No one will ever know she didn't die in her sleep. Christ, Michael, she was well into her eighties! She's been sick all week. What's more natural than for her to die in her sleep?"

He said nothing, but the look was still on his face. He shook his head slowly from one side to the other; the left side of his mouth curled in an expression of sourness. He let out his breath as if he'd been carefully holding it in. She saw him get to his feet and begin to turn away from her as if he were abandoning her. Frightened, she rose from the couch and put her hand on his arm, grasping it hard to stop him.

He whirled around, his hand sweeping out, catching her across her face before she was aware he was striking at her.

Light exploded in her brain. She felt herself falling backward. Her head struck the floor and the lights flared red and white and orange and blue, and the pain came. The whole side of her face felt enormous where he'd struck her. The back of her head ached.

She couldn't see. Pinwheels of light were shooting off amid the blackness. She heard his voice but she couldn't make out the words.

She felt his hand clench her upper arm, his fingers going almost all the way around it and she felt herself being hauled to her feet. His strong hand held her erect; she would have fallen down without its support.

"Dumb bitch!"

It wouldn't have been so bad if he'd shouted at her; he didn't. The words came out of his mouth in a harsh, hissing whisper.

She opened her eyes to see his face inches from hers. She had never seen such fury on it before. Fury and hatred and violence barely held in check. She knew what his violence could be like.

"Stupid! Goddamn stupid!"

He shoved her away from him with an angry gesture. Off balance, she stumbled, falling onto the couch. She lay there, afraid to move.

She saw him begin to pace back and forth across the room, going away from her, then turning and coming back. She saw him kneading the knuckles of his right fist with the fingers of his left hand. He wasn't looking at her. His head was bent and swinging back and forth as he paced.

She sat up slowly, pushing her long hair away from her face. Her left cheek throbbed from the blow. She put her hand up to touch it. Her fingers felt moistness. She looked at the tips. There was blood on them. It felt as if he'd split the skin over her cheekbone. She could feel the pulsing under her eye.

He stopped in front of her, towering over her. She was afraid to lift her eyes to meet his. She felt his hand come under her chin with steady pressure. She yielded to the pressure. Her face came up.

She knew it was going to be bad. Whatever she had done was very bad. Not because it was evil but because she'd done something that could hurt him. Whatever it was, it was wrong. Very wrong.

She heard him say, "No one will ever know?" It wasn't a question at all.

She tried to shake her head, but his fingers still held her chin.

"No," she mumbled. "No one will ever know. She looked just like she died in her sleep, that's how she looked."

"What do you think an autopsy will show?"

"I don't understand. Why would there be an autopsy? An old woman died in her sleep, that's all that happened."

"Because the law requires an autopsy whenever someone dies unattended by a physician."

"Oh," she said. "I didn't know that."

"What do you think an autopsy will show?" she heard him ask again.

"I don't know. Nothing, I guess. She just stopped breathing."

"Ruptured blood vessels," Michael said, almost patiently, as if he were explaining something to a child. "Hundreds of little blood vessels in her lungs. Broken. That's what happens when someone's suffocated. You might just as well have left a note behind."

"Is—is it possible they won't do an autopsy?"

"They have to," said Michael. He let go of her. "Can anyone prove you were there?"

"I—I think so. Mrs. Flint said she'd tell Arnold to leave the door unlocked for me, so I think he'd know I was there. Or, at least, that she expected me."

"Did he see you?"

"I don't know." She tried to think. "I didn't see him. He might have seen the car standing out front while I was upstairs talking to Mrs. Flint."

He stepped away from her. She could see he was thinking. She felt better. He'd hurt her and punish her and then it would be over and he'd take care of her. He wouldn't let anyone else hurt her. He never had.

"Maybe they can prove I was there, Michael, but there's no way they can prove I had anything to do with her death."

He spun back on her, rage inflaming his face again.

He grabbed her wrists and pulled them up in front of her face.

"You stupid cunt! Look at your wrists! Look at them! Don't you think the first cop who asks you questions will notice them?"

She looked at her wrists. She saw the short, irregular lines reddening them. Michael twisted his hands and she could see the backs of her hands. The skin hadn't been broken. The scratches were very small.

She said numbly, "They'll go away in a day or two."

He dropped her hands.

"She scratched you, didn't she?"

"I didn't feel it at the time." She stared at the tiny marks again. "They'll heal. No one will know."

"They'll know you were the last person to see her alive. Once they learn she died a violent death, they'll go over her body with a magnifying glass. You think they won't find human skin under her fingernails? It's one of the first places they look."

She tried to talk. She couldn't think of anything to say.

He went on. "It won't matter a damn if you have scratches that show or not. You've got a body full of skin for them to take samples from to match up with what they'll find. Now do you understand?"

Her mind wouldn't work. It was as if she heard the words and understood each individual word enough to recognize it, but she was unable to put them together to make sense out of them.

She said, "Michael," in a small voice.

She saw him staring down at her. He had let go of her wrists, but she still held her hands up in front of her. There was something strange about him. Not the cold, evil strange of the time she saw him bending over the sprawled body of Sandra Wilkes in the dark hallway. Nor the erotic evil strangeness of the time he had first taken her. No, this was different. It was as if he were totally impersonal; as if all emotion had left him, as if he felt no anger, no fury, no desire to hurt her or punish her.

It frightened her more than anything else.

"Michael?"

She said his name again, still staring at his face, seeing clearly the hard planes of his cheekbones, the shape of his beard and the width of his forehead and his eyes that had changed to a cold so penetrating she could feel its chill.

"Michael!"

She screamed his name.

Michael felt the rage in him expand. What he wanted to do was put his strong hands around Lisa Fialho's slender neck and squeeze until he felt the muscles and tendons and veins come together and felt the slow crushing of the gristle of her larynx in his hands. He wanted to feel her body bucking desperately under him; to feel the frantic, urgent thrashing of her long, lovely body and to watch her face turn blue and her eyes bulge. He wanted to see the ugliness her face would become, to smash at her with his clenched fists, to bruise her face, to feel the crunch of her delicate nose bones under his knuckles, to feel the hot, spurting blood from her nose and mouth.

He hated her for her stupidity. He hated her because she had gotten him into trouble. He hated her because she was a woman. Because she was slimmer and lovelier and more desirable than other women. Because she was shapely and soft and because the heat of her female body could so easily excite him and because when he went into her, no matter how strong he was, she was always able to drain him of his strength.

Mostly he hated her because she was a woman. And it was women that made men evil. Just like sister Maria Theresa had made him evil. Lisa had always reminded him of Sister Maria Theresa. (She didn't look at all like Sister Maria Theresa.) He had never known the color of Sister Maria Theresa's hair, for example. Or the shape of her body under the long black nun's habit. The nun's face had been rounder and plumper. Was that because her coif compressed the smooth flesh of her cheeks to make them look fuller? Always the pure white of the laundered, starched coif surrounding the clean, scrubbed skin of the nun's pale face, set off by the black habit. And her eyes. They were pale, like Lisa Fialho's eyes. Pale and cold and accusing.

Even when she punished him, her eyes never lost their remote, cool look. She could look into him. She could see into his mind. He hated that. She could see what he was thinking; all the dirty thoughts, all the thoughts he had about sex, about girls, about masturbating—he knew she could see them, and that he disgusted her.

When he was a little older, just before he left, he would lie in his bed at night and think about Sister Maria Theresa. He would imagine her coming into his room at night. She would take off her habit and undo her headdress and he would see her standing nude in front of him, with her long blond hair falling down her back before she got into bed with him, and then she would make love to him, teaching him what he wanted to know.

He hated Sister Maria Theresa. He hated Lisa Fialho. He had made Lisa Fialho do to him all the things he'd once imagined Sister Maria Theresa would do to him.

Now, feeling that hatred pour through him, he knew he was going to do to Lisa Fialho the one, final thing he'd always wanted to do to the nun.

He closed his eyes, waiting for the familiar darkness to come into his mind.

It would envelop him, and then it would seep out of him until it encompassed her, and he would feel that special exaltation for a long time.

And when the darkness went away, they would both be dead. Lisa Fialho and the nun.

—*No*, said Aaron's voice sharply. *Not again, Michael.*

He wasn't surprised to hear Aaron's voice.

—*I haven't any choice this time, Aaron.*

—*It's not up to you to sit in judgment on her.*

—*I'm not. I'm only protecting myself.*

—*It's wrong!*

—*She deserves it.*

—*That's not why you want to do it. You take pleasure in it, Michael. You do it for the pleasure alone. And the feeling of power.*

—*Is that why I do it?* Slyness in his voice.

—*Yes. I know you. I'm part of you. You can't lie to me.*

—*Then you know I want to kill the bitch! And you can't stop me. Not ever again!*

—*I'll try,* Aaron said. *I have to try. You know that.*

—*It won't do any good.*

—*I still have to try.*

—*Leave me alone!* The cry burst in his mind.

—*I can't.*

—*Why?*

—*Because we're the same person, Michael.*

—*No! You were my twin. I killed you once. I'll kill you again!*

—*I'm not your twin. I'm you.*

—*You're dead!*

She did not understand what was happening to Michael. She had been watching his eyes, feeling them on her, studying her, examining her. She knew he was thinking about her, about what he would do. Fear paralyzed her. She could not move. The cold thickness of total panic wrapped itself like a heavy stiff bandage around her body.

And then he was looking through her, not seeing her, his eyes focused on a point far behind her. She noticed the flick of the skin around his left eye. It twitched and then twitched again. Now the whole left side of his face drew up in a quick, spastic tic. It happened so fast she wasn't really sure she saw it, but then it came a second time.

She saw his eyes drift closed as if he had gone into himself, and she knew he wasn't thinking about her. Something was happening to him.

His eyes still closed, he said aloud, "You're dead!" and she thought he was talking to her.

Michael opened his eyes and looked at her.

"You're dead," he said again. This time looking straight at her, he said the words in a strange way. It sounded as if he were saying the words to reassure himself and not to tell her what he'd decided to do about her.

Michael stared at the pale gray eyes, at Lisa's beautiful pale face framed by the beautiful long pale hair. There was fear still in her eyes, but not fright or panic. She was staring back at him strangely.

She got to her feet, moving with her usual swift

litheness, moving warily as if he might leap at her. She shook out her hair.

"I'm going up to bed."

He nodded to acknowledge he'd heard what she'd said.

"I'm going to lock my door."

He said nothing.

"Don't come to my room tonight, Michael. I have a gun, and I'm afraid of you. I don't want to use it."

He watched her turn her back on him and walk to the stairs and up the stairs until she was out of sight.

God damn you, Aaron! The thought burned itself furiously into his mind.

Parked in the same spot he'd been in the night before, Charlie Daggett sat in the old Rambler, waiting. He'd brought a large Thermos bottle of hot coffee with him and sandwiches that Bernice had prepared.

He could see down the road at an angle. Not that he could see much in the darkness. He could see that the gate was half open.

Sooner or later, he knew, the Toyota would come out of that gate. When it did, he would follow it. He was very good at following cars so they were not aware of being followed.

He didn't know how long it would be before the Toyota came out of the gate. It might not be for hours. Or it might not even be that night. That was all right with him. He was prepared to wait.

Charlie Daggett was a very patient man.

CHAPTER SIXTEEN

Aaron!

It was all Aaron's fault. Aaron came and went in his head as he pleased. Aaron took over his body whenever he wanted to. His fists clenched in frustration and rage. He pounded them against each other. There had to be some way he could get rid of Aaron for good!

Now that Lisa Fialho was no longer in the living room, he felt his aloneness more acutely than he'd felt it in years. The high vault of the ceiling, the length of the room, its great width—all isolated him. The lights hurt his eyes. It was hard for him to think in the glare of the lights. He went around the room, turning them out until there was only the glow from one lamp. The darkness made him feel better, but now the room began to move in on him. He couldn't breathe. He went to the sliding glass doors that led to the deck and opened them wide. That was better, but not good enough. He walked out into the night onto the far end of the deck, pressing himself against the railing that ran around three sides of the house.

Wind in his face. Wind ruffling his short, dark beard. Night wind. Dark wind. Wind that came through the long night across the deep waters of the North Atlantic.

Smell of ocean. Smell of salt. Smell of kelp and fish, of decaying, black mussel shells cemented in clusters to the rough faces of rock, of crab shells and disjointed crab legs on the sand of beaches. The low tide stench of clam flats and seaweed beds exposed to air and rotting muck, ripe and rich, slimy black and bursting with life waiting with frightening, infinite patience for its turn to own the world a hundred million years from now.

His mind was on the ocean and the things that dwelt beneath it: the things that swam and the things that crawled and the things that lay unmoving, waiting for smaller things to drift past them and feed them, and the things that existed and died by the hundreds of billions—all of them in the deep salt waters of the oceans of the world.

He thought of the enormity of the life in the oceans and in the deep waters, in the bays and estuaries and sea marshes and salt flats.

Life swarmed in incomprehensible numbers. Blind, senseless, mindless but alive. Each living thing living and feeding on life even smaller than itself. The life in a bucket of sea water too great to be counted. How many buckets of sea water in an estuary? In a salt marsh at flood? In a bay? In just the North Atlantic alone?

His mind was bursting. The cold slime of fear oozed through his body.

Aaron was right! Life is stronger than death!

The soft night wind sliding past him, touching him, softly chilling him. Night darkness around him. Staring sightlessly into the farthest reaches of the night, not seeing the stars or the dark shadows of the few ships on the water, seeing only the enormity of the ocean stretching to the horizon in front of him, feeling fear at its great, implacable, relentless sweep against the land as if it would overwhelm it, smelling his own fear at his insignificance.

—*Aaron's wrong*, he told himself. *For every life out there, there is a death waiting. Death is stronger than life. I have the power of death.*

He thought he said, *There is more life on earth than ever before.*

He frowned. Was that Aaron talking? He hadn't mean to say that.

—*There is a death for every life!*

—*Life is stronger than death.*

—*Life is inexorable. Death is inevitable. Man is evil.*

—*Man is not evil. Man has a choice! Michael, why do you choose evil?*

His mind hurt. He could not take any more of this struggle. He wanted an end to it.

—*Go away, Aaron!* he cried out in panic.

Aaron left him. He was alone.

He wanted peace, but he knew there would be no peace for him, just as there was no answer. The wind was full of night sounds; the voices in his head were gone. He waited. He let the wind flow into him. When his mind became calm, he knew what he would do. He would go out into the town as he had gone out the night Aaron first returned to his life.

2.

When the headlights lit up the gates of the house from inside the grounds, Charlie Daggett took a last, quick gulp of coffee from the Thermos cup and threw the rest of it out the open window onto the grass. The Toyota swept through the gates and turned down the road away from him. He screwed the plastic top onto the Thermos flask and put it down carefully on the seat beside him so it couldn't roll onto the floor and kicked the Rambler into life. He waited a moment before he turned out onto the road and began to follow the red taillights. . . .

Michael was in no hurry to go anyplace special. He had no place in mind where he thought he should go or where he wanted to go. When he walked out of the house, he looked up and saw that the lights were on in Lisa's room. A momentary flare of anger at her burned within him just knowing that she was up there and unharmed. When he drove the Toyota out of the gates, he could just as easily have turned right onto the road. That way would have taken him through Pinchon's Bay to Gale Harbor and around the peninsula to Lawton's Race. Usually he liked to drive that stretch because the road twisted and wound narrowly along the shore. For some reason he turned left as he came out of the gates and took the road toward Harbortown. He knew, though, that he wasn't going into Harbortown.

About a half mile from the center of town, he turned onto Route 128 heading south. The highway was divided. He could speed up. He remembered that he hadn't been on this road since that afternoon with Sarah Flint in her Bentley. The image of the girl came into his mind. He remembered how it had been, how she had lain on the grass, lifeless under the blood-stained sheet and how he'd put his hands on her and how she'd come to life and sat up screaming into his face, her own face torn and ripped and pulsing bright blood from her mashed mouth.

Aaron!

Aaron's name burned his mind with its sound.

That was the time Aaron had come back after all the years he'd thought Aaron was dead and he was rid of him for good. That was the afternoon when the nightmare started, only he hadn't recognized it then for the horror it would become.

Aaron!

God damn him!

With an effort, he wrenched his mind from that train of thought. *It doesn't do any good to think about him,* he told himself harshly. He could feel the blood pounding in his veins and the tension in his chest so that it was hard to breathe. He made himself take slow and regular breaths. After a while, he was calm again.

Driving alone in the night helped. He liked to drive in the darkness. When the reflective sign that said CLARENDON—TURN-OFF, 1 MILE flashed in the beams of his headlights, he let the speed of the car drop down and made the turn. He came down the ramp from the highway, stopped momentarily for the stop sign at the foot of the ramp, and then turned right onto the old road that led to Hereford and Clarendon.

He was in no hurry. Once off the highway, even though he drove slowly, few cars passed him. About a mile after he crossed the Hereford town line, he saw the tavern and slowed down. He didn't know why he slowed down, nor did he question the impulse. It just happened. As he drove past the tavern, he knew that he'd been heading for this place, *this particular place,* ever since he'd driven out of the gates of the house. He went on for about a quarter of a mile before he found a side road to turn around on and head back.

The Rum Barrel was a one-story building of rough, unpainted shingled siding with a short ell at the south end. A wide, gravel parking lot went around three sides of the building. The parking lot was filled with cars. The windows of the building were small paned with louvered shutters nailed to each side, and the windows were seldom cleaned on the outside. Dim light spilled from them. He could hear the noise and the laughter when he pulled into the parking lot and turned off the engine. He stopped the Toyota just off the road on the far side of the lot. Even though there were spaces closer to the building, he made no attempt to use them.

Moments after he parked, another car came in off the highway to park on the other side of the lot. He didn't notice that the driver didn't get out of the car, or that the car was pointed at him so whoever was inside could see him, or that there were no other cars in between them.

He heard the noise die away. For a moment he wondered about it. Night sounds crept in through the darkness. It was warm. The moon was only partly full. Behind the tavern, there were open fields and trees edging the fields. He wasn't impatient. He didn't mind waiting. He didn't know what he was waiting for, except that it was right and that if he waited long enough something would happen.

Then he heard the guitar. It was very faint. He listened for a moment before he got out of the Toyota and walked across the gravel drive to the entrance of The Rum Barrel.

3.

Michael came into the bar, stopping just inside the door for a moment. First he was struck by the heat of the bodies, then by the beer smell in the air, the heavy-hanging smoke. The place was crowded with young people. The sports cars parked outside should have told him that, he thought. They were all wearing blue jeans and suedes and stencilled T shirts and ragged-edged shorts. Topsiders on their feet or sandals or heavy leather work boots. Beards and untrimmed hair and thick mustaches. They were aware of their youth. It made them a special group.

The girl sang only folksongs.

An old, straight-backed kitchen chair had been placed about a foot out from the wall across the room from the bar and at right angles to the line of booths. The small spotlight mounted on a ceiling rafter directly in front of the chair aimed a narrow beam at her. She sat erect in the small chair, on the edge of the seat, not using the support of the chair back, the guitar in her lap.

Her voice wound itself around the audience, weaving little strands that bound them to her until they were caught and bound so tightly they couldn't escape. Her voice wasn't like any they'd ever heard before. Joni Mitchell. Joan Baez. Laura Nyro. Carly Simon. She was different as they were different. She was an original. They knew it from the first words she sang. There was clarity in her voice, even though it was husky, and it carried easily throughout the barroom. To Michael she seemed to mock the words; there was secret amusement in her voice. A small, private smile on her face teased her audience; they couldn't understand why she was smiling in that strange way.

She sang:

. . . the crow that's black, my little turtle dove,
shall change its color white

before I'm false to the maiden I love,
the noonday shall be night . . .

They had been crowded around the bar and in the booths and they had twisted around to look at her. Now they were all facing her, trapped by that special quality in her voice.

A girl in a booth got out of her seat and came and sat down on the floor in front of the singer and gazed up into her face. The girl was very young, with frizzed hair and a loose embroidered blouse and a wide skirt. She pulled the skirt tightly under her bent knees. The young man who'd been with her in the booth came and sat down beside her.

One at a time, and then in groups, the others came and sat on the floor until there was a wide, deep circle gathered in front of the singer, young bodies on the floor, sprawling with the ease only young bodies have, sharing their own warmth and the pressure of other bodies pressing against them, touching along the length of a calf or a hip or leaning back against a supporting, bent knee. Sharing the experience of her singing with each other by their touching, their faces lit by the spill of light from the small spotlight screwed to the beam on the low ceiling in front of her.

She sang *The Weaver's Song* at them.

. . . one night she knelt close by my side,
when I was fast asleep.
She threw her arms around my neck
and then began to weep.
She wept . . . she cried . . . she tore her
*   hair. . . .*

Michael could see her easily over the heads of the crowd. The spotlight cut hard-edged shadows into the hollows of her face, emphasizing her gaunt cheeks. The line of her jaw was long and sharp and her teeth glinted white and even and shining as she sang, and when she lifted her head, the long tendons of her throat stood out along the line of her neck.

She lowered her head. Her hair fell over her forehead and down in front of the guitar so it blocked his view of her long, nimble fingers on the strings.

When she lifted her head again, she saw him. She looked directly at him. Her eyes reached across the room, locking into his. He held them, not letting them go, until he saw recognition come into them. When she started the next song, Michael knew it was for him.

> . . . *over the hills I went one morn,*
> *a-singing I did go.*
> *Met this lovely maid with her coal-black hair,*
> *And she answered soft and low:*
> *said she, "Young man, I'll be your bride,*
> *if I know that you'll be true. . . ."*

The light shone on her head and its part down the middle, dividing the black, straight hair, and the light shone on her left hand, chording, chording, the fingers hooked like an arthritic claw but very strong, the wrist bent, twisting and bending, the strong finger pads pressing down firmly on the strings and the music came out like her voice, clean and clear and exciting, but now something new came into it, the very faintest of discords so delicate they didn't catch it at first.

Michael heard it and knew what it meant. He'd reached across the room and put himself into her music. The dark was coming out of him. He wanted it to fill the room. The singer would help him.

> *. . . I will twine and will mingle my waving*
>   *black hair*
> *with the roses so red and the lilies so fair.*
> *The myrtle so green of an emerald hue,*
> *the pale emanita and islip so blue. . . .*

There was something wrong. The kids on the floor began to feel it in the air. They weren't comfortable any longer. Whatever it was, it reached deeply into them and made them aware of each other with discomfort. Imperceptibly they began to move away from one another.

Anne Goodwin was one of the three waitresses at The Rum Barrel. She was standing just behind Michael at the end of the bar. The crowd pressed her into him so her side was along his back. She felt the discomfort and irritation. She tried to move away but the bodies in front of her kept her jammed into him. She didn't like the way she was feeling.

When it became intolerable, she shoved her way through them and moved around the end of the bar against the wall. Denny Sloane was wiping bar glasses with a linen towel. No one ordered drinks when the girl sang. Anne Goodwin reached over the bar and touched him on the arm. He looked up and saw the expression on her face and left off wiping the glass.

She whispered, "What do you think of her, Denny?"

"I dunno. Why?"

"She's giving me a creepy feeling. You feel it?"

"No."

"She's not the same tonight," Anne Goodwin said. "Something's different tonight. I don't like her."

Her whisper was louder than she intended. Faces turned toward her in disapproval. She turned away from them, her face red.

Denny Sloane caught her arm. He leaned further over the bar and said into her ear, "If you're not feeling well, you can go home. I'll cover for you with the boss."

"You don't know anything," she snapped at him. "You're as much a bastard as the rest of them!"

She pulled her arm out of his grip, glaring at him furiously. She pushed into the crowd to get away from him. Sloane stared after her, puzzled, and then felt himself become angry. What he wanted to do was pick up a heavy shot glass and throw it at her. He could see it hit the back of her head and knock her down, stumbling and dazed. And then he thought, *Christ! What's the matter with me?*

She sang, "... *black is the color of my true love's hair* ..." and they understood blackness as they'd never understood it before. It frightened them. The deepness of the black became real to them. They looked at her black hair and the length of it. They'd never seen black so dark.

Something dark began stirring in each of them. Deep down, it began to move and roil and push its way slowly into their minds.

Michael sensed the change. The singer looked across the room at him again. She smiled at him, but her eyes were hot and hungry and they were asking him if she was pleasing him. The others saw the smile. To them it seemed as if she were mocking them with it.

David Newcombe sat in the front of the group beside his girl. She was leaning against his shoulder. He took his arm way from her. He couldn't understand the feeling that had been building inside of him. He didn't want to touch her, or to have her touch him. He couldn't take his eyes off the singer. He was so close he could have leaned forward and touched her. He wanted to touch her.

He felt desire for her grow in him until it was almost overwhelming. The pictures began in his mind. The desire was angry and vicious. The pictures he had of her were foul. He wanted to degrade her. He wanted to take her alone, in a field somewhere, in the dark, to take her violently, to smash her, to make her cry out to him, to rip the clothes from her thin body, to drive into her with his own naked body until he wiped away the smile on her face.

He became angrier because he knew that even if he could reach her, even if he could put his hands on her, no matter where or when, she would mock him and it would be she who would deplete him, and she would continue to mock him with the look in her eyes. . . .

Wilma Enwright was on the edge of the group, her legs stretched out straight in front of her, leaning back on her elbows. Only after a while was she aware of the way she was feeling about the girl on the chair in front of her.

She wanted to make love to her. No! She wanted the girl to make love to her. . . .

She saw herself lying nude on a wide bed and the girl nude and coming to her and reaching down so that her long black hair fell down to hide both their faces and inside the curtain of black hair she would open her mouth to the girl's mouth and writhe against her to feel her warm skin and the pressure of breasts against her own and hands touching her between her thighs. She could feel the heat of her response and the incredible, mounting intensity of it, and then the girl was gone and there were men holding her down and laughing crudely and rough hands on her and the men taking her. . . .

She knew she wanted what they would do to her and that she would enjoy it, the girl . . . the men . . . the terror and the excitement of being violated and the fierce desire for more.

She felt sick inside because of her thoughts, but the thoughts wouldn't go away. The pictures grew clearer in her mind and her excitement continued to mount. She crossed her legs, pressing them together, and closed her eyes and let herself swim into the pictures totally. . . .

> . . . *run to the rock, the rock was a-melting,*
> *run to the sea, the sea was a-boiling,*
> *run to the moon, the moon was a-bleeding,*
> *run to the Lord, Lord won't you hide me?*
> *run to the Devil, Devil was a-waiting.* . . .

She looked at Michael. Her lips bent into a small, twisted smile. Then she turned her head and smiled at them and they felt the malice in her smile and the bite in her voice and her eyes mocked them coldly and cruelly and made them feel small and dirty.

Nancy Banek was on the floor, sitting crosslegged at the back of the group. She said to Connie Easler, "She's a real bitch!" and was surprised to hear Connie whisper back, "You're the bitch! Shut your fucking mouth!"

The girl got off the kitchen chair. Standing, she looked very small and fine-boned. The spotlight was on her face and brighter because she was closer to it.

She struck a chord on the guitar and then another and then began the song, never taking her eyes off Michael.

> *. . . Michael, row the boat ashore . . . hallelujah!*
> *Michael, row the boat ashore . . . hallelujah!*
> *Michael's boat is a gospel boat. . . .*

They'd never heard the spiritual sung that way before, not the way she was singing it now, and they didn't know what to think about the expression on her face.

She finished the spiritual and walked through them. They moved aside to let her through. Guitar in hand, she came up to the bar to stand in front of Michael. Then the two of them walked through the young people to the door and outside.

They watched her leave. No one applauded. There was fury in their eyes, and envy, and desire, and frustration, and all the dark, foul feelings were churning closer to the surface.

They felt hate. . . .

CHAPTER SEVENTEEN

Charlie Daggett saw them come out the door. He wondered who the girl was. He couldn't tell much about her because of the dark and the distance. She was short and very slender. They walked away from the tavern toward Hietala's car; she moved easily, with a gliding motion, her legs hidden by her long skirt which flowed across the pale gravel driveway like a dark shadow.

It was the Mary Palumbo thing all over again: Hietala going into a bar and coming out with a girl. He wondered how Hietala had picked her up and what he'd said to her to make her come with him. It didn't make any difference. It could just as well have been that the girl had picked him up. He knew Mary Palumbo would have done that. Girls were bolder now than they were when he was young. He didn't understand them anymore. At times like this, he was glad that he and Bernice didn't have any children. He'd have killed a man like Hietala, going off with his daughter.

He watched them cross the parking lot to the Toyota. He knew that they'd get into it and drive off, and he'd follow them. He was going to get Hietala. He knew that. The feeling was strong in him, and he had to push it down because it was too soon to start savoring his victory.

He saw them come up to the sports coupe and stand beside it. He put his hand on the ignition key, ready to turn it. Hietala and the girl were standing beside the car. They seemed to be in no hurry to get into it.

Daggett took his hand away from the key. He wondered what the hell they were talking about for so long. . . .

From the moment in the bar when her eyes had lifted and met his across the room and he had seen the recognition in them, Michael had felt the dark feeling well up strongly in him. It had never been so strong as it was now. This was even better than it had been with that girl in the Harbortown bar, when he'd stood in the doorway and willed her to look up at him and to leave her friends and come to him and she came.

This was better. He didn't know why. There was something different about this girl. The Palumbo girl hadn't been able to help herself. This girl came to him because she recognized something in him and wanted to come to him, and, at the same time, whatever it was in him that she recognized, he found in her and wanted her because of it.

When they came up to the Toyota, he made no move to get inside. The girl stood patiently beside him, the top of her head not quite reaching his shoulder. He put his hand on her arm. It was incredibly thin. Her bones were delicate. When he put his other hand on her ribcage, it spanned her side from just below her armpit to her waist. Through the thin material of her jersey, he felt the hard, curved bones of her chest; his fingers fit into the spaces between her ribs.

He touched her face. Fragile. Everything about her was fragile.

In the dark she tipped her face up to his. The mocking smile was still on her lips. She wasn't afraid of him, he knew.

This one was different.

Her eyes challenged him. She hadn't spoken. He wanted her to speak first. The silence went on for a long time while something flowed between them and they learned about each other and tested each other.

Finally she spoke.

"I'm Lilith."

"Michael."

"I've been waiting for you to come along, Michael. I didn't know when you'd come, but I knew you'd come. It's been a long wait."

"Yes."

"I know what you did in there."

"What'd I do?"

"You made them hate each other."

"I didn't do anything."

"But you can, can't you?"

"Yes."

"Strong things?" she asked devilishly. "Really strong things?"

"Yes."

"Like what?"

She was pressed up against him now, the guitar laid aside on top of the hood of the car.

"What can you do?"

He felt a tremor go through her thin body. She was tense with excitement, quivering like the strings on her guitar.

"Tell me," she said. One of her hands reached up to his face, lightly stroking his beard, touching his mouth with her fingertips, sliding them along his lips, waiting to feel his answer on his breath.

"Dark things," she said, her eyes brightening. "You can do dark things, can't you?"

"What do you know about dark things?"

"I'm a witch," she said seriously and importantly. It would have been ludicrous, except he knew she believed in what she was saying.

He put both hands on her thin face, holding her cheeks with his palms. Staring down at her face, he saw now that she was younger than he'd thought. The harsh light and sharp shadows created by the spotlight had aged her face. She was about twenty, he guessed, and she would know all the jargon. She would have read all the books. Witch and warlock and coven and incubus and sabbat and how to read a tarot deck to tell the future, and she'd probably attended more than one black mass where they frightened themselves by enacting the devil's rituals. Diabolism in darkened lofts and old barns and deserted fields. The casting of spells, incantations muttered at midnight in the dim, flickering light of black candles. Children playing at things they didn't know about, trying to fill themselves with excitement that came from playing with evil.

As if she were reading his mind, Lilith said, "Merry meet."

He found himself answering, "Merry meet," and Lilith smiling at him and pulling his head down to her and kissing him on the lips. It was a dry kiss. Her lips were thin and dry.

"Will you come with me tonight?" she asked. "Now?" He felt the dry heat of her breath on his mouth.

"To the coven?"

"Yes. We're meeting at midnight."

He nodded, knowing she meant witches' midnight, that hour halfway between sunset and dawn.

Lilith pulled her face away from him, still holding his head in her hands, staring into his eyes. Eagerly she said, "Show me a dark thing. Give me a sign of your power."

Anger stirred in Michael. She was a child playing at things she didn't understand. Until she had spoken, he'd thought she shared something with him and that thought had pleased him greatly, satisfying something deep inside of him. She shared nothing with him, he knew now. Nor could she ever.

"A dark thing," she said again, urgently, pressing against him. "Show me!"

I will show you! Oh, yes! I will show you something that isn't an imagining or a pretense or adult children masquerading in old clothes, play-acting, pretending!

I will show you what evil is, and what fear is, and fright!

With one hand, Michael opened the car door. He shoved the girl into the car and slammed the door behind her. As he ran around to the driver's seat, he swept the guitar off the hood with a short, savage, angry blow.

"The sabbat's in Adam's Cove tonight," she said, her eyes filled with excitement. "Is that where you're going?"

He made no answer. He started the car, and turned right onto the road, accelerating. Lilith reached over and put her hand on his thigh. She felt the heat of his solid leg under her palm, the muscles in his thigh moving as he pressed on the accelerator and let up, braking for the curves, back to the gas pedal again. She was excited and tense and frightened. Nothing in her life had ever before been like this. She smelled her own fear and sensed the power radiating from him in great, surging waves. She knew she was helpless. The feeling stimulated her.

Charlie Daggett watched them drive off. He thought, *Okay, now the son of a bitch has picked up a girl. So where the hell is he going?*

He saw Hietala's car turn right. That meant he was going back toward Harbortown. Where was he taking her? To Sugar Island? Not at this time of night. The tide was in. He wouldn't be able to get to it unless he swam. To the cemetery? He didn't think so. Back to Adam's Cove? He didn't know. All he could do was follow them.

He turned out of the parking lot only a moment after the Toyota, following the red glow of the coupe's taillights down the twisting, country road.

He didn't feel particularly excited. He'd known all along that sooner or later he was going to get Hietala. Tonight had turned out to be the night, that was all. It could have been a few days earlier, or a week or two later. It wouldn't have mattered. Long ago, once he had decided that Hietala was the man, he knew he would get him.

Patiently he followed the taillights of the Toyota back onto the main highway that led to Harbortown.

The road to Adam's Cove led through Harbortown. The shortcut goes directly through the heart of town to the waterfront and around the harbor to the peninsula on which Adam's Cove is located. Michael took the shortcut. He came off the rotary onto the avenue that led into town, slowing down even though at this time of night there was no traffic.

He drove across the railroad tracks. The streets

were narrower now. They twisted and crossed each other at odd angles here in the old part of Harbortown. The houses were old three-family wooden tenement buildings, most of them in need of repair and paint and all of them exuding the smell of failure. This was where they came from to stand in lines at the unemployment office.

They passed Paoli's old market that was now The Shrine of the Second Life. Lights were on in the shrine. The front was lit up. Michael noticed that there were groups of women standing in front of the building talking to one another. They were dressed in their best clothes. There were no men among them. The plate glass windows of the shrine had been painted halfway up with blue paint. Light shone from the top half of the windows; the paint on the bottom half showed thick amateurish brushstrokes. The door was open. Women stood in the doorway, a dark cluster of heavy figures.

On impulse, Michael brought the car to the side of the road, sliding it against the curb.

Lilith was surprised. "Why are we stopping here?"

"Let's go," Michael said, getting out of the car.

On the sidewalk, he took her by the arm. The women in the doorway looked at them as they approached. They recognized Michael, and cleared the doorway for him, some of them agitated by his presence. They looked away from his face quickly. Two of them crossed themselves; the others saw the gesture and crossed themselves, too.

Inside the door, Michael paused for a moment. The rows of folding chairs were almost all occupied. At the foot of the polychromed Christ statue which stood in the alcove at the front of the shrine, candles burned in tall glasses. Dozens of candles had been placed on the floor in front of the statue, each of them now burning, the wax melting slowly into pools of clear liquid inside the glass holders. The light they gave off was bright. It lit up the statue and the draped walls of the alcove in which it stood. The wooden walls were covered with blue paint, heavily applied. It was the same paint, Michael noticed, that their husbands used on the rusting hulls of their fishing vessels. There was a lot of that paint in Harbortown.

In front of the statue, three women crouched on their knees, praying.

The room fell silent as the women became aware of Michael's presence. Heads turned toward him. They saw Lilith and stiffened. It was wrong of him to come with a girl, especially one like her, with her wild, long hair and her wild, slender body. She didn't belong in the shrine. Lilith shrank under their hostility. Michael held her arm tightly, pulling her into his side.

One of the women, Gina Abruzzi, bolder than the rest, came up to him and knelt at his feet. She touched his trouser leg gently, in supplication.

Michael realized that the women had gathered at the shrine to give thanks for their husbands' lives. For a moment he wondered if the vigil had been going on without interruption since their pilgrimage to him. He looked around at the heavy, somber, middle-aged faces and knew that it had.

"Pray for us," called out a voice from somewhere in the room.

Others took up the chant.

"Pray for us!"

"Pray for us!"

"Pray for us!"

The room became a murmur of gentle, insistent sound pressing implacably against him with a force that was almost physical. The chant went on and on. It enraged him. He knew it was meant for Aaron and not for him.

The voices and his anger became too insistent. He could deny them no longer. Behind him, the women crowded in from the outside. Pulling Lilith by the hand, he strode down the short aisle between the folding chairs to stand in front of the Christ statue. For a moment, as he faced the statue, he gazed up into the face of the Christ. He saw the dark hair and the beard and the sad, dark brown eyes. He turned away to face the women in the room. The women who had been standing in the doorway and those who had been outside on the sidewalk had moved into the shrine, packing the small room tightly.

"Pray for us!" called out a voice. Loud, harsh, stronger than the rest, it came stridently over the chanting of the others.

Michael held up his hand. Lilith edged away from him. The women in the room stared at her with anger. She was afraid of them. She was afraid of Michael. She wanted to run from the room. She did not dare move; she was afraid that if she tried to get through them to the door, they would set upon her and tear her apart bodily.

She looked to Michael for help, her mouth opening to ask him to get her out of the room. The words died in her throat. She saw his face above her; behind it was the face of the Christ statue, and she saw that they were the same. Feature for feature, they were identical. Panic froze her body in place.

"Pray for us!"

Michael held up both hands. The sounds died away. There was silence in the room.

He looked around at them.

He wanted to shock them, to take each one of them and shake her with both strong hands; to hurt each one of them as she had never been hurt before. A wild rage surged up inside of him. He felt himself tremble at the raw intensity of the hatred in his chest.

"Have you prayed to Him?" he asked them, gently, controlling himself so that he showed no emotion in his voice. "When you were troubled, did you pray to Him?"

"Oh, yes! Yes!" They cried out to Michael. "Yes!" It was like a catechism they had learned; they were pleased to show him how well they had learned it.

"But you came to me," he said, his voice still gentle, chiding them only slightly.

He saw that the words didn't mean anything to them. They hadn't understood him.

"He couldn't help you, so you came to me."

This time he made it a statement. Now he saw that a few of them were beginning to understand. On some of the faces, expressions began to change. One woman crossed herself hurriedly.

He went on, his voice low and controlled, but carrying throughout the room, now letting the sharp edge of his sarcasm cut into them.

"Did you enjoy seeing the blood come out of the palms of my hands and from my feet and from my side? What did you think when you saw the blood and the pain? Did it give you pleasure to think that a man was bleeding for you, suffering for you?"

They weren't sure what they were supposed to think. They had never thought about things like this before. What he was saying puzzled them. It frightened some of them. Here and there, a woman slipped to her knees onto the floor and bent her head. Others stared at Michael with dark, hurt eyes.

Few of them were young. Almost all of them were overweight. Their dresses were gaudy and cheap, styled for another culture in another country. They sat uncomfortably on the hard, small folding chairs set in rows, not knowing what had suddenly taken place to change the prescribed routine of the vigil into this horror they were hearing. They breathed in heavy, corseted breaths, bosoms heaving, the heat of the room making them sweat heavily under their armpits and between their thighs. Fleshy bodies, slow minds moving slowly toward anger because he was making them think about the unthinkable.

Michael hated them. They were animals. Subhuman. They had poured all of themselves into this shrine. Now he was desecrating it for them. He wondered how far he could go before they turned on him. There was no wrath as vicious and brutal as that of a woman. The thought of the danger he was exposing himself to excited him.

He looked around the room slowly again, taking his time, making them meet his eyes so that each woman thought he was talking directly to her.

"Two thousand years ago," he said into the silence, "you went to see the same thing. It was like a carnival. The man was a criminal, executed like a criminal, crucified between a murderer and a thief, executed in a way that was reserved for those who broke the law. He was no better than the other two, but He showed you more pain and more suffering than anyone else ever had, and so you worship Him to this day. Are you going to worship me, now?"

Gasps came, first from one part of the room and then another.

A voice cried out, "He's only testing us! He's testing our faith!"

"Am I?" Michael smiled maliciously at them. "Then listen! From the beginning there has been only the power of good and the power of evil, and we belong to one or the other. Take your choice. Pray to the one, pray to the other. There is no difference between them!"

Anna Baldasino rose heavily to her feet. She pointed a finger at him. "Blasphemer!"

Michael laughed at her. "I remember you. You knelt at my feet and cried out to me. You tore your face bloody. Who was the blasphemer then?"

Shaken, Anna Baldasino sat down; she hid her face in shame.

Michael stared around at the shocked, stricken faces.

"Blasphemers? All of you are blasphemers. You came crawling to me on your knees! You knelt down before me in the dirt of the road! You grovelled to me!"

Now he spat the words at them. "You'll pray to anyone or anything if only you get what you want. You're not devout! You're superstitious! You're not pious! You're selfish!"

Michael turned to the statue. He moved around the candles to stand beside it on its small dais. He touched the statue, rapping against its side with his knuckles so that it gave off a hollow sound. Women cried out at the sacrilege. The sound of their cries filled the room.

"Plaster!" Michael shouted over the noise. "Paint! Something you made yourselves! Something someone made for you! Is that what you worship? A giant doll!"

He spun around to face them, this time on the far side of the candles so the light shone upward onto his face from below, his features elongated and saturnine.

"Why did you come to me?" he demanded. "Why?"

They were terrified now, on the verge of panic. He saw their terror. It pleased him incredibly to see them that way.

"You came to me because He—" he rapped again against the side of the polychromed, plaster Christ, "—because He couldn't help you, and that's all you've ever wanted from Him! '*Give me! Give me! Give me!*' is all you ever say to Him! You asked Him for help and He couldn't help you! So you came to me! You knelt in the dirt of the road at my feet, and you prayed to me as you had prayed to Him!

"Well, which of us is the more powerful? Which one of us gave you what you begged for? *Answer me!*"

Their fright washed over him like a hot, liquid wave, filling him, expanding him to gigantic size.

In his mind, he called out to Aaron, shouting:

—*Aaron, see what I am doing! I am stronger than you, Aaron! Here's the proof! Look at them!*

Out of the corner of his eye, he saw Lilith standing, trembling, her eyes fixed on him. He read her fear.

—*You asked for a dark thing,* he said to her in his mind. *Is this thing dark enough for you?*

He saw the women waiting.

"I don't pray to Him," he cried out to them. "When you prayed to me, it was not He who helped you! Do you understand what you've done? Do you?"

One of them did. A low, plaintive wail broke from a desperate throat. Now the others picked up what it was she understood. The faces in the room filled with shame and horror as the women became aware of what they had done, of the sin they had committed, of the blasphemy and sacrilege they had perpetrated.

"So much for Him!" Michael gave the statue a disdainful shove with his arm.

The statue swayed, moved past its point of balance, and, as if it were a deliberate, planned gesture on its part, the Christ continued to fall, falling in slow motion, falling over, seeming to fall forever.

It was as if every one of them expected the statue, at the last minute, to bend its knees under the plaster robe and to step over the bank of candles on the floor in front of it. When the statue fell with a crash onto the candles, they were surprised.

Candles smashed and scattered. Glass from the candleholders flew. Women screamed, leaping to their feet. Michael stood erect on the small dais where the statue had been standing, his laughter reverberating through the small room.

"Here!" he shouted at them. He leaped forward, seizing Lilith, pulling her back onto the dais with him, holding her in the crook of his left arm so that she couldn't get away from him. "Here! You want something to worship? Worship a human being! Worship beauty!"

Half turning, he clawed at the neckline of Lilith's blouse with his right hand, ripping it down the front. In two swift moves, he stripped the remnants of her blouse from her, leaving her nude from the waist up. Lilith struggled in his grasp, screaming.

"Look," he shouted at them. "Here's something for you to pray to! Pray for a body like this, if you're going to pray!"

He tore Lilith's skirt away from her and then the last, small flimsy garment she wore around her loins. Now she was totally nude, except for the sandals on her feet.

He paid no attention to the burning of the candles. Flame from the scattered candles began to lick at the bottom of the drapes in the alcove. Fire began to mount the folds of the dry material.

A woman screamed, pointing to the flames. Michael turned. He looked at the fire that was now moving quickly up the panels of cloth. He laughed—a wild, manic sound.

The fire substituted its own fear for the one they had been feeling, and the fear of fire was the greater. They knocked over chairs, scrambling to get to the exit. The women rushed to get to the door, but the chairs they had knocked down got in their way, tripping them, making a barrier in the narrow aisle. The first few who got to the door jammed the opening in their struggle to get out. The others pressed hard against them. Now no one could get through the door. All of them were screaming: high, shrill animal screams of panic. They tore at each other with their fingernails and beat each other on the head. They seized handfuls of hair, pulling desperately to gain an inch of precious space closer to the door. They bit into flesh with strong teeth until blood filled their mouths. Blind, senseless, they fell upon one another. They knew fire. They knew how swiftly it could sweep through a tenement.

Lilith felt the heat of the flames on her naked body. She struggled violently in Michael's grasp, trying to get away. He slapped her across the face.

Her eyes bulging with fear, she struggled even harder. Michael picked up her small body in his arms and threw her over his shoulder. He turned to face the room. In the wall to his right, he saw the outline of a door. It had been painted the same shade of blue as the rest of the walls. None of the women had noticed it. They could only think of getting out the same way they'd entered.

By now the flames had engulfed the cloth panels. The alcove had become a roaring pyre of flames. Michael pushed his way through the few stragglers who were too weak to fight the others in the mob beating on each other to get out. He stepped over fallen chairs. A woman threw herself at him, screaming imprecations, her eyes wild, saliva spewing from her mouth in sprays. He slapped her away and continued toward the side door.

The door was padlocked. It was so old that even the padlock had been painted over. He hesitated momentarily in front of the door, wondering where it led to, and then decided it made no difference. He raised his leg and kicked at the center of the door. A panel shattered. He kicked again. The door broke loose from its hinges. He grabbed the door, now held only by the hasp, and pulled it to one side. The cool air of the alleyway blew in on him.

Behind him, the air stirred the fire so that it leaped forward and upward toward the front of the store and toward the ceiling. The women at the rear of the mob felt the heat of the fire. Screaming, they threw themselves even more desperately on the ones in front.

Michael flung himself through the doorway, Lilith on his shoulder. He was suddenly in the alley then, in the cool darkness, running down the narrow length of it, running away from the fire, away from the shrine, away from the women.

Inside he felt a glow as intense as that of the fire. He felt strong and enormous.

Panting, he stopped for a moment to take Lilith from his shoulder. He held her in front of him, nude, holding her by the back of her head and by one arm. He shook her, pushing his face into hers.

"You wanted to see a dark thing?" he shouted at

her. "Was that dark enough for you? Was that evil enough for you? Or do you want more?"

Lilith began to scream.

When the Toyota ahead of him pulled over to the curb, Charlie Daggett slowed down and then drove past it. He went to the end of the block and came back down a parallel street for several blocks before he turned back onto the main street again. He parked diagonally across the avenue from the shrine. By the time he got there, Michael and Lilith had already entered the store. Daggett could see Hietala's empty car. He saw the women who had been standing on the sidewalk when he drove by the first time go into the store. He turned off his headlights, settling himself down for another wait. This time he had something to think about: What was Hietala doing in The Shrine of the Second Life?

Charlie Daggett heard the noise; raw, mindless, violent, high-pitched screams came tearing out of the shrine. He saw a woman stagger out of the front of the shrine, falling to her knees on the sidewalk. A second woman fell beside her, tripping as she stumbled out the doorway. He saw a cluster of bodies struggling in the narrow opening of the door, blocking off the light. He saw them jam together, three or four women all trying to get through at the same time, pounding at each other, their faces contorted with panic. A woman tried to crawl between their legs. Her shoulders tripped the woman above her and the doorway was blocked solidly with their flesh.

Daggett flung open the door of his Rambler, and raced across the street to the storefront, drawing his revolver as he ran. The light coming out of the upper half of the painted storefront windows was yellow now, yellow with tinges of red and orange from the flames in the back of the shrine.

As he ran, he reversed his gun in his hand, grasping it by the barrel. He came up to the windows, smashing hard at the plate glass with the heavy, steel butt. The window cracked. He smashed again. This time, the window shattered, huge shards of glass dropping like guillotine blades onto the sidewalk to shatter again into smaller fragments. Furiously he attacked the jagged edges of the glass that still remained in the window frame.

"This way!" he shouted to the women inside. "Out the window!"

He ran around the women on the sidewalk, now sitting up but dazed, to break the glass in the second window. Glass cut the back of his hand as the window shattered. He ignored the sting of the cuts, pounding desperately at the brittle, keen icicles of sharp glass that jutted up from the bottom of the window frame.

Again and again, he shouted into the store for the women to come out the window.

Some of the women at the edge of the mob inside the doorway heard the glass shatter and saw Daggett smashing away to give them a chance to escape, and they left off their fighting to climb over the fallen chairs to the window. They tore their skirts and ripped their stockings and the glass cut long, brutal slashes in their legs, but they climbed over the windowsills onto the sidewalk, still screaming in panic, still striking out at one another in their haste to flee the fire.

At first there were only a few of them, and then more. They came climbing out of the windows like a dark flood of burly animals, screaming and cursing, flailing wildly and blindly at anything in their way, knocking Charlie Daggett back off the sidewalk.

He pushed his way back through them, ruthlessly now, not caring if he hurt any of them. They had lost all control. Fights had broken out on the sidewalk. They grappled with one another, friend fighting friend, clawing, scratching, pulling hair, screaming bitter curses, still in the grip of panic and hate. There were other women inside. Daggett knew he had to get to them. There was no one else who could save them from the fire. Like mindless creatures, they were still trying to get through the blocked doorway.

He flung the heavy bodies aside brutally, charging through them to get to the open window. As he stepped over the sill, he saw Hietala emerge from the alley, pulling the naked girl along with him toward his car.

I'll get the son of a bitch some other time, he thought and then the thought went out of his mind, and he was in the shrine, the smoke stinging his eyes, almost blinding him.

The lights had failed. The interior was now lit only by the flames raging up the walls and curling bright, hot, beautiful fingers of fire along the ceiling. The fire now made sounds of its own; there was the steady roaring of the flames, the crackling of paint and dry wood exploding into fire, the roaring noise from the inferno that the alcove had become. Wax from the candles had melted along the floor and ran into the cracks in the planks.

Daggett used his strength to hurl the women at the back aside. Some he knocked down. Others he flung to one side. Now only the three in the doorway were in front of him. He seized the larger of them, bent his head into her back and lunged forward with all his strength, driving with his legs the way he'd learned to smash into opposing linemen when he'd played football in high school. He still had the strength. He broke her loose, out of the doorway, both of them catapulting onto the sidewalk, the concrete knocking the breath out of him, tearing the skin of his face and forehead.

Dazed, he got to his feet. Women were now running out the doorway. Then the doorway was empty. But Daggett remembered seeing others inside in the few moments he'd been in there. They had been lying on the floor unconscious. He took a breath and plunged back into the flames and the smoke.

He didn't know how many of them he could get out before the fire got to them. All he could do was try.

CHAPTER EIGHTEEN

Michael drove down to the waterfront, Lilith crouching nude in the seat beside him, her body shaking uncontrollably. The narrow, short side streets to the docks were dark; only the car headlights lit them up as he drove through. He turned into the huge, empty parking lot behind the largest of the fish-packing plants. The plant was empty at this hour of the night. Empty and dark. An enormous, five-story monolith of a building with only a few windows barely lit by the few night lights burning inside.

At the far end of the parking lot, the long finger of a wharf jutted out into the dark oily water of the inner harbor. Two draggers were tied up to the wharf, bow to stern. Across a small stretch of water, there was another pier with smaller boats tied to its pilings. The air smelled of decaying fish and salt and ocean. The smells were strong in the warm summer night.

Michael parked the Toyota close to the end of the building in the darkest of the shadows. When he opened the passenger door, he found Lilith curled into a ball, hugging her knees, her face burrowed into the crevasse of her arms and thighs, trying to retreat from herself. He drew her out of the car, her eyes blank, her face slack.

She stood in front of him, the wind blowing against

her long, black hair, her face turned down and away from him. He saw how small she was and how much he towered over her. She was incredibly delicate.

"Come," he said to her, commandingly.

She didn't move. She heard his voice. She heard what he said. Her body refused to respond. She felt his strong fingers come under her jaw and lift her face. She closed her eyes, refusing to look at him.

"Open your eyes," he said.

Her eyelids lifted. His face was above her, looking down at her.

"I will take care of you," he said, and she believed him. With a tiny, mewing sound of relief, she flung herself against him, her arms wrapping around his waist, her face against his chest. She felt him stroking the smooth, naked slope of her back.

"Come with me," he said again, moving away from her. She walked along beside him, yielding herself completely to the authority in his voice, not noticing the sharp broken planks of the wharf under her bare feet, not caring that she was naked.

They walked to the end of the wharf. Now they were directly behind the great, looming mass of the fish-packing plant. There were no windows at all in this huge, back wall of the plant. The wharf ran along its base like a wooden sidewalk above the water of the harbor. The water rose and fell gently. A tall-masted schooner lay at anchor by itself in the middle of the harbor.

The night was still and warm. The summer breeze caressed Lilith's naked body, moving softly over her skin, calming her with its gentleness. Lilith heard the lapping of the small waves against the pilings of the wharf. She reached out a hand to feel the rough, splintered wood of the piling.

Michael didn't move. She wanted him to say something to her, but she didn't know what it was she wanted him to say. She looked up at him. Moonlight fell on his face, cutting deep shadows under his eyebrows and under his cheekbones above his beard. His hair was black in the moonlight. His beard was black. His forehead shone in the light.

She was aware that he was staring at her. She wanted to tear her eyes away from him. She couldn't. She saw him staring unblinkingly into her face, measuring her. His eyes moved over her naked body; they were on her breasts and belly and crotch and thighs, but there was no lust in them. They were cold and distant. When he put out his hand to touch her bare shoulder, she shivered. Her fear came alive again, and along with the fear came a strange, dark yearning for him. The yearning was so strong she began to cry. Helpless, she sank down on her knees in front of him, embracing his strong legs, pressing her face against his thighs.

Michael felt her arms around his legs, felt how thin they were, how delicate and fragile. It stirred the darkness in him.

Now Lilith raised her head. She wanted to see his face again. She saw him looking down at her and the pitiless brutality in Michael's eyes struck her deeply. She felt a quick, hot response surge up inside her. She felt the intense excitement of helplessness. She wanted to give herself to him, to be taken violently, to be used and punished and hurt, to feel the keen pleasure of total submission. She saw that Michael was aware of her thoughts and she was not ashamed. The thought that he knew what she was thinking and feeling excited her even more. Quivering, she reached up to embrace him around the waist.

Inside Michael, the dark feeling swelled to bursting. The girl kneeling abjectly at his feet was an abomination to him. He wanted to destroy her.

He was aware of his power, of the power given him at his birth. In a moment he would destroy her, but right now, for a little while, he wanted to savor the feeling of power inside him. Never before had he felt it so intensely as now.

He felt Lilith touch him between his legs.

Vile! Vile!

She was lewd and evil, the stench of it hung over her monstrously.

Like the girl in the bar who came to him brazenly and unashamed, offering her body in ways that were sinful to him.

Vile!

Like the young blond girl on the street who got into his car, eager to give up her virginity to him.

Vile! Depraved!

He closed his eyes to call up the darkness for her death.

And then the shout burst in his mind like a clap of thunder, its sound stunning him.

—No, Michael!

He put his hands to his head, hurting, holding his skull cupped in his plams, his palms on both sides of his head.

—Not again, Michael!

He'd never heard Aaron's voice so loud before. Nor so strong. Nor so angry.

Aaron was furious. Aaron's voice was a trumpet pealing in his brain. Aaron's voice was a ram's horn calling down on him all the forces in Aaron he had always been afraid of.

—Never again, Michael!

Aaron's voice flailed at him, stripping him of the power he had felt only moments before. He wanted to scream. Aaron was god. Aaron was good. He had fooled himself, he saw that now. Aaron was stronger than he, had always been stronger, always would be stronger. Aaron's voice rang out stentoriously in his head, echoing commandingly throughout every crevice in his mind.

He flung himself against Aaron in his mind, struggling to kill him as he had once before killed him. He fought against Aaron with all his might. They came together, the two of them, tearing his mind apart with their violence, and they wrestled against each other with all their strength.

Lilith looked up in fear. The figure whose legs she was clasping in her arms loomed tall in the darkness. Unmoving. Tense. Catatonic. Something had happened to him. He was no longer looking at her. His face was lifted to the night sky and there was terror on it.

She pulled away from him, moving one step at a time, but she felt no need to flee. She didn't understand what was happening.

Lilith heard noises from the wharves nearby. Across the finger of water that lay between the pier she was on and the next dock, small spills of light snapped on, reflecting on the oily surface of the water. She heard an engine start up far away on the waterfront. She heard voices shouting at each other in Italian. It puzzled her until she remembered that the fishing crews came to their vessels before dawn to go to sea.

She saw Michael still standing rigidly, his head now thrown back to the night sky, his eyes closed. She wanted to go to him, to comfort him. He looked as if he needed comforting.

He was losing. No matter how strongly he fought, Aaron was stronger. No matter what wiles he tried, Aaron countered them. Aaron was impervious to his tricks. Aaron had a strength he had never known him to be capable of before. Aaron was exhausting him. He knew that he would lose. The thought defeated him.

He lost.

Aaron opened his eyes. He looked at Lilith. She smiled tentatively at him and was warmed by the small flicker of his lips in response.

Aaron went over to the edge of the wharf. He stopped beside a piling, his hand on the rough top of it. He looked out over the expanse of still, black water. In the night the water of the harbor was still and black, its surface slick, and the boats in the harbor rode still and unmoving. There was a great sadness in Aaron; he knew what he had to do, and he knew, too, that he should have done it long ago; that he could have no mercy on either Michael or himself. He could not go on fighting Michael forever.

Michael would come back again. He was not strong enough to keep Michael from taking over their body. Michael was evil. Michael had always been evil. Now the evil in Michael was more powerful than it had ever been and it was growing. For a time, for a short time, summoning up all the strength he had, he had defeated Michael, but Michael would slip into their mind again, and Michael would take over their body again, and Michael would do evil again and kill again and destroy again.

Whatever the cost, he knew that Michael had to be stopped, and he knew that the cost would be great. A deep, ineffable sorrow came up in him. He wanted to cry for Michael because he loved Michael. He wanted to explain to Michael what it was he was going to do, because it was something that had to be done and that he was doing it out of his love for Michael. He hoped that Michael would understand.

He began to prepare himself.

To the east, the horizon had begun to pale with the first light of the false dawn. In the shelter of the breakwater, boats lay at anchor, almost unmoving in the still water. In the middle of the inner harbor, the tall-masted schooner sat as if it were solidly and permanently in place. Along the docks and wharves, the sounds of the fishing crewmen grew louder. Here and there a donkey engine started up. On some of the ships, the diesel engines had been turned over and their deep, chuffing sound spilled into the damp air.

Aaron stretched and looked around him at the harbor. He saw Lilith and smiled at her lovingly.

Lilith saw his smile and felt his love for her and loved him back with all of her being. She wanted to run to him and to have him hold her. She had never felt love as great as this in her life. It had the purity of light and it shone in her mind clearly and cleanly.

She saw Aaron pull his jersey over his head. He bent, taking off each sneaker in turn. He unbuckled his belt, dropping his slacks and stepping out of them. Now he was a naked as she. Lilith came to him, standing in front of him, looking into his eyes. He placed his hands on her shoulders and drew her to him slightly and bent and kissed her on her forehead. Lilith was happy.

Aaron turned away from her. He stepped to the very edge of the wharf and dove into the water. Lilith ran to the piling, peering down at the water, waiting for his head to emerge. She felt no fear for him. She felt completely and totally calm.

Aaron came to the surface and began to swim. The morning chill of the sea water was cold on his body, but the cold didn't bother him. He swam strongly, without haste, tasting the salt water in his mouth, feeling it slick back his hair and his beard and cooling the heat of his body.

He came up to the schooner, catching the line of a fender and pulling himself onto the deck. He breathed deeply, taking in great gulps of the air, his chest swelling with each inhalation. His skin was cold from the water and the chill of the morning air on it. He had never felt so alive, so keenly aware of the water drops on his skin, of the wind ruffling his beard, of the salt smell and the smoothness of the deck under his bare feet. It would be a day, he knew, to live to its fullest because of the joy that would be in it. It made him sad.

He moved to the bow where he found a short coil of line and unfastened it. He looped the line over his shoulder and made his way back along the deck to the ratlines going up to the peak of the mainmast.

Slowly, carefully, he climbed the ratlines to the crosstree.

Lilith stared out at the dim figure moving on the deck of the schooner. The light was getting brighter now. She saw him stand and stretch his body, his arms wide, reaching. She saw him walk to the bow of the boat and bend down and then move back to the main-mast. She saw him more clearly as he began to climb the ratlines, moving higher until he finally came to the crosstrees.

It was hard to see what he was doing exactly, but after a while, she began to understand, and when she did, she began to cry.

It took him a while, and it was difficult, but when he was through, the line he had taken from the bow of the ship was fastened around the mainmast just above the crosstree and around his chest and a loop of it was around each arm of the crosstree. He hung from the line, one arm in each loop, the weight of his body pulling heavily against the line, the sharp pain of the cord around his chest biting into his flesh.

Michael's voice was in his head. Michael said:

—*Aaron, don't do this.*

There was nothing for him to say to Michael. Nothing that Michael would understand.

—*Aaron. Please, Aaron!*

The voice went on begging until he said finally:

—*I must. There is no other way.*

Michael heard the great sadness in Aaron's voice and the great regret, and he knew it was for both of them. He wanted to plead with Aaron, but Aaron was pushing him out of their mind. He was helpless in the face of Aaron's great determination.

It was still not quite day when the brilliant light filled Aaron's mind. He closed his eyes to welcome its brightness. Never before had it shone so brightly or with such intensity or clarity. Never before had it surrounded him with such grace and peace of mind and well-being.

He felt the wounds beginning to open in his palms

and on his feet and in his side. He felt the warm blood begin to run from him. From his palms, from his insteps, but mostly from the great wound in his side.

After a while, the brightness of the light began to fade and the darkness began to seep in, but it was a different kind of darkness than he had ever known. It was a final darkness. It welcomed him into it and he was soothed by it and comforted by it.

Michael came to him. Aaron saw that Michael was no longer troubled. No longer filled with anger or rage, and for the first time in his life Michael was at peace with himself. He held out his hand in welcome. Michael took his hand and slipped into their body. They were joined now. Together.

The conflict was over. They were finally one as they had been at birth.

On the horizon the first rays of the morning sun broke out of the cloud bank, lighting the tall masts of the ship, touching his body so that it shone with an eerie radiance.

Throughout the harbor, wherever they were on their vessels and on the docks, the fishermen stopped their work.

The sounds of the donkey engines died away. In the bowels of the ships, the diesels were shut down and the men came up onto the decks to stand at the rails in silence.

Everywhere, every face was turned toward the tall-masted schooner riding at anchor in the middle of the harbor, and every man, wherever he was, felt a great peace come into him.

CHAPTER NINETEEN

All morning they came. They came in powerboats and
sailboats and in dinghies and in rusted, steel-hulled
draggers and trawlers of every size. The lobster boats
came. The fishermen brought their wives and children to their fishing boats. They were dressed in their
best clothing. The fishing boats anchored close to the
schooner. The women from The Shrine of the Second
Life were there. None of them had died in the fire.
They came to taste the bitter pleasure of their revenge.

When the harbor-patrol boat came, the fishermen's
wives would not let them board the schooner. Not until they had had their fill of revenge and spite.

Almost all of the people in Harbortown who could
came down to the docks. They brought field glasses
with them so they could see the crucified body hanging helplessly from the cross of the yardarm.

On the bow of the dragger, *Agatha Rose,* Enrico
Cardozo and Sam Gaspar had mounted the scorched,
burnt plaster statue of the Christ taken from the
shrine. The paint had blackened on the back of the
robes and on the back of the head, but the face still
shone brightly because it had fallen face down and
been protected from the fire. Women knelt on the fore-
deck of the ship around the Christ statue, the wind

billowing the cloth of their black dresses, their faces rigid, their voices loud in a continuous litany of prayer to the statue, their backs to the man hanging high on the mast of the schooner only yards away from them.

On all the fishing vessels, the decks were crowded with women and their men and their children. All of them knew about Michael's appearance at the shrine and of the fire, even those who hadn't been there. There was a constant murmuring among them. Occasionally a woman would go to the rail of a vessel to stare up at the body and to call out loud curses against it and to spit into the ocean.

Hatred burned in the air around the schooner.

It was not until late afternoon that the harbor patrol was able to board the schooner and cut the body down.

2.

It was a week before Charlie Daggett returned to work. His hands were bandaged from his burns. His left cheek was blistered. His eyebrows had been singed off.

He had driven out to The Church of the Second Life in Adam's Cove the day before to find the woman who had been living with Michael Hietala. The building was locked. There were no cars in the garage. The front gate had been left wide open. It was apparent to him that she had been gone for several days. It was no great matter to him. As far as he knew, she wasn't wanted.

His desk was cluttered with mail. He finally got to the one from the Boston city hall. Awkwardly, his hands paining him, he tore it open, ripping the envelope to get at the copy of a birth certificate.

He scanned it, but not with much interest.
It read:

Name of child:	*Michael Aaron Hietala*
Sex:	*Male*
Mother:	*Mary Hietala*
Father:	*Unknown*
Place of birth:	*St. Theresa's Home for Girls*
Notes:	*Mother died at birth*

The paper no longer had any interest for Daggett. He crumpled it up and threw it in his wastebasket.